THE CP SEX FILES

by

LESLEY ASQUITH

Published by **CHIMERA**
ISBN 9781780807164

Remember - always practice safe sex.

INTRODUCTION

The letters contained in this book have been selected from the many received in reply to my requests placed in appropriate adult publications. It was for explicit and relevant CP and S&M experiences from willing male and female participants.

The resultant correspondence showed that those who indulge, both in the giving and receiving of punishment and humiliation, rallied to extol in full and lurid detail the acceptable pain/pleasure virtues of their sexual preferences.

In turn it provides us with unique insights into a most secret and intriguing subject. The following pages contain a fascinating compilation of individual experiences involving men and women of all age groups and social backgrounds.

Explicitly detailed writing came from every level of society, the one factor in common being the great interest in CP and S&M practices as an important, even major, part of their usual sex lives.

My sincere thanks go to all uninhibited enough to contribute, who wrote so vividly of such varied and intimate sexual sessions and experiences.

Lesley Asquith
London, 1999.

PREFACE

Are our wildest sexual wishes and fantasies too way out or downright shameful, no doubt considered perverted by many, to be discussed openly? I've been fortunate (or bold!) enough to try out and experience my more unusual desires, hence my writing to Ms Lesley Asquith's survey.

It's the perfect way to divulge our secret preferences and to air taboo subjects. Having my carnal cravings fulfilled through extra-marital affairs makes me a more contented wife at home, with a loving husband who is not highly sexed none the wiser for my infidelity.

A strong craving to be dominated and strictly disciplined has been with me as a demanding part of my nature since first being spanked by a boyfriend for flirting before him. He was older than my sweet sixteen, married and macho, and stood no cheek or nonsense from me whatever, despite my pleading.

Lowered across his knee, my panties were hauled down. Bare bottom warmed as never before by a rapid flurry of hard and painful smacks rained down on my tender cheeks, I was left in no doubt who was my master as I squealed and sobbed, but left on fire inside, made lewd by his dominance and the spanking. I'll call myself May from Wakefield, and wish you good reading.

CHAPTER ONE
Dominant Male

Married over twenty years to Freddie, our union had settled into a routine and anything but passionate arrangement. We were seemingly content; as the years passed more like friends than man and wife. The sexual side of the marriage had never been great, though I suspected it could be better. Maybe that was my fault for not tempting him more, although Freddie seemed not to care. My husband seemed content to be in no need of sexual relief, yet I found copies of explicit picture magazines in our spare room.

Featured were nude girls bound up to walls, ceilings, beds and chairs, being punished by canes and whips or spanked over the knee of dominant looking men or women. I put this down at first to the sort of thing men looked at, then found myself going back to look at Freddie's secret horde when he was out. I began to get an idea that my husband found this material arousing, for to my great surprise it had the effect of making me masturbate.

I had never before pleasured myself to gain relief, had never before experienced a climax in my life. My mind began to fantasise Freddie tying me up and whipping me, then supposedly forcing himself on my helpless naked body. It was shattering to find I could have repeated orgasms while masturbating. After the spasms ceased I was ashamed of my lewd behaviour and dirty thoughts. Of course, I told myself, I would never do such things, or allow myself to be tied up or punished. It made me wonder, however, whether mild Freddie harboured such thoughts and brought himself off by hand thinking about the same things as I.

We'd switched to beds in separate rooms, and Freddie used the spare room as a den, housing his computer there as well as all the sexy books he didn't know I'd found. To add extra shelves to the walls, he employed a carpenter. When he came I was struck by how handsome the boy was, tanned and with a body-builder's physique. The summer days were hot and he worked stripped to the waist. I found myself admiring his broad muscled chest whenever I went to the room with coffee for him.

Phil was twenty-four-years-old, unmarried, and joked that he was still playing the field. I told myself I was getting too familiar with the hired help. I made him lunch the second day and ate mine with him in the kitchen. While we ate he questioned me about my marriage. I blushed when he mentioned he'd uncovered a load of sexy corporal punishment magazines. I was embarrassed by the way he grinned and stared at my rather over-developed breasts. When he had left I took a shower, and thought about the boy smacking my bottom and making me have sex with him. Of course, that brought on the desire to satisfy myself with my fingers.

On the following day I took up his coffee and he asked me if I was into the sort of things pictured in Freddie's magazines. He remarked I had the kind of upholstered bottom that would be ideal for spanking. My guilt must have showed for I turned bright red, too quickly to deny I'd never want such things done to me. He took me in his arms and kissed me, his tongue in my mouth and his hard body pressed to mine. Despite the shock, I found myself responding for a moment before I thrust him away and shrieked, 'How dare you?'

'Because you want it,' he said forcefully, ordering me to undress while I stood trembling, starting by his hand unzipping the back of my dress. He drew it roughly over my head, then said I must continue for he'd wanted to see me without my clothes from the first day. When I protested, left in my bra and briefs only, he sat on the edge of the bed, pulled me across his lap and drew my briefs down over my feet. I screamed and struggled, only to be held fast and warned to behave. Then his hard palm began to slap my tender bottom cheeks until I begged for mercy among my cries, saying I'd do whatever he asked.

'Strip, like I said,' he commanded curtly, and I unhooked my bra and handed it to him. Standing naked before a young man about the same age as my lawyer daughter made me excited enough to faint. His eyes devoured my bared breasts and pubic region with its heavy growth of hair. Outrageously aroused and ashamed by having such feelings, wanting him and knowing the spanking had an unbelievable effect on my desiring to be fucked, I forced myself to beg him to let me dress.

He shook his head and kicked off his jeans and underpants, his socks and trainers, until naked himself. I tried to force my eyes away from his hugely rampant penis, but couldn't, knowing I desired it to penetrate me. Made then to fondle the hard stalk, I tried to suppress the feelings surging inside me. I'd heard ribald tales of milkmen and tradesmen making love to wives. This can't be happening to me, I thought, recalling my husband and daughter, and how much I loved them and not him. But I realised he'd taken his hand from mine and still I continued to stroke and rub the iron-hard rod of flesh in my grasp.

To increase the torment and my helpless mounting excitement, he made me repeat lewdly obscene words about how big I had made his prick grow, and how much I was loving holding it. I felt its hot throb transmitted up my arm, tingling my breasts and tightening the nipples.

'Kiss it, bitch,' he then ordered degradingly, and I found myself doing as compelled, even putting my lips over the big bulbous knob. He jeered at me that I was wanting to suck it, and said he'd return the favour before he fucked me. I knew he meant to kiss and lick my vagina, something I had secretly hoped for. I heard myself begging him to do it like a wanton slut.

He laid me out on the thick carpet, first sucking hard on my nipples before pushing his face between my thighs and probing my vagina with his tongue. I groaned in pleasure, a climax shaking me, my first other than by masturbation. Then he moved between my thighs, which I gladly widened for him. I guided his stiff young prick to my cunt and it was a glorious release to take his thick stalk and jerk back to his thrusts. Using words I'd never said before, I urged him to fuck me, fuck me hard and long, not wanting it to ever finish.

He asked me if my husband ever fucked me as good. Shamelessly I told him no. Violent orgasms shook me repeatedly. I clung to him with my arms and legs,

4

then he drew out suddenly, his hot cream spraying my breasts and throat. 'Can't have you made preggy,' he joked. 'You don't look the sort that's on the pill.' I grabbed for my clothes, burning with shame and in utter humiliation running from the room. He followed me, saying I needed spanking and fucking, only that my husband should be the one to do it. I was hot-blooded, he said, and needed fucking as well as being ruled with a strict hand.

When he returned the next day he questioned me as to whether I'd informed my husband about our session. When I said no, he did what I'd secretly hoped he'd do.

He roughly ordered me to strip. I called him 'Master', as it seemed to be right and I actually wanted to, feeling very sexually submissive. He said I'd receive extra strokes for that, as the title was due to my husband only, and as a loyal wife I should know that. This time I was made to bend over an armchair, naked bottom raised and my wrists bound. He'd brought a whippy riding crop to use on my bum, making me whoop as he stung the defenceless buttock flesh.

He then fucked me while I was in the same bound position, a deep penetration from the rear making me come at least three times.

When he left that day, his work finished, he made me keep the riding crop, saying I should present it to my husband and tell him to use it on me. Left alone, I determined Freddie would be given the chance to punish me for my adulterous behaviour.

He came home and I served dinner, awaiting my chance. After all, if he liked seeing pictures of females being spanked, surely the real thing would be much better?

I waited until he'd gone to his den to use his computer. My excitement mounting, I stripped naked, and with the riding crop in my hand to present to him, knocked on the door.

Let me end by saying the sexual side of our marriage is now all-important. Dear Freddie knows how to keep me sweet, and at the same time enjoy his role as dominant master. It improves a stale marriage no end!

Mrs J. K., Sheffield.

CHAPTER TWO
Maid to Obey

Students nowadays have a punishing time making ends meet on student loans and overdrafts. I come from a thrifty Scottish background. Although I fully intended completing my college studies to become a teacher, I had no desire ending up in debt for years as so many do. I had to make enough money somehow.

Although looking prim and proper, I am a nineteen-year-old girl who since the age of sixteen has been turned-on sexually by the thought of being dominated, spanked or worse. I once was told off and humiliated in front of my class for cheating. This very humbling experience excited me. Although cringing with shame I was also enjoying being paraded before my scornful classmates, so much so that to add to my public disgrace I peed my knickers in front of everyone, including the boys in my form.

Thinking back on it makes me so horny that I masturbate, and I add the scene of me being made to touch my toes for the teacher to cane my bare bottom. I had other equally early fantasies used to aid my frequent self-pleasuring. A father-figure older man had me across his knee for a knickers down spanking, or would order me to take off all my clothes. He'd have rough sex with me which I supposedly didn't like, but this fantasy made me have multiple climaxes while masturbating.

Then sometimes it was a woman (my fierce spinster French teacher) who had me across her knee, parting my bum cheeks to play with my cunt and bring me off. The threat of a beating made me lick her hairy vagina, something I knew I would like to do in time, but more so with a dominant lesbian lover making me obey her. I began to have doubts about my sexuality, whether I wanted men, was gay, or bi-sexual. I thought of women having me as often as I did men, tying me over a chair and leathering my behind, as well as fucking me with strap-on dildos - even in my forbidden hole. I lived at home and my parents had no idea of my nature.

I found a willing older boyfriend when seventeen and he paid me for sex like a prostitute, which thrilled me too as it was degrading. Terry liked to tie me up, to a chair or on the bed in his flat. I always fought him when he wanted sex, struggling until his prick thrusting inside my greedy cunt made me beg him to fuck me. He enjoyed making me suck him, coming in my mouth always. If taking a bath together, he'd stand up to pee over me. Very well endowed, he went to California hoping to be a stud in porno videos.

In a magazine Terry left when I took over his flat, I saw an advert from a Madam X offering strict discipline to wayward boys in her house of correction. I phoned and asked if she needed an assistant, thinking it would help with my financial situation. A husky voice at the other end of the line said she had hard-up housewives, shop girls, out of work actresses and a waiting list of females wanting to work for her. 'So what's special that I should consider you?' she asked. 'Come and let me see you.'

She was as I'd imagined: big built, bosomy, with make-up plastered, and laden with jewellery. She said I looked too young and sweet to be taken seriously as a strict disciplinarian. More the type to be dominated. She had clients, men and women, into smacking botties and being sadistically inclined who paid well. 'If you were a masochist,' she added, 'I could get you work enough to earn you a small fortune, never mind pay your way through college.'

I assured her I was that type, loving spanking, whipping, humiliation, bondage, the whole bit. So she led me through to a room resembling a torture chamber with chains hanging from the ceiling and walls, whipping posts and heavy wooden contraptions with manacles and leather straps attached. Clients were there chained to the walls or strung up to the ceiling. Two were on their knees polishing the floor while they were whipped by large women dressed in black rubber or PVC; just bras and tiny briefs and boots. All were armed with whips or canes, paddles and tawses, and all wore black masks.

One whining client was led on a dog's lead fastened to a metal studded collar, his back striped from his mistress's whip and worse indignity, a tail sticking out from his bottom hole. I heard he was to be taken to his kennel and made to eat dog food from a bowl on the floor. As I watched, fascinated, my future employer laughed at my expression. 'See what you'll be letting yourself in for, Alison?' she asked. 'Before I let my clients loose on you, I need to know you're a true submissive, willing to endure indignities and suffering but inwardly relishing it. I'm going to hand you over to my girls. You won't fool them.'

'Of course,' I agreed. 'They can do what they like...'

'Don't tell us what we can or can't do with you, bitch,' one of the dominant women snapped. I was made to undress while they made disparaging remarks about my girlish boobs, the light fuzz on my pubes, and my marble-white bottom made to whip and redden.

'I expect she's a virgin too,' announced one with menace, and I saw she now wore a monstrous strap-on dildo. 'We'll soon alter that.' Nipple clamps were attached to me until my breasts hung down under the weight and it hurt dreadfully. I whined in pain and was jeered at as a baby. One then cracked a cane on my bum.

'This one's a pussy cat,' she remarked, 'so she'll now get a cat's tail and a nice collar that she'll wear whenever she's near any of us.' Ordered to my hands and knees, I had a jewelled collar locked around my neck with a bell attached. Then I gasped as I got a stinging crack with the cane for moving as my buttocks were roughly prised apart. I complained as I felt a cigar-shaped object pushed up my back passage. Turning my head as I heard my tormentors laughing, I saw that a cat's tail was attached to the object up my bottom.

A crack of a whip across my cheeks made me crawl ignobly as ordered, and with each strike I had to meow loudly. In a side room I was led into a naked man was handcuffed to a frame and he cried out pitifully for mercy as a black girl flogged his behind. I was tethered over a similar wooden frame, bottom up, and all my mistresses beat me in unison with the whip, cane and riding crop. Until I stopped begging the thrashing increased, then the sound of my screams were muffled as I was gagged.

Relieved when the beating stopped and the gag removed, I was alarmed to note that now all three women wore dildos. I was told I was not to express pleasure if getting aroused. That was not for submissives to enjoy, it was for the pleasure of my female fuckers. If I dared to climax, that would lead to punishment far worse than I'd experienced. But when the first oiled dildo slid into my cunt, already pulsing from the heat of my thrashed botty, I could not ignore the erotic sensations rippling through my body and began to moan and jerk. It became patently obvious from my uninhibited convulsions that I was in the throes of multiple orgasms as the three women fucked me without respite.

The feel of the latex pricks thrusting up me felt exactly like a real stiff flesh and blood cock penetrating me and I reacted accordingly. I called out lewdly to be fucked, never minding the consequences in my lust.

At last unshackled from the whipping frame, fucked until I was lost in a haze of sensuality and exhaustion, I fell to the carpet sated as never before from so many sapping climaxes.

'On your feet, and go fix your make-up, slut,' I was told, and I saw in a mirror that my mascara had run with the tears I'd shed. I used the mirror to inspect my bottom with the cat's tail fixed into my rear hole. My cheeks were scarlet, smarting like they'd been brushed with stinging nettles.

'What did I tell you to do?' asked the woman who'd told me to fix my make-up. 'And what are you doing?'

I said innocently that I was inspecting my striped bottom, and got a hard smack on my face for not obeying her order. I was made to lap milk from a saucer and curl up in a basket. Later I was told I'd passed the set tests and would be employed as a genuine submissive.

Such is the demand for the likes of me, I was whipped by a client that evening and made to suck his prick and have his jism shoot into my open mouth as he came. How I fared from then on in my new career, sent out at times to the homes of wealthy dominant folk, both male and female, I'll let you know in another letter. I've been manacled, bound, dildoed, whipped and spanked until my poor bottom was too sore to sit down upon. But at least I'm paying my way through college without taking a loan.

Alison, Leicester.

CHAPTER THREE
Star Treatment

I used to be an accountant with a prestigious firm that handled the financial affairs of personalities famous in the world of entertainment and sport. At the time I was settled with a nice wife; a quiet young woman of thirty-two, mother to our two girls, whose life was dedicated to homemaking and family. I had no wish ever to indulge in way-out sex like wife watching, bondage and spanking, and I'm sure Joy was of the same mind. What happened was thrust upon us. I have to admit here, however, that such sexual games can appeal to our baser instincts and can be erotic viewing, especially with a loved partner involved. It makes for a better understanding of couples who indulge and are uninhibited, and who find such activities addictive.

Years ago I was sent to London on business and took the opportunity to take my Joy. A village girl, busy mum and wife, it meant a break while her parents kept the children. It appeared I had been a help with the tax problems of a famous actor, known for his roles in Hollywood movies. He was also notorious for his wild living and affairs. He was not American or British, but colonial, if I may use the term. Through my work for him my quiet wife and I were asked to an afternoon party at the star's London apartment.

We felt awed by the people around the bar in the spacious lounge, many recognised faces of film, stage and television. Joy and I stood drinks in hand, content to take in the scene, my wife in a simple print dress that hugged her rounded figure, the picture of wholesome health, unlike many of the painted creatures around. Pressed with drink, enjoying a complete change of routine, she became slightly tipsy and relaxed. The big star was surrounded by admirers, but we didn't expect to meet him. He wore a white shirt with a cravat, expensive slacks and slip-on loafers. Joy remarked he was even more handsome than he appeared on the screen.

It was then she was approached by a minion, now known as a minder, I suppose, who said his boss would like to meet her. I at once nodded my approval, knowing she had liked his films. As she was led away, I said to the man beside me at the bar that Joy was flattered. 'How nice of him to meet his unknown guests,' I said, and saw him smirk.

'Better watch out, he no doubt fancies the look of such a wholesome unspoilt wench as a change from actresses,' he said. But Joy was gone, led away out of sight.

The room was full, the air filled with cigar smoke. Looking around, now at the bar by myself, I could not see my wife or our famous host. I passed an hour wondering where she'd been taken, a time spent chatting with the barman. Then I saw the actor back in the room surrounded by admirers, but not a sign of my wife. When she did appear later she walked unsteadily, her hair disarrayed and her eyes glazed as I helped her up on the tall barstool next to me. I had to hold her as she wobbled, and she winked at me as if she'd never felt better. She was unused to drink, of course. I asked if she was all right.

'I've just been fucked and spanked,' she giggled. As much a shock to me was to hear her use the 'F' word, never in her vocabulary. 'He fucked me and then smacked my bottom for being a very wicked and horny girl, and a married one too. It just seemed to happen.'

Dumbfounded, I stared at her as if seeing a different person, and wondered what to do about it. 'My bottom is on fire,' I was aware of her tipsy voice announcing gaily.

Our host was as before, in a circle of beautiful women, seemingly unconcerned. 'Did - did he rape you?' I asked, which brought more out of character giggling.

'Of course not,' she said blithely. 'I told you, it just happened. He fucked me the back way too, and kissed my pussy like I want you to. Don't go on, dear, it's done and I did enjoy what he did to me.' That irked me as much as anything.

'We're leaving now,' I said, marching her off.

In our hotel room I felt an unexplainable mix of outrage and strong arousal thinking she'd been with another man. She got out of her clothes to shower, but unashamedly naked lay sprawled on the bed with her smile showing she still savoured the fucking. 'I suppose he gave you more drink?' I suggested, to excuse her lapse.

'He fucked me and I wanted him to,' she said huskily, as if proud of the fact. 'If you think I've been bad, then you give my bare bottom a good spanking like he did. Otherwise, love, you fuck me as well. The back way too if you want...'

Unable to resist, I threw off my clothes and got between her thighs as she guided me into her already juicy quim. As never before she thrust up to gain full penetration, grasped me in her arms with her legs locked around my back. Excited by her allowing sex with the lecherous actor, I worked my flanks and did all I could to fuck her to a frenzy. 'I'm a bitch, a dirty slut!' I heard her scream. 'Make me come and come, and then beat me for being an unfaithful wife.' Her climax was such I thought she was having a fit, her spasms continuing as I pumped my seed up her.

On recovering together, kissing lovingly, I wanted to know if it had happened by chance at the party. Of course he had seen her, fancied her curvy wholesomeness, and guided her into a large bedroom, so it was obvious what he had in mind. Not so obvious was how my wife would react to his advances. Once alone he gave her champagne, kissed her eyes and told her she was beautiful. It was like a scene from his films and light-headed, she allowed him to lead her to the bed and lower her across it, pressing long and passionate deep tongue kisses to her mouth. Protesting that she was a wife and mum, she trembled as he undressed her until she was stark naked before him. His mouth was everywhere, on her tits and nipples, between her thighs with his long tongue in her palpitating quim and his lips suctioning on her clitoris.

He'd thrown off his clothes and made her suck his stalk until thrusting it up her now very receptive cunt. Deep in her and iron hard, his movements slow to begin with, he worked her up to a frenzy until she was bucking her body to his, crying out that he was making her come and must not stop. After she had climaxed at least twice, he withdrew and rolled her over, using the back entrance to relieve himself as he drenched her innards. It was then, fooling about kissing and fondling, that he'd pulled her across his knee and spanked her for being a naughty wife.

She whispered to me that she was after we'd fucked ourselves to satisfaction, suggesting that I smack her bottom for being the unfaithful wife she was. I thought at once that she'd enjoyed the spanking and the thought appealed to me too. It made me feel very macho, and I sat up on the edge of the bed and ordered her across my knee. I didn't spare her, really enjoying whacking her plump arse cheeks and turning them rosy red. It was good too telling her she was a slut, a tart, and any more fucking about with other men and she'd get leathered until she begged me to stop. Then we slept, only to awake excited and fuck again. Never had we done it twice in a day since our honeymoon.

At another of his parties we found we'd been invited early before any guests had arrived. Once more she was taken to his bedroom and I didn't stop her. His minder said to me that my firm did much business with his boss, so it was wise to keep in with him. He gave me drink after drink at the bar, but my mind was elsewhere and I also had an erection thinking of what my Joy was doing.

'So he's screwing your wife,' said the minder. 'Seems your missus wouldn't want you to stop them. Let's go see.'

He led me to a bathroom and removed a picture from the wall. One of those two-way see-through mirrors was strategically placed behind it. I saw Joy tied to the bed face down, bumping her bottom up to the actor who was mounted above her. Reluctant to stop viewing, I watched my bound wife get well and truly fucked from the rear.

Later he released her, sat down and made her suck him back to hardness. Then I saw Joy mounted on him, her back to us and buttocks spread as she straddled the man and ground down on his cock. She was spanked again too before going to shower with him and join me later in the lounge.

The cocky actor clapped my shoulder in passing during the party. I told Joy to wait until we got back to the hotel. Her arse would sting through contact with my belt, and she'd do everything I ordered like a good little submissive wife.

It's in the past now, but I've had a new and exciting wife from then on. Sometimes we see the randy actor, dead now through high living, in a film brought back on television, and I see Joy smile.

Can't give you my name and address, but this is no lie.

Anonymous, Surrey.

CHAPTER FOUR
Fantasy Floggings

Your advertised appeal for CP experiences have elicited this response and brought back memories. It was in the so-called and promiscuous 'Swinging Sixties' but it was only in my daydreams that I got what I desired sexually. A randy teenager at a rather posh all girls school, my nature dictated that I be made to obey a strict master or mistress, and be severely disciplined and made humble. That way would give me the highest sexual arousal, I was already aware. It featured in my fantasies when diddling myself to climax (at least once a day).

Now I'm Judy, single and in my fiftieth year. Gladly still a randy female and bi-sexual, I've had corrective and bondage sex with many male and female partners. But as a teenager none of my boyfriends were assertive, or interested in doing what I wanted. To play with my growing tits and pussy, fuck me in what always turned out to be a quickie with over-excited boys, it was no wonder I got more satisfaction having sex with girlfriends at boarding school. The dormitory at night was a hotbed of horny teenage lesbian loving. Fingers, candles, bananas were used; breasts were fondled and nipples sucked; in the absence of boys we improvised.

One girl took delight in spanking me over her knee, using her hairbrush and a cane and belt to chastise me. Knowing I got a tremendous thrill from being dominated by her, she made me pay for the privilege and hand over my pocket money for her services. This gave me a feeling of being degraded and used that I liked, as did the girl making me lick her plump hairless quim, often in front of classmates who wanted me to do the same to them. Girls definitely had it over the boys. I recall romping in the nude with a boy during the school holidays while my parents were out. I longed for a spanking followed by a fuck made torrid by my bum having been warmed.

I was sweet sixteen with my maiden's bottom ripening and made ready for a good smacking. With my need desperate, I draped myself across the boy's lap. Bare buttocks tilted and offered to tempt any male worthy, suggesting I deserved punishing for I had kissed other boys, he looked at me amazed by my perfectly normal request. So, lying naked across his knee didn't do the trick. He said I was stupid as I confronted him with my sprouting tits and wispy-haired quim. What a lulu he was, I remember!

So even then I was an imaginatively sexy girl and being submissive was my thing. Fantasising and bringing myself off saved me from exploding. A favourite was of me being caught frigging myself when alone in the dorm, working a vaselined courgette up my cunt when Miss Ross the gym mistress walked in. Screeching, 'You are a depraved wretch, a wicked girl!' she thrashed at my naked form with the cane she carried. There really was a Miss Ross; a buxom young teacher who all the girls had a crush on. Ordered to her study, on my knees begging not to be expelled, several randy alternative fantasies would spring to my fevered mind as I played finger-fuck to bring on successive orgasms.

One was to be made to lick her out, or be fucked with a dildo she kept in her study along with manacles, whips and riding crops from the school's stables. I'd also dream of being stretched over her desk, with knickers down, bare bottom tilted. Standing right behind my upturned bum, legs astride, she'd see my fig-like cunt and tight little arsehole. The thought thrilled me to my core, the whippy cane she held swishing through the air as she thrashed my bottom. She'd demand to know who had fucked me, which girls I had licked out, then the flogging ceasing, I'd shudder at the delicious sensations I felt as Miss Ross stroked her fingers up the outer lips of my puss.

She'd enter me, a finger probing in the moist spongy flesh of my secret inner sex, while she told me not to respond knowing I couldn't prevent working my bottom back to her fingering. I was sodden, each in-and-out movement of her fingers making embarrassing squelchy sounds. Such thoughts never failed to give me strong orgasms. Her study became the scene for all my fantasies. I'd be made to strip and be questioned about my sexual thoughts, called dirty bitch and minx-slut for having such a lewd mind. With my wrists tied and myself fastened over a chair or the desk, I'd be strapped with her whip every confession I made. I was also tied face up, legs parted and my cunt struck with a leather belt. All this gave a randy schoolgirl tremendous sexual relief.

So it fits that I was ready for the real thing when the chance came. I enjoyed riding and even mucking out the stables as the rough men who worked there eyed my tits and bottom, which I liked. I went there one evening to find it deserted, but then I heard a moaning sound, like a woman in bliss, for it was the same as I made when coming. I crept up the rows of stalls with my mind excited at the thought of seeing someone being fucked, a local girlfriend of a stable-hand, I guessed. Looking through a knothole in the boards separating me from the next stall, one of the men was fucking a woman, but not a local girl. It was Miss Ross, on her knees in the straw with her broad bare bottom curved and the workman's prick thrusting into her cunt, stretching her cleft. 'Fuck me, smack my arse!' I heard her scream and the man struck her bottom with a loud crack as he jerked into her, both squealing their pleasure as they came.

Intrigued by the prim and proper Miss Ross getting fucked and crying out for her arse to be slapped, I wondered if all the men were fucking her. One evening I went on the pretence of booking a ride next day, hoping to see the gym mistress getting fucked, but only two stable-hands were there. The younger one said I could have a ride anytime, he'd see to that, while his mate said he'd be glad to oblige too. I knew what they meant, and feeling I was being made fun of as a naïve schoolgirl, told them they could go fuck themselves. The men said I was asking for it, and I said they couldn't fuck me like they did Miss Ross, for they weren't up to it. I'd deliberately made it a challenge, and then both were kissing me, feeling my tits, and I said they'd have to tie me down before they did what they liked.

My struggles were token efforts and I was stripped naked, my wrists bound with a leather harness strap. I was pushed down on my hands and knees in the straw and the two men said it was time I was taught a lesson, for they well knew I flaunted my body before them. I screamed as I felt my bottom get a flurry of smarting slaps from one, while his mate used a handy jockey's whip, stinging flicks that had me howling for mercy. But my cunt throbbed with arousal, the heat in my thrashed buttocks making my whole pubic area tingle with sensations and my nipples stiffen as I felt on the brink of coming. I knew for certain then that I found it thrilling to be degraded and punished. I shouted out as I'd heard Miss Ross do, 'Fuck me, smack my bottom, I want you to...'

I wanted them both to fuck me, bracing myself on all fours to take the first prick ramming into my greedy teenage cunt. First there was another indignity as they squeezed a tube of cream used to treat bruises on a horse's ankles into my cunt; and even worse, pushed the tube's nozzle into my tight little virgin bum hole and creamed that. Crouched over me, I felt a huge stiff shaft stretch my quim, even as his friend stood before me and fed his hardened stalk into my mouth. Later, both fucked my anus, and then laughing, left me to struggle out of the wrist bindings and get back into my clothes, which were strewn around me. The session really was a romp in the hay, going on until dark and making me late for returning to school. I crept in covered in bits of straw, spunk between my breasts, and even in my hair, the advent of the pill saving me from pregnancy, no doubt.

Future visits to the riding school often meant rides without a horse being involved. Often I left with a tender bottom, not always the result of being in the saddle, but more likely by the correction I craved as a confirmed masochist. It's been that way for me ever since, so your readers can take it as fact that we do exist out there. Presently I am the submissive sex partner of a married couple strongly into S&M, both of whom delight in making sure I'm kept faithful by constant spankings and whippings. On weekends we sleep together to make a threesome, both the husband and wife using me as they wish to gratify their sexual desires.

Melanie K., Winchester.

CHAPTER FIVE
Wimp Watcher

I saw your advert for CP experiences. I'm writing to add my bit for all those weak-kneed husbands like me who get their kicks seeing wives being severely disciplined and shafted by macho and well-endowed studs. A bonus in my case is that being a complete wimp, thriving on humiliation, my greatest thrill is watching my wife and dominant lover performing before me. Even when I'm told to clear off out of the room, in a frustrated state of ecstasy I am aroused enough to wank over the sounds of my wife's cries when she's being spanked or fucked, my imagination running riot.

The arrangement suits me, so think what you like, for that's how I get my thrills. Over the years my wife, Jean, has accepted the whip and the prick from a variety of masters, whose ages have ranged from eighteen to a hugely hung virile black stud of sixty. She's approaching forty and stacked with fine big slightly pendulous tits, a plump hairy snatch greedy for cock, curvaceous figure, and a well-rounded fleshy arse made for smacks from a strong male who demands obedience or else. At present she is being screwed by Tom, a young ram with eight thick inches she has to take in her mouth or cunt when he calls.

But others never get a look in when the most dominant of all her partners is around. Neville is a mature and very well-endowed overbearing type. He doesn't wait for an invitation when he wants a fuck, but just turns up. Once when I complained about this I was bent over a chair, trousers down, and had my arse leathered with my own belt until sobbing for mercy and had promised he could come and fuck my wife whenever he wished. You can't experience anything more degrading than this as a husband, but I loved the excruciating pain/pleasure such inflicted indignities give. Jean too was excited, knowing this brute of a guy was going to take her and thrash her backside unless she pleased him.

A self-employed television engineer, I saw how impressed my wife was when Neville installed our new set. Flirting and bending close as he worked, it was a ploy to let him ogle the deep tight cleave of her large milk-white boobs. I figured him as the macho type as he chatted Jean up crudely without caring her husband was present. I got excited thinking of him fucking her, having his way, whatever it was. Saying I had to go out, I left them to it, my mind in an erotic turmoil about what might be taking place if I'd guessed right about him. I was not to be disappointed.

On my return I found the lounge deserted and the new telly working. Upstairs I found Jean spread-eagled naked across our bed, a dazed look in her eyes and a blissful smile on her face. It told me that here was a woman who'd been satisfactorily bonked. Her nipples looked erect and raw from strenuous chewing and sucking, her parted thighs revealing a cleft glistening with their juices and remaining parted from taking a prick of considerable girth. She looked at me proudly as she half rolled over to show her buttocks were striped and bright red from being punished quite severely.

'He fucked me,' my Jean said. 'I told him I was a very happily married woman, but he said that was rubbish. I'd given him the come-on, and he marched me upstairs and ordered me to strip for him. When I refused he put me across his knee and gave me a really painful smacked bottom. So I did what he said, and you were not here to stop him, you feeble wimp.' Of course we were both turned on by the event, and pleased Neville was so sexually demanding and dominant. I was told, to further excite us both, that he'd made her suck him, and she could hardly get his brute of a cock in her mouth. 'He said I was a great fuck,' Jean added to humiliate me, 'and you were a creep for not keeping me in check or fucking me properly. But you never could, Ronnie...'

This was true, and what with my small dick and the problem of premature ejaculation, I wasn't much of a husband, although no doubt earning a salary far greater than what Neville made.

Once he'd found us, he returned to fuck her like I wasn't there, leading her up to the bedroom as if his right. He arrived once as she was about to take a bath, so he got in with her. I saw him fuck her from behind at the basin. Late one night as we watched telly, he strode in and fished out his prick, ordering Jean to do what was necessary with it. There in our lounge she went down on her knees and sucked him off as ordered. I've gone upstairs to find him fucking Jean while she was on all fours on the carpet, after a sound spanking to keep her obedient.

At times his arrogance pissed me off, but my wife thought him so masterful that she worshipped him; and that from a woman who bossed me unmercifully. He took her on a holiday to the South of France without asking me, the time they were away keeping me in a ferment thinking what they were up to. The holiday pictures she brought back to taunt me with showed her nude on the beach. And all the time in the hotel room, she sneered to explain he was shagging the arse off her as well as caning it frequently. Saying she loved his big cock in her mouth, between her tits, up her cunt and wherever else he had poked it.

However she delighted in degrading me, Jean could get her comeuppance too if she annoyed Neville. On her birthday we were going wining and dining in a posh hotel and she'd got all dolled up to show off her new dress, hairstyle and make-up to her sister who was hard-up, which Jean enjoyed doing. As we were leaving the house Neville arrived, saying he'd come for a fuck with his slut. For once she was not pleased to see him, her mind on the evening planned. They argued in the hall until his anger mounted, grabbing her arm and marching her upstairs despite her vehement protests. I stood at the foot of the stairs, hearing a shouting match above.

'You'll do as I say, bitch!' I heard Neville bellow. When it went quiet I ventured up to stand by the open bedroom door. Jean stood stifling sobs, but was meekly undressing. Neville sat on the edge of the bed, his glare enough to make my wife obey, looking fearful as she unhooked her bra and slipped off her panties to be naked and extremely fanciful with her nice big tits swaying as she trembled before her master. I saw Neville merely indicate his knee and she docilely lay across it.

'Please don't, Neville,' she begged abjectly, delighting me that she was so submissive. 'Not my bottom. Last time I couldn't sit, you'd spanked me so hard. Don't smack my bottom, please. I'll suck you and let you fuck me whichever way you like...'

'I'm going to do that anyway,' Neville laughed. 'When I come to fuck you, you fuck! There's other women I can fuck instead, you know.' This brought a howl from Jean, a howl that turned to a screech as he whacked his palm in stinging strikes to her upraised buttocks. I danced a jig with joy as she wailed and struggled, begging for mercy, promising anything. He thrashed her until she went limp, only her shoulders lifting as she sobbed in her humiliation. Then he dumped her off his lap to land with a dull thud on the rug, her arse cheeks scarlet from the spanking. Neville strode out of the bedroom, brushing past me and announcing he'd go elsewhere for a fuck, with my wife pathetically crawling after him on her knees, begging him to stay.

Recovering in time, she noticed me grinning at her downfall. Rising to her feet with her fine tits bobbing, she majestically said that if it appeared to be uplifting watching a bottom being spanked, I should try it. As she sat back on the edge of the bed, her anger evident, she made the same sign Neville had made, indicating that I go across her knee, adding grimly that I would see how I liked it. I had no doubt I would, the idea appealing to a confirmed masochist like myself. Trousers down with my underpants around my ankles, bare bottom up, I docilely lay across her knee. To add to both our pleasure I howled, cried and begged as her hand cracked down on my arse. Reaching for her hairbrush to use, she increased the pain inflicted until I was really begging for mercy and relieved when she dumped me on the floor as Neville had done to her.

At her feet, between her legs, my ordeal was not yet over. To complete my humbling she widened her thighs and thrust out her hairy snatch, sharply ordering me to lick it, to make her day by tonguing her to a climax. I loved to hear the mewing sounds she made as she built up to her climax, jerking her cunt to my face as I lapped at her drenched furrow. A stiffening of her body prior to helpless convulsions of her hips told me she was coming off against my lips.

Dressing again, we went off late for our dinner date. On our return she was mellowed with wine. I was told I could sleep with her that night, a rare treat. 'I shall need your tongue again,' was the reason she gave.

This is one man's account of being subservient to a dominant wife who in turn is submissive to other men, who spank her and fuck her while I'm sometimes allowed to watch. I wouldn't change Jean for any other woman, as I was married before to a girl who was no fun at all; a prude, and nagging with it. We are happy with our way of life, entertaining her boyfriends. No doubt the neighbours may think we entertain a lot, but they can have no idea of what goes on behind our closed door. Their bad luck that they haven't been invited!

Ronnie, Manchester.

CHAPTER SIX
Career Dominatrix

The flat was a dream, within walking distance of college, the shops and beach. It was perfect for a girl with no car and about to study at music school. But like most dreams the flat was out of reach, or should have been with the rent demanded. Yet in a moment of weakness I moved in, praying for a miracle to happen and somehow find the money.

The cash I'd saved playing with a group was dwindling fast, despite frugal living. The kind of money I needed would make me take work in a strip club if I knew where to apply. I had the body; firm breasts, good thighs and buttocks; a strong healthy girl. I shuddered to think of a future relegated to a shabby and cheapo bedsit, and the rent was due when the phone rang.

'Angela?' asked a furtive voice. 'Are you free? This is me again, Roger. I've been really naughty and need correction. I do deserve a good spanking.' I said I wasn't Angela, hardly able to suppress a giggle that such people existed. But he wasn't put off, asking me if I were available. 'If you're in that line, you know, dominating and punishing,' he added nervously, 'I really do need to be reminded to obey and taught a lesson. Have you Angela's equipment, if you've taken over from her?'

'That's for me to say,' I replied, my voice harsh. I knew a little about types who paid to be punished and humiliated. At school my best friend's father had a collection of girlie mags hidden in his garden shed which we found. Most were of men and big breasted girls sucking and fucking in every way; impressive stuff for two teenage virgins to discover. What excited, or at least intrigued me most, were the few fetish magazines all about bondage and domination, with men and even women tied up to be spanked or whipped, made to crawl and beg like inferiors.

The thought of me, a girl, lording it over a weak male and inflicting punishment on him greatly appealed to me. Janice, my friend with the father who hid his mags, was sympathetic when I said I fancied smacking someone's bare bum. Perhaps she was being kind or was the submissive way inclined, but she volunteered to lie across my lap and let me spank her. I fantasised doing it to her father, spanking him for hiding his magazines, picturing him with a tremendous erection, and having to masturbate to calm down.

'Will you correct me, Mistress?' the weak voice on the phone asked, the excitement in his tone growing. 'I - I've had a wank thinking about the man next door, which makes me wonder if I'm gay. What would my wife think about that, or if she knew I dress up in her clothes when she's out?'

I told him he really was mixed up and ought to have such ideas thrashed out of him. It was horny talk and having an arousing effect on me. I found I enjoyed the feeling of power it gave to talk to such an obsequious character.

I called him scum, dirt, filth, told him his wife deserved to be informed of his low nature, surprising myself at the fury of my tongue-lashing. In return I heard him whimper his pleasure, begging me to correct him that day. He nervously asked what he must call me and I told him Mistress Kay.

'How much did you pay Angela for being corrected, creep?' I shouted. He meekly said fifty pounds, and I doubled it, deciding that's what he desired, an assertive mistress. He was told to pay cash.

He said he always did and would park his car well away from the flat, entering by the back door through the garden as usual. 'You will make it worth my while, won't you, Mistress Kay?' he stuttered. 'I do need a good thrashing for my behaviour. I've been unfaithful to my wife as well.' I was to learn later that he had no wife, but like all submissives wanting to be punished they lied about their misdeeds to get a proper hiding as if deserved.

'Stay on the line while I question you to find out if you're worthy of my time, you wimp,' I ordered. 'So you like a girl thrashing your arse? What else turns on an incompetent loser like you?' I needed to know what to do when he arrived.

His voice was a sob when he said Angela often tied him up and left him while she went out shopping with the money he gave her. If he wasn't tied he was expected to clean the kitchen and toilet, and thrashed really hard if the work was not to her satisfaction.

'She sat on my face and made me lick her if I was not quick to obey her,' he whined. Made to stand naked in a corner, he was smacked over her knee if he dared get an erection. He admitted that if he lost control and ejaculated, Angela whipped him severely. I could feel my cunt moisten and soak my briefs as my arousal grew.

'I'm surprised you could get an erection, let alone come,' I scoffed at the caller. 'Do you fuck your wife, you sad bastard?'

'She has a toy boy lover who fucks her for me,' he said. I told him that would be necessary for he wasn't able. Saying I now expected him to arrive with the money, I added, 'Don't you dare to keep me waiting.' He then said his name was Roy, and I enjoyed a surge of power saying he wouldn't know what had hit him when he was under my sway.

I put on my only lacy bra and tiny briefs to receive him, wishing I had a suspender belt and black stockings to complete the ensemble. If regular clients called, I'd get such things as PVC thigh boots and canes and bondage gear.

But it wasn't only for money I hoped to succeed as a strict mistress. Meting out verbal and physical punishment was already a powerful aphrodisiac. I felt incredible horny! Roy sounded very educated, arriving nervously apologetic and bolstering my courage as I surveyed a little man of about forty in an expensive suit. I demanded the money right away, and once paid I was willing to beat him mercilessly with the rent worry relieved. I led him into the lounge clad only in my overflowing bra and brief panties.

'Lower your eyes, don't you dare ogle my body, you lowlife pervert,' I told him viciously. 'Why are you not undressing?'

'I - I wasn't told to, M-Mistress Kay,' he pleaded. He then began dutifully to strip, and when naked and trembling, trying to cover his erection with his hands, I stood menacingly close with my tits under his nose.

'You disgust me,' I snapped, knocking his hands away so that his prick stood to attention. I gave it a good hard swipe with my hand, then ordered him to turn around and try to touch his toes. Taking the belt from his discarded trousers, I doubled it in my hand and as he whimpered in fear, I struck him.

That first swipe at his bum felt so good that my arm worked overtime belting him. Squealing, he began to hop around the room, so I followed, whacking the pale flesh of his arse into great red weals. 'Down!' I ordered, and he scampered around on all fours as I flogged him. When I allowed him to stand up his quite large and thickish dick looked more rampant than ever. I insulted him for being so out of control, but in truth, highly aroused as I was, I really wanted to suck it, nurse it between my tits or have it buried deep up my pulsating cunt. But I had a job to do, money to earn, and so well that he'd return for more treatment. My torment was as much as his!

To keep him helpless and scared, I marched him through to my bedroom and tied him to the corners of the bed, using old tights from my stocking drawer. I was deciding if a mistress made her slaves fuck her during corrective treatment, and was coming to the conclusion, why not? While helpless before me, I slipped a pillow under his bum while he cowered. By then, desperate for relief, I squatted over his face, aiming for some satisfaction by rubbing my swollen sex lips over his nose and mouth. The first probing of his tongue in my cunt made it too good to order him to stop. To appear to be in command, I ordered him to lick me.

With my cunt throbbing and his lips sucking greedily on my responsive clitty, I leant forward to drape my teats over his rearing stalk, tit-riding it, then forgetting myself and next it was in my mouth. The hardness and heat of the toothsome stalk made it imperative to have it up my cunt. Even then I screamed, 'You'll pay for this, you dirty beast,' as I impaled myself on his prick. Only when we had both come did I resume command, giving him an ear-bashing for daring to fuck me, as if he could have helped what I did.

Once untied, I had him over my knee for a real good slippering of his arse, sending him on his way thankful, full of praise for my methods of correction, and vowing to return. This though I had him squealing and sobbing as I thrashed his already well-bruised behind. From that day on my phone continued to ring with clients eager to pay me large sums to humiliate and beat them, or leave them bound up for hours while I study piano, or prepare a meal for later. I equipped the flat with bondage gear, canes and whips, and got myself kinky leather bras and panties, becoming very professional.

One weakness I have is my inability to resist getting too sexually aroused and satisfying myself on my helplessly bound clients. My fame has spread, and even some women come to be spanked and to be allowed to tongue my cunt. It may be I won't make a famous concert pianist, but I have become a very successful dominatrix.

Kay, Liverpool.

CHAPTER SEVEN
Beat Me, Daddy

My live-in girlfriend and I are very much into bondage and discipline, liking nothing better than a bout of across the knee spanking or a caning in our living room or bedroom. This depends on where we happen to be when she plays me up, or where I send her to await my arrival and some deserved punishment. I know she deliberately provokes me at times, as the devious little minx does love being dominated.

I put a reason for it being she had no dad at home when she was growing up and missed a father's guidance and dominance in the home. She's told me she envied girls whose fathers were very strict. Eileen is seventeen, with a well-developed figure. I'm twenty-eight and she no doubt enjoys the fact that I'm her missing father-figure. She loves me to wear my policeman's uniform. Always I call her 'girl' and she refers to me as 'daddy', which is almost an allusion to the taboo subject of incest. With her frivolous attitude, she is like my daughter.

But at other times she's a rebellious bitch, flirtatious and showing me up before my friends. For being cheeky I know it will be ordained that her panties will be removed as soon as we arrive home. Then, ordered to bend over the whipping chair or my knees, I'll spank or slipper her deliciously girlish bare bottom until red and sore. She'll howl for mercy, beg me to stop, promise she'll never let me down before my friends again.

If she's been really annoying, flirting with boys her own age at the pub or club, or making remarks about my age, on our return home I'm really mad and the wicked girl knows it. She knows too she'll get the leather strap I keep for serious offences, and will be bound by the wrists and strung up to a hook in the spare bedroom ceiling. Balanced on her toes, she'll shriek apologies for her behaviour as I leather her back and buttocks. Then I let her down, blubbering her eyes out because I order her to remain in the spare bedroom, to stay there sleeping alone until I decide she has become deserving of my company, and properly obedient.

This can be fun, for often when I'm asleep in bed she'll come into my room. The next thing I know I'm awake with the duvet drawn aside and Eileen is greedily sucking on my prick to get back in my good books. Or she'll crawl into bed with me and hold a nipple to my lips to nurse me. Again she'll plead that she'll never play me up again. But we both know that's not what we want!

It's not as though we don't have hours of torrid fucking too. In fact, Eileen is the most lustful female I've known of any age, always horny for sex, especially after being disciplined. No doubt a warmed backside turns her on despite the sobs. She'll come to me on her knees after a caning or spanking, showing her striped bottom tearfully. She'll climb up to lie across my lap to plead to have her blistering bum soothed. The cunning little minx then hands me the jar of scented oil she keeps for such a time, tilting up her apple-cheeked arse for anointing. Well, with that sight under my nose, you can guess what develops.

After a sound spanking or caning, or even a good telling-off, she can't wait for me to fuck her. All the time I'm smoothing the fragrant lotion onto her fiery bare buttocks, the teenage temptress is gyrating her sweet tush so that my greasy fingers oil up her quim. Add that to the way she parts her legs and reaches back to separate her bottom cheeks, starts calling on me to fuck her and fuck her and fuck her, and you can see how she's on heat after a whacking. She doesn't want it any other way but in the heat of the moment, both of us mad with lust.

Not for her the gentle touch and leisurely strokes, but having every thick inch of my rampant meat rammed up her barbarously and knocking the breath out of her. I take her to the brink of an orgasm and pull back, leaving her clamouring to be finished, to be made to come, forgetting herself and calling me a beast, a sadist, and ordering me to thrust my prick hard up her cunt again until she has her usual repeated climaxes. This goes on until I'm ready to give in and fuck her until we're both completed sated.

Although a father-figure to her, she wants to be my wife as well.

She's young, and I want to give her the chance to be sure I am what she wants. A treasure, when I come off duty, collapsing in my armchair, she'll kneel to unlace my boots and remove them. A glance at me and a nod in reply gives her permission to unzip my fly and give me a nice suck-off before putting my dinner on the table. But not if I come home to find she's been watching the telly all day and nothing is done. Then it's a spanking on her bare bum, which invariably leads to a good old 'table ender' with Eileen on her back among the plates and sauce bottles.

CP and S&M fun certainly improves our sex lives, but what I caught her doing the other day shook me a little.

I guessed she masturbated, though that was one thing she wouldn't admit. Why are females so secretive about such a normal practice?

I was on police duty, but when passing our house I popped in for a coffee. I heard the definite whack of a leather belt coming from upstairs, and even her crying out. Immediately I thought the masochistic little cow had someone else up there doing my job. Furious, I mounted the stairs to throw out the guy and give her a deserved caning.

But on going into the bedroom I found her naked on the bed with a vibrator up her cunt and whacking her thigh with the belt, getting off on fantasising about being beaten.

For her impatience in not waiting for me to arrive home, I took the leather strap from her and finished the job, tanning her backside. While doing that she jerked about, undulating her body in a mighty come.

She loves such experiences, so I'll continue to give her what she craves. After all, it's what I crave as well. It's between consenting adults what we do, so what business is it of anyone else?

P. C., Norfolk.

CHAPTER EIGHT
Ena's Treat

A bookkeeper, I was retired but still did work for a few favoured old clients. A young lad had taken over a group of small supermarkets when his father died. He asked me to a party he was throwing to celebrate a successful year. I'd worked for his dad for years, and that's why I was invited. He said I'd better leave the wife behind because there'd be porno videos and a stripper. I've no secrets from my wife, Ena, and when I told her about the party, she insisted on going too.

It wasn't to keep an eye on me, but that she really liked the idea of such a night out. She's a handsome forty-two years young, and shapely still, with big firm tits and an arse to match; rounded cheeks that wobble as she walks.

Arriving at the host's large house, we felt (at least I did) somewhat out of place as all the guests were male and looking very young, none of them much more than teenagers.

However, we fitted in, with me well aware that the boys were eyeballing Ena's big tits. She was enjoying the fact as the bitch had deliberately worn a dress with a low neck, revealing a deep cleavage between acres of creamy rounded tit flesh. The lads got unruly with a supply of canned lager, and randy watching a horny video with an S&M theme; bound victims being whipped and fucked. The biggest cheer went up when a mature naked woman was put across another woman's lap to be noisily spanked.

When the stripper arrived she proved to be a skinny slip of a girl, her tits the type described as fried eggs. She flounced about and got naked in a half-hearted fashion, demanded her money for the 'entertainment' and left. Everyone said what a let down as the viewers (including me) had looked forward to seeing a show of voluptuous tit and cunt. My Ena, who'd had a few vodkas and was merry, agreed, and added she could do better herself for nowt.

I didn't think she'd meant it literally, but all the lads now insisted that she prove it, and do better. I had no qualms about my wife revealing her goodies.

On our hols in Spain she obviously enjoyed going topless and I'd seen how men eyed her 40DD breasts. So when she got to her feet and began to undress I knew she'd be good.

At home I'd seen her flouncing around to music, playing a striptease dancer when undressing for bed. Now it seemed her big chance had arrived. She swayed to the music like a pro stripper, peeling off her dress and seductively baring her gorgeous tits as she peeled off her bra, draping it over the head of a lad young enough to be her son. She lowered her panties, turning to waggle her cheeky bottom at the appreciative audience. It was a defiant gesture from a woman saying: 'How'd you like that, boys?' and her bare arse was blatantly asking to be smacked for her nerve.

It was not long in coming, for as she waltzed by alternately jiggling her big boobs and mooning her bum at the lads, I got an urge to grab her. In a moment she was laid across my knee, arse up. Encouraged by our audience, I got in a flurry of hard smacks to redden her cheeks before she escaped my clutches, going back to the centre of the floor, surrounded by young admirers to dance naked for them. I'd learned a couple of things; one, that given the chance my wife was an outrageous exhibitionist, and two, that I'd discovered the thrill of spanking a bare arse and intended to do lots more of it with my wayward missus.

I could tell by the goggling group, and their lustful looks, that Ena had shown an older woman could more than compete for their attention. I heard one admirer say she'd made the paid stripper look like a boy. Present, and more or less the guest of honour, was a black seventeen-year-old star footballer, the target for signing as a professional by top league teams. I thought him an arrogant youth, assured of a well-paid and glamorous future. He threw off his shirt and jeans, socks and trainers, showing a fine athletic body and a rearing prick. It looked iron-hard, as big as the monster dicks we'd seen earlier in the porno video.

Gliding sensually to the music, he closed in on my wife and she clasped him to her naked body, their mouths locking in a torrid kiss. The onlookers, including myself, began shouting 'Fuck her! Go on, fuck the bitch! Shag her useless!'

I heard Ena laughing, urging him to give her that lovely big black cock, but did he think he was up to shagging her useless? Cushions were tossed on the carpet and the boy lowered her on her knees. Knelt before him, she caressed his prick and balls, giving the big rigid stalk a long slow kiss, her cheeks hollowing as she sucked.

Clearly eager to fuck her, much as he was loving the deep-throat she was expertly giving him, he pushed her down among the cushions, positioning himself between her spread thighs. She circled her legs high around his back, locking her ankles, all the while holding his truncheon-like prick and directing it to the moist flaps of her outer sex lips. With a moan of pure pleasure, she thrust her pelvis up as he heaved his flanks, the entire length sliding up her cunt and stretching the entrance wide to accommodate the length and girth.

We were privileged to view a mighty fuck. My full-bodied mature wife mounted and deeply penetrated by a superb specimen of black youth. Both soon became so lost in lust they fucked like animals. I heard Ena screaming out for him to fuck her harder, deeper, that he wasn't to come but keep on fucking her. 'You can come to my house and fuck me any time, son!' I heard her grunt as his prick worked into her. The rapid undulation of her torso told us we were witnessing a woman in the throes of repeated climaxes while still wanting the fucking to continue.

When her black youngster shot his lot, jerking frantically as he rammed into her, he was pulled aside by a lad eager to take his place. As he climaxed another boy was on her and up her cunt while others were on their knees around her. Both nipples were being sucked at the same time, and a cock was being fed to her lips as she twisted her face to suck the better. The next thing was seeing her rolled over to be taken doggie-fashion by the black lad, his cock resurrected in my wife's mouth. It was obvious she enjoyed the position, her bottom gyrating back to a youth's belly as he shafted her on all fours, braying like a donkey in her delirium.

Spunk in her hair, over her tits and cloying her pubic hair, she was helped to a bathroom and had no end of volunteers to soap her tits and between her legs. As many willing hands helped to dry her. All agreed she'd been a great sport, and had made the party. Before dressing she flirted with all the young men, let them feel her big tits and cunt, and suck on her nipples.

Driving her home soon after she said dreamily that what had happened was her fantasy come true; lots of young men fucking and sucking her. Even the spanking I'd given her was something she needed, and I should keep it up and punish her whenever she misbehaved.

I said that her conduct that night warranted a good hiding, and she was going to be disciplined once home. There I ordered her to our bedroom, to strip and bend over the bed, awaiting my arrival. Actually I was glad she'd had a ball sexually; as a good wife, mother, and young grandmother, she deserved a fling. But it was good too ordering her about, pleased with myself as a domineering husband, proud of the way she'd obeyed me.

I found her dutifully bare arse bent over the bed, and doubling the belt from my spare trousers, walloped her good. Her yelps were music to my ears and she begged forgiveness for being a slut.

But that was just the beginning. I worked on auditing the books in a newsagent's out of town a day later, away all day. Arriving home I found my wife dreamy-eyed and in her dressing gown, just out of the bath. Seeing me, she handed me the belt I'd whupped her big arse with, so I knew a confession was forthcoming, to be followed by another disciplining. She admitted the young black footballer had called, as she led the way up the stairs to our bedroom. There she slipped off the dressing gown, and left gloriously naked, she leaned forward across the bed. What did surprised me was that her bottom was already marked crimson from a beating.

'So let's hear it,' I said grimly. Ena said she answered the door, surprised the boy had taken the trouble to find out where we lived. Then all day, with a break for a snack at lunchtime, which she'd prepared while remaining nude, they'd screwed and sucked on the bed she was leaning across before me. Despite his youth he was into kinky stuff.

He'd dragged the dressing table beside the bed so they could watch each other fuck in the mirror. Then using her dressing gown belt, he'd tied her hands to the brass headboard and sat over her, having a tit-ride in her cleavage and making her suck his prick on the upsurge. Each time he got sucked hard again the erection was used to fuck her to more orgasms, leaving her limp.

Finally untied, she was rolled over and he took pleasure in calling her a faithless married bitch for fucking with him and the others at the party. He told her he was punishing her on her husband's behalf, as I wasn't present. Using the back of her hairbrush, he'd spanked her until she was begging for mercy.

It was then, his jism over her tits and belly, she ran a bath while he dressed. Entering the bathroom to relieve himself, as a last dominant gesture the arrogant young sod stood and peed over her breasts.

That was the last we ever saw or heard of him except that booze and women led to his downfall as a footballer, and he ended playing for non-league teams. As for Ena, when I arrive home to find her waiting to hand me the belt, I know it's show time! Do you know of a better welcome?

D. D. S., West Midlands.

CHAPTER NINE
Sucker for Punishment

My first wife was a naturally randy slut, into everything sexy. Well almost everything, she wasn't into domination or stuff like spanking, but was big on fucking, sucking, exhibitionism, lesbian loving, starring in amateur video porn and having affairs all the time. This suited me, having such a sex pot as a partner, as it allowed me to enjoy regular wife-watching sessions during threesome (and more) romps with male and female guests. She gave a great tit-ride and blow-job, knew every possible sex position, and was vocal on the job, demanding deeper penetration. Rose was my idea of a good wife.

I eventually lost her to one of her many lovers; a rich bitch woman who, like her, swung both ways. They departed for the South of France with a strap-on dildo and an assortment of sex toys in case the supply of suitable men occasionally ran out. Me, I was grateful for the years of a highly entertaining marriage she'd provided, so held no grudge, and Rose went with my blessing.

Not expecting to find such another, and not settling for less, I played the field. But finally I met and fell for Ellen, who had good breasts for tit-riding, a nice mouth for sucking dick, a pouting cunt for licking and fucking, and she allowed me all these things necessary to a guy. So I married her.

Things cooled as they do, and our marriage got routine. I was not to know it was my fault, because she didn't tell me what she was in to and what turned her on the most. A teacher, she went back to being a tutor at evening classes. Being a thicko, I didn't think what was going on when she told me her ex-boyfriend also taught in the same school. She'd told me about him before we married, saying he had been possessive and jealous (things I am not), and was strict with her, treating her like a slave and punishing her whenever she displeased him in any way. I thought she'd be glad I wasn't like that.

Then she began returning home later and later, telling me she and her students went to a pub for drinks and more talk. This suited me as by then I had a bit on the side, a neighbour's wife. One night I was in bed when she came home after midnight. Not my style to ask where she'd been, I put on the bedside lamp to chat and enjoy watching her undress, looking forward to fucking her. A well-built busty woman of twenty-eight years, she was well worth admiring. As her bra was removed she stood before me with her breasts thrust out as if inviting inspection. I saw the rounded soft flesh covered in bites, big purplish blotches on her milk-white skin. The big nipples, still thick and erect, looked tender and raw from extreme sucking.

Before I could say anything about this, obviously the work of an avid lover, she turned from me to reveal a well-striped bare arse, each curved buttock bruised by a caning. Somebody sure as hell had walloped her good. Call me an odd-bod, but it amused me to think somebody she was having it off with had stood no nonsense from my wife. Ellen could have her awkward moments, and throw the occasional tantrum, so I actually envied whoever had been annoyed enough to teach her a lesson. I decided too that I'd been too easy on her, rather fancying the idea of spanking or caning her lovely arse for any future misdemeanours. I pictured her across my knee for a sound smacking, and the thought aroused me to get a real stiff boner on.

She slipped into bed naked, cuddling into me with her boobs against my chest, sobbing and begging forgiveness as she admitted she'd been unfaithful. On the nights she'd been late getting home she'd been with the ex-boyfriend. She insisted on confessing all, and with her soft body nestled against mine I was extremely randy and wanted to hear. By sympathising with her and saying we could all make mistakes, be led astray, I hoped to get all the lurid details about him fucking her, forcing her to do all the lewd acts he demanded, with the threat of a caning or spanking to keep her in order.

I was not so naive that I didn't know about domination and discipline being part of many people's sexual practices - probably more than is thought. It struck me that my wife's ex was in to CP and S&M to heighten his arousal. That she had gone back out with the guy also told me that Ellen must have enjoyed the submissive half of their relationship. She should have told me, the silly bitch! Certainly with my previous wife I'd have never believed in domination and correction to pep up our sex, but then we'd never needed it. She didn't have to be strapped to a bed or a chair, or bent over to be spanked or whipped to get us in the mood. But if my new wife did, I was already warming to the prospect. And was it so kinky? Who would say that the wife-watching sessions I'd enjoyed was so normal?

As I'd guessed, she blubbered it was her ex-boyfriend who was knocking her off as well as striping her pretty bum with his hand, a leather strap, or a cane, at the least sign of disobedience. If anybody has to do that, I told her, I considered it *my* job if she was in to caning and spanking. She murmured, 'Yes, darling, you must keep me in order. I can be such a bitch, so unworthy of you. Please fuck me, dear, show you forgive me.' I told her she wasn't going to be let off that easily, and I fucked her really savagely as if in retribution for her being so unfaithful. I warned her I'd thrash her at the least sign of stepping out of line in future. She started to have an explosive orgasm that made her entire body jerk wildly out of control, mouthing lewd orders to fuck her horny cunt and other crudities never usually in her vocabulary, so excited was she.

It was obvious the threat of punishment was an aphrodisiac so powerful to her that she was having multiple climaxes. Isn't that what every man wants his woman to be like? To be randy and ever ready for it, with the added pleasure of spanking her bare botty before, or binding her to a bed to be entirely vulnerable to your evil designs? That is surely a bonus. Once recovered from our fuck, to make sure she understood what I meant, across my knee she went to receive a smacking.

On the very least excuse, I now paddle her pliant cheeks frequently. I also sorted out the ex-boyfriend, making sure he kept his distance in future. It was a civilised discussion when I met him over a drink. After all, he'd put me in the way of a good thing. I was given the cane he'd used on Ellen to keep handy.

I've now got myself a respectful wife, one who even admits she's overspent her housekeeping so that a spanking is in order. I've made videos on my camcorder of disciplining sessions, showing her stripped, bound, blindfolded, while being punished by whip or cane, as well as being fucked. It would do well as a marketable video, but though not for sale, is not just for our eyes alone. We now have a circle of friends into CP and bondage, dominant men and women both, with our submissive slaves waiting upon us, in some cases to be exchanged during visits or club meetings.

It's a way of life that suits Ellen and I admirably. We have even been on arranged CP and S&M visits with like people on the continent, and have an invitation to attend a group meeting in the Los Angeles area of California. When a German couple stayed a week with us, it was the wife who was dominant, keeping her wimp husband well-whipped and made to do all the housework and cooking during their stay. I'm writing this in good faith, hoping it is of use to your survey.

J. & E. S., Cornwall.

CHAPTER TEN
Slave Training

Twenty-two and of West Indian origin, one of my best masturbation fantasies as a girl was of me being sold as a slave to a plantation owner. Both he and his son would fuck me, as did his foreman and the huge black slave who was chosen to give me children. Such a fantasy was a great aid to achieving strong climaxes when self-pleasuring myself. I imagined being whipped for trying to run away and tied to the wheel of a cart when caught, available to anyone who went by and wanted to fuck me.

It was obvious I had a streak in me that found pleasure in being mistreated. As well as the imaginary whippings and bondage, I also found it thrilling fantasising about submitting to others for sex, often by a dozen men who paraded me naked around a pub or club and fucked me while others watched. Other times I'd be performing as a stripper in the club, forced to give a lesbian show to the audience. Sometimes I worried about the regularity with which I had such thoughts, plus the resultant arousal which would lead to me playing with myself until I came off, sometimes more than once a day.

My way-out slave girl scenario seems absurd in the cold light of day. Sometimes I worried about it and told myself I was not really that way; submissive and wanting to be dominated. No doubt the high sex drive I had, which made me want to seek relief with a daily orgasm or two, made me think such wild thoughts. Then I met Jonathan, a young man working in the estate agents where I found employment. The only black girl in the office, the staff went out of their way to be friendly. All but Jonathan.

He wasn't being racist, just standoffish and very strict in overseeing my work. The other girls working with me said he was a sadist and a brute, and as the boss's son had used his influence to take them all out. I got the idea that to secure their jobs, they'd all been fucked by the arrogant slob. They never admitted this, but did say he'd reduced a mature married woman member of staff to tears, sobbing all over the office before the others. I thought only a real bastard could do that, like the people in my fantasy, so I allowed myself to be willingly bullied by the office tyrant.

The mature woman still worked in the office and I saw by the way her eyes followed him, no matter he treated her like dirt, she worshipped him. I even envied her for that. It was accepted that Jonathan had been fucking her. Besotted with her toy boy, she was distraught at the cruel way he'd dumped her after getting all he wanted. She was plump, nice looking, and it was said he'd taken up with her after being bet he couldn't fuck her on a date. Another fact the office girls were delighted to tell me, was that he'd take the woman out to empty houses on sale during office hours. It was to take instant photos of the properties to put in sales brochures, but pictures taken of the lady in lewd postures when in the nude had been boastfully shown around to a favoured few male colleagues who'd said they'd seen them.

Evidently, from the evidence of the instant pictures, the rat had not only fucked the besotted older woman, but had bound her with cords to beds or chairs, there to undergo perverted sexual practices and sado-masochistic rites. This included correction in the form of bottom smacking across his knee, and severe canings and whippings with a riding crop. Some pics had featured her sucking his prick or taking it up between her ample titties. It was also said he'd had anal sex with her, the naughty back passage route. But however he'd treated her, it was obvious to me she'd have gone back and done whatever he asked if invited. And I understood how she felt, being that way myself.

I looked at him in a new light and he took the hint. I had fallen for him, as there was an aura of cruelty and arrogance about his manner. Alone with him in the rest room making coffee, he took my wrists and pinned me against the wall. Unable to move, he kissed me with his tongue down my throat. Next time he ordered me to make coffee, he followed. Pinned to the wall again, he put his big erect cock to my crotch and jerked it against my mound, and I was 'dry-fucked' until I became aroused and he jeered at me as I groaned and shook helplessly in a strong climax. Sometimes in the office he'd squeeze my wrist, but I dared not cry out in pain. He'd bend, with others working close, to whisper how he'd fuck me. He enjoyed hurting me, but suspected that I didn't mind.

One night I was ordered to remain late as he lectured me on what he claimed was sloppy work. Rather than be reported to his father, I nervously agreed he could punish me by whacking my black bottom with a wooden ruler. He allowed me to keep on my tiny briefs as I bent across his desk for six (and more) of the best. They were so flimsy my bum was as good as bare. The spanks really stung and I cried, which pleased him, the beast.

Invited out for a meal with him soon after, I met a group of his friends. A woman told me they all knew Jonathan was training me to be his slave. It was her husband who said I should visit their house, as they'd warn me what to expect if I took up with Jonathan.

I went next evening and was shown into a room in a large Georgian house. It was fitted out for bondage and correction practices, so I knew my hosts were into CP and S&M. Jonathan was there, so I also knew I'd fallen into a trap, along with others present to be made into slave material, both male and female. There were obviously effeminate naked boys and maidenly girls waiting on their masters and mistresses. The slaves served drinks and snacks. Others were fettered in old-fashioned stocks or fastened to the wall by wrist and ankle manacles. The room had permanent fixtures for trussing up victims, and I soon realised they were going to be put to use in my case.

Jonathan and another man took hold of me, and although I'd often fantasised such a scene, I screamed out loud in protest and struggled. Forced to my knees, I was brought before a masked man who all addressed as Master. He said I was to undergo a trial to be made a good slave. I'd allowed Jonathan to spank my bottom in the office, let him kiss and rub against me, which apparently proved I was good slave material. Stripped, tied and gagged, suspended from a ring in the ceiling with my toes barely touching the floor, my bare breasts, cunt mound and buttocks were flicked with the tails of a whip until I had confessed all my past sexual sins, which included masturbating to fantasies of being enslaved.

Released, swearing I'd strive hard to be a good and obedient slave, I was made to remain on all fours, and cut with a riding crop as I was made to crawl into another room like a whipped dog. It was evident as I scuttled around on my hands and knees, with anyone I passed at liberty to cane or whip my bare buttocks, that training sessions were in progress. The wife of our host was busy tutoring a beautiful girl in female sex by fucking her with a big strap-on dildo. On a similar couch opposite, a glamorously made-up she-male with superb silicone boobs but still well-hung in the dick department, was ordering a pretty girl to suck on 'her' rampant stalk before, I had no doubt, using that same prick on the girl's sweet hole.

Others, of both sexes, were having buzzing vibrators worked into them, just as I was by Jonathan while still on all fours. He said he was loosening me up before fucking me doggie-fashion.

An effeminate white youth got on his knees in front of his dominant black boyfriend. He knelt to lick and suck on his master's oversized prick. Soon that monstrous ebony cock would be going somewhere else other than down the girlish lad's throat, I suspected; no doubt between his pale arse cheeks. As I hazily took in the whole scene around me, following a deep fucking from the rear by Jonathan that gave me a tremendous orgasm, I was lifted to my feet. I was told I'd done well and was taken to shower with him.

There would be other more severe tests, I was warned. Meanwhile I was a man's slave and sexual plaything. I was ordered to keep him happy, which meant whippings and canings if I didn't. Called to his office, I knew I'd be across his knee or the desk for a hard spanking.

We sleep together when he tells me to and I sometimes share him at night with another girl, or even the mature married woman from the office. He spanks us both when he makes us put on a lesbian show and claims we don't put our whole energies into it. It pleases him to sit up in bed with two females crying because he's spanked our bums like naughty girls.

I know when he tires of me I'll be dumped. But I have my own plans. I'll get a slave of my own, black, white, male or female. I'll enjoy the change, being dominant, for I've been taught well and know I'll enjoy what being in command entails. I am building up equipment for that day: bondage gear, canes and an assortment of whips, vibrators and a good strap-on imitation dick of solid latex, just like the real thing. It's black too, to go with my colour! To make up for the spankings and indignities I'm enduring from Jonathan, someone is really in for it when I have a slave of my own. Any volunteers for the post?

Aimee, Kensington.

CHAPTER ELEVEN
Surprised Straying Wife

Sarah never had a clue, thinking as usual that the coast was clear and I was far away. A cleverly worded note, printed out on a computer, similar to the letter I'd found from the lover she'd been secretly meeting, brought her home early from work. I had to wonder what excuses she was giving her boss. Suspecting she was having it off on the side, worse still I'd learned she was using our home for the romps. In our marital bed, the deceitful bitch!

After employing a female private detective to investigate, and learning it was always at our house she entertained the guy, the trap was set. This time Sarah was going to find herself with a different kind of playmate than the one she was expecting. I'd let it be known I'd be off on firm's business all day, in a town miles away. Confident of my absence and the genuineness of her lover boy's letter, she came home on cue and went up to our bedroom, as I'd gambled on happening.

I'd been told she left the front door unlocked so that the married guy she was screwing could enter and join her. In the bedroom was a spacious built-in cupboard where I'd earlier concealed myself, leaving the door open a mere inch but wide enough for me to see all I needed. From my hiding place I watched amazed as she drew open the bottom drawer of her dressing table, a space I thought she used to keep towels and linen. I'd never looked in there or thought I had reason to.

But from that drawer she brought out stuff I recognised as items of correction and domination, laying them out on the bed. I had not a clue such gear as cords, handcuffs, sex toys and rubber underwear existed in our house. I was as ignorant too that Sarah was into CP and S&M sex. I burned with resentment watching her strip off to prepare for her lover, a bitch who rationed my sex to a weekend fuck as if doing me a favour. She stood nude admiring her pointy tits and tufty quim before stepping into the black rubber panties with the crotch cut away to reveal her pouty cunt with its split lips.

Next she fitted on the rubber bra, tight enough to enhance the cleavage and force up her tits, the taut nipples protruding through holes designed for just that. The act of preparing for her lover to arrive had made her randy, judging by the way her nipples peaked. I stood in the closet, still coming to terms that my bitch of an unfaithful wife was into specialist sex, and the very kind I'd fantasised having with her but hadn't dared mention.

Before the dressing table mirror one hand tweaked and pulled her nipples while the other hand stroked up and down over the lips of her cunt. She threw back her head and laughed delightedly at her image. I was furious; it was as if she were laughing at me, the dumb bastard who didn't know what his wife was up to. Yet despite my anger, the thought that she'd prepared herself for another man and seeing her playing with herself in that kinky outfit, gave me the biggest erection I'd ever known.

31

She sat in the chair we kept in the bedroom and continued to play with herself, now using a buzzing vibrator picked up from the items laid out on the bed. Intent on titillating her cunt, she went into shock as I stepped out before her. Frightened and blubbing tears, she asked what was I doing there, claiming that I'd caught her in her masturbation ritual. I called her a lying whore and an unfaithful slut who would pay for two-timing me.

Wasting no time, as she was dazed, I used the handy cords and straps to tie her firmly to the chair, lashing her wrists behind the tall back and her ankles to the front legs. Her sobbing was for real, but more in humiliation and anger at being found out. In answer to her demand that I release her, I enjoyed saying she was in no position to demand anything. It was not my usual way of talking to her. I'd always been easygoing, so this alarmed her, as I added I'd decide what to do with her.

I taunted her that as it was evident she went in for bondage and correction, being tied up for a whipping or caning, she didn't really ought to mind what I intended. She became genuinely concerned, whining that her lover only spanked her in token fun punishment, begging abjectly that I didn't hurt her, promising to be a good wife in future and always be obedient to my wishes. 'You bet your sweet arse you will, bitch,' I positively revelled in telling her forcefully.

Laid out on the bed were such goodies as a springy cane, a nine-tailed whip, and the sex toys and bondage gear I've already mentioned. What surprised me was the thickness and size of the big vibrators and dildos, showing me what a cock-greedy slut my Sarah really was. I spotted a pair of small white plastic balls, the two spheres joined by a thin chain a mere inch or so long. These I knew were advertised in magazines as Japanese Love Balls, and when popped into a female were sure to arouse.

Another matching pair that intrigued me was nipple clips with weights attached. As I wickedly lifted these items and gave Sarah a lewd grin, she blubbered that I was being mean and cruel, that it wasn't like me. 'It fucking is now, you dirty cow,' I said, puffed up with the power dominating gives. I clipped the nipple clamps on and she moaned that they hurt, and the weights added to the pain in her sensitive boobs. She squirmed, now promising me anything; that she would suck me off, which she knew I liked, or whatever I wanted to do.

But she wasn't getting off so lightly. I chose a vibrator that had batteries, switching it on to play the rotating head up and down the moist lips of her quim. Although she protested, I could sense she was holding in an urge to push against it and have the plastic cylinder enter her cunt. Then she squirmed in the chair, her low moans telling me that she was now too aroused to resist telling me to fuck her. Much as I wanted to, I casually refused, saying she would stay tied up until I decided when to release her. Again she offered to suck me off if I'd release her.

It was getting quite dark so I drew the curtains. As an afterthought, just for the hell of it to see how she would react to them, I pushed the love balls far up her cunt channel, the inside so sodden that they went in easily. As I switched off the light and went to leave the bedroom, she begged me not to leave her in the dark, tied up and with those balls up her twat. It was another move I enjoyed in my quest to dominate her.

I took a stroll to my local pub and ordered my usual lager and a bar snack of bacon rolls. People I knew nodded and we had the usual small talk. One woman there with her husband asked me how Sarah was keeping, and why she wasn't with me. I said my wife was unable to come, being tied up at home. It amused me no end to think of the disloyal bitch left tied up in the pitch dark and wondering when I'd return. In time I went back, deciding whether to use the cane or whip to teach her a lesson for deceiving me.

As I released her she got on the bed face down, as ordered and without argument. Wary of the new me, she'd decided I was not to be messed with any more. I raised her bottom up, the better to cane, by placing a pillow beneath her crotch. Each strike was a real pleasure to deliver, as were her yelps and pleading to be spared. With the love balls still inserted, each writhe of her arse as I caned her was accompanied by an orgasm until I stopped and she lay limp and gasping. Turning over to face me, she begged me to pull the balls from her and put my prick in instead.

As she'd asked so humbly, I fucked her good. Begging my forgiveness later, she said I should have been more domineering with her. It had meant her having an affair for us to find out what it took to make our marriage more lively and fun. Now she knows her place and the boyfriend is history. I make regular use of the equipment he bought to discipline my wife, ensuring that she won't stray again. I've even added one or two items to the collection of corrective and bondage gear. I'm always finding a reason to use it.

Douglas, Tyneside.

CHAPTER TWELVE
What the Master Wants

No doubt it's the submissive nature I have, always desiring my will to be totally overcome by a dominant man. This in turn results in heightening my sexual arousal to becoming wanton lust. Caned when at school by the strict nuns who taught me, the sting in my bottom warmed me right through to my tight little hairless virgin cunny. I loved the delicious throb it started in my pussy and even brought on my first orgasms. Needless to say I was often deliberately naughty and made to bend over for caning. That act of submission thrilled me too.

It was supposedly punishment to be dreaded by us girls, but I knew what I liked and what turned me on. Acting mild and passive, I crave things seemingly done against my will. I only make out it's against my will because that increases the pleasure of what's being done to me as punishment. Even now I protest and squeal whether being spanked or fucked. But the first men in my life were weaklings, kind and considerate types who left me cold, not a bit of rough among them.

I always resisted their fumbling advances, hoping they would lose control and ravage me. Although I'd struggle, it wouldn't have been rape for I'd have welcomed it, being apparently forced. But pleading 'no' to them when I meant 'yes' always stopped them, the wimps. My dream was for a he-man, a macho stud who knew how to lay down the law with a girl. One who'd pull down my panties and put me across his knee to spank my bare bottom if I gave him any cause. Then, without asking, fuck me while put on my elbows and knees on the carpet.

When I met Mike I knew he had a bad reputation for treating his women as inferior beings. On our first date I said something he considered was answering him back. Sitting in the driving seat of his car with me beside him, he hauled me unceremoniously across his lap. Skirt lifted, he ripped off my flimsy briefs before smacking my bottom painfully hard. Still smarting, I was then made to sit up over him facing his chest while his big hard prick was embedded up my cunt.

He had my tits out, chewing on my nipples in turn while I had that thick stalk of rampant flesh up me. Of course I came, and he did also without caring, drenching my innards with his hot sperm, making me glad I'd gone on the pill. Then after he'd given my bottom such a spanking and my cunt such a fucking, he made me lick his prick clean before returning it to his pants. Not a word of thanks did he give, no indication that I was a nice tight fuck or anything. What a lout.

'You - you fucked me,' I said. 'Who gave you permission?'

'I don't need any with sluts like you,' he laughed, adding that from the gyrations of my arse and the way I'd come, he knew I'd loved every inch of it. Embedded in me as he was, I'd actually climaxed several times, my first multiple come. No doubt the spanking had made me randier too. He guessed that, saying I was a proper horny bitch, no doubt always on heat and a girl who hawked her cunt around to any who'd fuck it.

I found being called such names a turn on, again something to do with me finding pleasure in being humiliated, and treated like a tart. I found my knickers on the floor of the car, too ripped to be worn again. He said I was not to wear any knickers or a bra when we went out.

'Who says I'd go out with you?' I dared say. In reply he seized my hair, kissing my mouth aggressively. He then threatened me, warning, 'When I whistle, you'll come running, or else. As long as I want you, you're my whore, get it?' Then, as if to show he meant all he said and had power over me, he actually pushed me out of his car and drove off.

I was left miles from home on a cold dark night. My feeling was of both fear and excitement that he could be so indifferent to my fate, yet got a thrill, having a sneaking admiration for him being so masterful. Waiting hopefully for him to return, I grew cold and aware he had no intention of coming back for me, realising he hadn't been kidding when he said he was off to meet another woman. Knocking on a nearby door I had to humble myself, admitting my boyfriend had dumped me and could I please phone for a taxi?

That in itself was cringe-making enough, especially when the woman of the house showed no sympathy for my plight. But by then I knew being humiliated, used and abused, was what turned on my kind of masochist. Much to his sour wife's annoyance, who'd have pushed an obvious floozy like me back out into the dark night, her old husband offered to drive me home. Once along the road from his house, he stopped the car. 'If you've missed out on a fuck, I'd be glad to fill in for your boyfriend,' said the lecherous old sod.

I was tempted. No doubt he never got a ride with his miserable bitch of a wife, and I thought it a chance to get back at her for the way she'd been so contemptuous of me. But fearful of it being known I was unfaithful to Mike, I didn't let him fuck me. For his cheek in tapping me up, I told him he could lick me out if he was into sucking pussy. 'My favourite eating place,' he assured me. It was wicked of me, knowing he'd be cleaning out Mike's jism. I had no knickers on, of course, lolling back in my seat with wide parted thighs. Eagerly, he buried his face into my crotch, his busy wet tongue reaming out every nook and cranny of my twat. He mumbled that I had the juiciest tasty cunt he'd ever licked, and he certainly had the tongue for it, making me come strongly.

Agreeing to let an elderly stranger eat my pussy was yet another manifestation of my submissive nature, degrading myself by being so available, deserving of punishment. When the cunt-licker dropped me off near my flat, I was thrilled to see Mike's car parked nearby. That feeling changed to fear when he came over to drag me out from beside the old chap. While gripping me by the hair, he scared the man by demanding what was he doing with his slut? The car roared away and I was left to face Mike's wrath alone; apprehensive, but my tummy churning with arousal.

Marched indoors into my flat, he ordered me to strip naked. Taking off his belt and gripping it tightly, he then whipped me around the room until my bottom stung and I was pleading for mercy. This kind of treatment, plus being used sexually purely to satisfy his own selfish ends, is what every slave craves if loyal to her master.

When not needed by him, and lonely weeks would go by without a call, I engaged in fabulous masturbation imagining being chained and whipped, my submission fantasy stronger for his actually doing such things to me. At times, risking his anger, I'd call him, begging to be beaten, fucked, anything, as long as he still regarded me as his property, his slave.

He was expert at keeping me down, worthless and degraded, a bittersweet sensation I both loved and hated. When introducing me to a circle of his male friends in a bar, he told them I was a dirty bitch who loved sucking cock. I cringed as the men grinned and said they'd be glad to let me eat their dicks. One even took out his and said degradingly, 'Chew on this, love.' I looked at Mike for help, but he said nothing, allowing his mates to make crude remarks. He knew that shaming though it was for me, I felt a stirring in my cunt, an excited throb, and my panties becoming sodden with the juices of arousal.

With Mike's approval I was marched out to the pub's car park and made to go on my knees with the men lining up in the dark to stand before me. One by one they came on making my jaw ache until it seemed I'd sucked on endless stiff cocks and been made to gulp down mouthfuls of thick glut. Thinking back on my convent school training, doing what would have been considered 'dirty' and a 'mortal sin' only makes me more erotically aroused by what I'm made to do. Without shame, I asked to be fucked, by any one of the men I sucked. Three of them had me up against a car.

I obey Mike implicitly now, doing what is ordered or paying the price. This can be a spanking or caning if I complain about being offered to others for sex. I want to be faithful to him. I'm sure he accepts money for my services, which thrills me too, thinking he's my pimp and I'm his prostitute. Once walking in the park we passed three elderly men sitting on a bench. One who knew Mike remarked what a pretty girl he had. On Mike's order I was made to open my coat and lift my skirt. With no panties on, as his instructions, I showed all I have. Mike told the delighted old men to feel me, and he laughed as I was shamed.

At a party he claimed I was a professional stripper, and I was ordered to perform in the centre of the room. Once naked, he told me to sit on the men's knees and rub my breasts in their faces. My nipples were sucked raw, my cunt fingered, and it ended with the men clamouring to screw me. The fucking and sucking, no doubt, sometimes with two men at me at both ends, made me respond and have visible climaxes. For this exhibition, Mike thrashed me later for being a shameless whore. I was then strapped to my bed by my wrists and ankles while he went out to spend the night with another woman.

I ask for what I get, and must like it. More than one video has been filmed of me when I'm having sex with others or being 'corrected' by my master; across his knee for a spanking, caning, or being thrashed with my own slipper. Mike tells all his friends that I'm his slave by my own choice, when they ask how can I stay with him. I answer it's because I will do whatever he asks and be faithful, happily kept in my place by his frequent use of the cane or whip, and my need for his super lovemaking.

Jean, Sheffield.

CHAPTER THIRTEEN
Old Time Romping

Don't think it's only in this age of sexual enlightenment and freedom that way-out sex has been practised. No doubt since the dawn of time kinky men and women have done their thing, with CP and S&M introduced to enliven many a sensual session. Do look again at that stuffy neighbour and her ancient husband. Who knows what they once did behind closed doors? I was the kind to knock them as old fogies, but not any more after a recent discovery.

My wife's dear old gentle Aunt Jenny had passed away. As the nearest relative to the eighty-something spinster lady, Marje, my other half, inherited her aunt's house and a little money. We had to see to the funeral arrangements and insurance claims. It was decided to sell the house, so we had to clear it. The local Sally Army was to get the furniture. While I was up in the dusty attic sorting out stuff to take to the council refuse dump, I came across a shoebox filled with old photographs.

They were still quite perfect black and white prints of all shapes, postcard size and even enlargements. All evidently taken before World War Two, they showed a very pretty buxom Aunt Jenny as a girl with her equally attractive sister, Kath. Snapped at a seaside resort recognisable as Scarborough, they posed eating ice cream, riding on donkeys, and other holiday snaps. Even in the bathing costumes of that era (hardly bikinis!) one could see that the wholesome-looking sisters were superbly built in the tit region and curvaceous everywhere else - two real beauties.

Pictured with Jenny in a few shots was her fiancé Len, an amateur photographer of some skill. He was later to become a Jap prisoner-of-war and never made it back to Jenny, poor bastard. She never married and lived quietly with her sister. We thought of her as a nice old thing, hardly a sex-pot or a very horny or sexually adventurous lass.

Certainly she'd been a looker, as the old pictures showed. It was with interest that I glanced through the collection, then at the bottom of the box, found a sealed envelope. Intrigued as to why it had been stuck shut, I opened it and got quite a shock; a pleasant one, I must add. Still mainly in black and white, although a few had been flesh-tinted, all crisp and professionally taken as well as enlarged, I saw a young and nubile Jenny smiling back at me wickedly. Naked as a jay bird, starkers, gloriously in the bare buff, she would have graced a *Playboy* centrefold.

Her perfect breasts were like large melons, firmly rounded with big nipples enhancing the marble spheres. Curvy hips, and a forest of hair on the prominent mound between her thighs, showed a most fuckable wench. With fiancé Len as her secret snapper, no doubt he had dipped his wick often with the mischievous young model. In fact, I was to find that lucky Len the lensman had twice the fun. In the next picture I examined, Jenny and her beautifully built sister were both posing in the nude.

Another pic had the girls with their backs to the cameraman, both smiling impishly over their shoulders while sticking out two amply rounded lovely bare bottoms.

In others the subject became erotically pornographic. Jenny was bending over a chair being shafted from the rear by a lad I took to be Len, wearing nothing but his socks, and I presume using a time exposure for the shots. He'd need the same in the two following, which were of Jenny in the act of gobbling his dick, or someone's dick! It was in close-up and the greedy girl's cheeks were drawn in as she sucked on a mouthful of hot cock. Then I wondered if sister Kath had taken over as snapper when Len was in action.

Jenny and her sister were seen in quite a few naughty and surprising poses after that. The first to tickle me was of both girls bound hand and foot by cords and lying naked on the floor, side by side. It seemed a spot of early bondage fun was taking place. There were others in the same theme, the two girls with their gorgeous tits bound up, or blindfolded and gagged as tied by the wrists and ankles to upright wooden chairs.

Each picture told a story of three uninhibited young people daring to do what came naturally without shame or guilt. Randy buggers they were too, hence one or two shots of the girls laid back with legs wide to show off their hairy minges, and even with both lasses masturbating, with fingers or carrots or bananas. It seemed, although engaged to the lusty Len, Jenny didn't mind her sister sharing his sizeable dong. On her knees with hands bound behind her back in a classic S&M pose, Jenny had long inches of Len's cock in her mouth. A similar pic showed Jenny tied up the same way, as if being forced to take in the stiff stalk being pressed to her lips.

The sisters were also pictured while laid across Len's lap, magnificent bare buttocks up as he simulated spanking their bad little bums, although it seemed the cheeks were bruised. In all these rude poses it was evident how the girls enjoyed being naughty, and what fun they were having. Smiling at the camera in every case, the sensuous nature of this pair of minxes was plain to see.

Len's life may have ended early in some tropical Japanese prison hell, but I held in my hands evidence that he'd enjoyed precious moments that few of us are privileged to have. That was two pretty sisters, both willing to be his models in his kinky photographic shoots.

I have no doubt he fucked them both. The pictures were masterpieces that would enhance the glossy pages of any modern magazine featuring bondage and discipline subjects. One particular shot of the two naked girls strung up by the wrists to hooks in the ceiling of a barn or shed, awaiting a flogging, was a work of art. The game-for-anything sisters were stretched on tiptoe, with their arms so raised it lifted up their magnificent boobs.

I did say the pictures *were* masterpieces, for my wife considered they were shocking and destroyed the sexy ones. And this after me pleading to save them, the puritanical bitch. She needed to be bound and have her arse spanked for that sacrilegious act of vandalism, for she hasn't the uninhibited nature or the sexy imagination of her feisty maiden aunt. Bad luck for me, her husband!

Graime, Sunderland.

CHAPTER FOURTEEN
Across the Desk

My marriage to Vernon was good, of its kind, but never very exciting or fulfilling. Obsessed with his work and cricket, he became content with his lot and uncaring of mine. I began to feel frustrated. Left for weeks without sex, I fantasised and found what excited me most was imagining being forced to do another's bidding, dominated sexually and in other menial ways. Thus, while I masturbated, always in the bath, I pictured women as well as men doing kinky things to me which made me blush with shame, as well as become incredibly aroused and climax violently.

My two daughters were teenagers and at school all day, so I went back to work as a private secretary, and soon advanced to the position of personal assistant. My boss was a very attractive woman called Karen, and we became friends. Some years older than I, she was smart, confident, and had a good figure. We went out for drinks or a meal at times, always to places that were meeting spots for females. I suspected that gay girls and lesbian women congregated there, but Karen was married so I thought she took me where it was nice to visit for drinks and meals.

I found myself drawn to her, feeling for Karen differently than I'd felt for any woman friend. Apart from my fantasies, I'd had no sexual feelings for women, yet I was strangely attracted and falling under her spell. The warm glow I had on seeing her was the same as being in love. My heart pounded when she entered the office. With her breasts almost touching mine and her sweet breath on my face, I longed to take her in my arms and tell her that I loved her. I was confused, but never expected anything sexual to come of it. We were both married women, so I dismissed the idea completely.

Karen had never made a sexual advance on me, but I must have yearned for it, for one night I had a vivid dream that we were having sex. She entered the office, locked the door, and ordered me to strip naked before her. She asked why did I think she'd taken me to gay bars? Why hadn't I reacted, because she knew I wanted her? For being so slow to recognise we could be lovers, she forced me across her desk, smacking my bare bottom hard with a plastic ruler until I cried and agreed to do as she wished. As I remained bent over, she first fingered my sex and then knelt before me to lave it with her tongue. She undressed and I was made to suck her breasts and sex, then we rubbed ourselves hard together, pubic bone to pubic bone. Making love in the dream, I awoke shaking in the midst of a powerful orgasm, waking my husband.

Then, a few days later, something happened which I could hardly believe. After my dream I had to force my eyes off Karen when in the office, which she noticed. Rising from her desk she drew me to my feet and held me, and kissed me lightly. Then the kiss became torrid between us, wet mouths open and our tongues meeting in passion. Held close, she whispered she had longed to do that, and I said the same. Her lovely breasts crushed against mine, and I returned her kiss more ardently than I ever had with any man. 'Make love to me, Karen,' I said. 'Fuck me...'

She moved me until my back was against a wall, continuing to kiss me with her tongue in my mouth while rubbing her pubes against mine in a grinding motion. I tilted my hips to get the full pressure of hers. Unbelievably aroused, I began to shake violently as I swiftly climaxed, my first by another woman. As if in a continuation of the erotic dream I'd had, the spasms of my orgasm still pulsing in my sex, I begged her to beat me. 'Punish me for having such wicked thoughts about you, my darling,' I was mumbling, besotted with her. My whole mind and body in a turmoil, I went to my desk as in the dream and leaned across it, bottom raised.

'Is it guilt you feel, Lynda?' I heard her say softly. 'Do you want me to beat it out of you?'

Later I learned she thought I felt guilt about betraying my husband, but the guilt I felt was for behaving so lewdly and having sex with one of my own kind - a woman. She asked again if I wanted to be beaten, which now I know was because as a dominant person she liked inflicting pain. To answer her, I drew my dress up over my stocking tops, saying I needed to be taught a lesson by her. Crossing to the door, she locked it and returned to me. Rolling my dress further up over my waist, she drew down my briefs over the cheeks of my buttocks and lowered them to my ankles.

'Such a sweet bottom, Lynda,' she said as I lay across the desk, shivering in anticipation of a spanking. I knew I really wanted to be beaten.

'Your lovely bottom deserves kisses as well as discipline,' she told me. 'It shall have both now that we are at last lovers.' Then, just as in the dream, and I suppose because it was the handiest and most suitable object, she picked up the plastic ruler on my desk and began to spank my bum with it.

If I'd imagined a few light playful smacks, I couldn't have been more wrong. Karen set to with a will, the ruler thwacking noisily across both cheeks and making me howl in pain as my poor bottom smarted. I was sternly ordered to make less noise or it would get worse, so clenching my buttocks and gritting my teeth, I tried to bear the pain. It continued long after I wanted it to, the pain acute, but Karen was now obsessed with punishing me, enjoying inflicting more stripes to my reddened cheeks. She got carried away, crying out that she'd see I suffered for making her fall in love with me. I was a slut, a scheming bitch, she told me, that I'd get regular thrashings to keep me loyal.

Bottom cheeks burning and in a torrent of tears, I fell sobbing into her arms when the spanking ended, swearing undying love to one of my own sex. I'm sure now the punishment came to an abrupt end only because the plastic ruler snapped in half as she whacked me so furiously. I was warned that such thrashings would be regular if I displeased her, then I was sharply ordered to draw up my briefs and get back to work. She was once again my boss and standing no nonsense, even if we were now lovers. I worshipped her for such dominance over me.

I sensed she had beaten and dominated submissive women before me. Later, having dinner at home with my husband and two daughters, I wondered how they'd react if they knew I'd been made to come having sex with another woman. And that I'd also been bent across my desk and had my bare bottom severely spanked, had me excited merely thinking about it. I was so aroused I later masturbated while in the bath, reliving the session with Karen, the memory so vivid I came over and over on my hand.

Sex with her became a several times a week ritual as the year progressed.

Called across to her desk at times, I'd find her lolling back in her chair. Devoid of panties and showing off her exceedingly hairy vagina, I'd be ordered to tongue and suck it to bring her to a strong climax. If in a mood, she'd cane me while stretched over her desk. At other times while bent before her with bared bottom, she would prise apart my cheeks to make me come strongly with her probing tongue. The sixty-nine position for us to lick each other simultaneously was another innovation to make use of behind the locked door of our office. Who needs husbands? she'd joke to me when we lay exhausted by multiple orgasms.

Avidly sucking and tonguing to bring each other to repeated climaxes was not all we did. On business trips together we shared a bed. At such times a 'must' to be packed in her suitcase was a big and very realistic strap-on vibrating dildo. With this I was introduced to woman-to-woman simulated fucking. At times I got to be the 'male' and fucked Karen. She was certainly not just a 'man-on-top' lover, knowing positions my husband never dreamed of.

The regular correction of being spanked across her knee, or bent over for a caning or strapping with a belt, was a ritual that continued along with our sexual sessions until her husband retired and Karen went with him to live in their second home in Spain. I only have memories now. I long to meet another woman who would dominate me as well as being my lover. So far no luck in a chance meeting, so I'm going to advertise for one. I've tried a strict woman mistress and liked it. I hope I find another Karen.

Lynda M., Glasgow.

CHAPTER FIFTEEN
Not So Innocent

I was past the age to learn new things about heightening sexual stimulation, I thought. But to my immense surprise and delight a girl in her teens showed me how naïve I was, teaching an old dog new tricks about sexy fun and games, including bondage and correction. We'd met through my relationship with her mother. Shirley knew I was bonking her mum. She had her own flat, but visited her mum one day when we were washing up the dinner dishes. At least, it had started out as washing dishes.

When Shirley walked in I had her mother bending over the sink, her rubber gloves gripping the taps to steady herself. I'd rucked up her dress under her armpits and drawn her knickers off. Then I was shafting her strenuously, up on tiptoe to give her all the cock I could, both of us grunting and gasping in pleasure as my rampant dick ploughed the juicy furrow of her grasping cunt. It had been that best kind of fuck; unexpected. Standing behind her at the sink with the tea towel, I'd playfully felt up her pliant bum cheeks. Carrying on washing the plates, she waggled her bottom back, laughing as she said she'd give me two hours to stop touching her up. Encouraged, I went in under her dress to feel and stroke the prominent bulge at the crotch of her panties, feeling it hot, sticky and moist.

With my prick solidly rising to the challenge, it was only natural to ease down her drenched briefs and let her step out of them. Directing my knob to her cunt lips, one thrust and I was deep up her tight receptive love tunnel like a hot knife through butter. She gurgled her pleasure and leaned further forward over the sink, dishes forgotten. Parting her feet wide, tilting up her apple-smooth arse, ensured the very deepest penetration of my six inches of hot stiff cock.

Fully engrossed in such enjoyable carnal capers, we did not notice we had a spectator until hearing giggling from the direction of the kitchen door. Turning our heads together, we both saw young Shirl observing our torrid shagging. Too late was the cry, for both her mum and I were at the point of no return. I grunted and buckled at the knees as I shot a salvo of spunk way up her farthest internal recess. Shirl's mum croaked and whinnied as she shook bodily in a series of wild convulsions.

Adjusting our clothes, we shamefacedly said we thought we were alone. Shirley laughed and said she hoped her mum was on the pill. From where she stood it looked like we were trying to make her a brother or sister. Should have brought my camcorder, said the minx, it would have been a classic.

However, her mother broke up with me soon after that. Her ex-husband appeared back on the scene and Marion decided to give their failed marriage another chance. He was a useless bum, but I think she only felt sorry for him. I was sorry to lose such a horny woman, and had intended to marry her myself.

Anyway, I was at home in my bungalow some time later when young Shirley called. Invited in, right away she told me I'd been an idiot to give up her mother without a fight. The shifty guy, Shirley's stepfather, was borrowing money off her mum, and had tried feeling up Shirley as well as her younger sister.

'He's on his way out, mum's wising up to him, you want to get in there if you want to win her back,' I was warned. Shirley then blamed me for not being assertive with her mum. 'You've got to put your foot down, be dominant, show her who's boss,' said the confident teenager. 'If necessary, spank her bum to keep her in line. She needs a strong man to rule her. And to fuck her,' the little minx laughed, 'for you know how my mother likes taking the cock, and your big hard one especially.'

I told her now she was getting personal, but she just laughed and sat down on my lap with her arms around my neck.

'Don't say you're not missing your regular nookie with her?' Shirley teased. 'Until you get back with her, you can have it off with me, if you like. After all, she wouldn't want you turning to another woman, would she?'

I laughed at her cheek, asking if she wasn't another woman, what was she?

'You know very well what I mean,' she answered seriously. 'This would be keeping it in the family.'

I tried to slide her off my knee, feeling my cock rising as she writhed her bum into my crotch, but she clung on. With her pretty face close to mine, breath sweet on my lips, and the hard cylinder of my prick nestled between the cosy cheeks of her arse, I was a goner when her mouth covered mine and her tongue wormed inside. She whispered I could do as I wanted; any way-out sexy thing at all wouldn't shock her. Adding that she had wanted me to fuck her since seeing the way I'd shafted her mum over a sink full of dishes, I stood and carried her through to my bedroom. There we threw off our clothes while still kissing and touching, desperate to get fucking.

I'd forgotten at my age how silky smooth a young girl's skin is, how firm her maturing tits. The horny little bitch was all for it, climbing over me to feed her nipples to my lips, then rolling over to drag me on top of her. She circled my back with her legs while guiding my rampant cock into her tight little juicy cunt, and at once urged me to fuck the arse off her like I did with her mum. I told her I'd fuck her rigid, thrusting up her snatch to the balls while she talked dirty to increase our lust.

It started regular sessions between us, mostly in her very upmarket apartment, I wondered how she could afford. She loved to be spanked before having sex, her favourite position being on elbows and knees for rear entry penetration. Like mother, like daughter, I told her. She liked cock sucking, cunt licking, and my mouth on her nipples during foreplay, but got extra hot being ordered to bend over or go across my knee for a good spanking. One day, flaked out on her bed after a long slow fuck, my prick being sucked to bring me up to shag the greedy little bitch again, I remarked she was extremely naughty doing that to the bloke she wanted to marry her mother. That's how I learned she liked her bum being smacked.

She giggled as she agreed, saying if I were half a man I'd have walloped her arse like naughty girls deserve, and her mother as well for dumping me. So that first time I smacked her bottom and enjoyed it, as well as discovering she got a big thrill out of being punished. She liked it so much that she played me up just to get a thrashing, at times handing me a variety of whips, canes and tawses that made me wonder where they came from. She then showed me her secret room where she earned her living dominating men clients, hence being well able to afford the apartment. But although she degraded and beat them, she always felt the need to be dominated and punished to be sexually fulfilled herself.

With her panties lowered and her shapely bum offered up, I'd whack her until I began to doubt I could hurt her enough. 'Harder than that! Smack my bottom harder!' she'd screech, until her arse must have stung agonisingly. It came as a revelation to me that I looked forward to dishing out spankings and canings. I became very severe with her, finding fault so I could beat her. It also turned out that I made use of the bondage equipment in her flat, tying her to the bed or a chair, having her at my mercy. It was obvious she liked being submissive, and told me it was what her mother needed; to be dominated by a strong man. 'For that reason,' Shirley said. 'Why do you think I've trained you so well?'

I'd been visiting her for several months when a letter came from her mother, a request to meet me again as she'd thrown out her ex-husband for good. 'Be firm with her this time,' Shirley advised, laughing. 'Don't take chocs or flowers. Take the cane or strap you've used to whack my bum so often.'

I considered the little trollop's advice worth taking, so warned her mother when we met that any further nonsense, even just looking at other men in future, and she could expect to be severely corrected. I would demand obedience at all times, I added, delighted to see the way she nodded, as meek as one could want when telling me she only wanted to please me, be my woman for always, my wife hopefully.

Boosted by this show of deference, I pushed my luck, testing her abject pleading attitude and asserting my dominance. 'For the way you dumped me,' I said sternly, 'I intend to show you how it will be if you fuck me about in future, Marion.'

Nodding again to show me she'd agree to anything, I knew I had a servile subject on my hands, accepting me as her lord and master. Starting our resumed relationship as I intended it to go on, I ordered her to strip off right there in her cosy living room. Naked before me, I then told her to kneel before me, to suck my cock to stiffness and give it a squeeze or two between her tight cleavage.

Doing that willingly enough, she got randy and begged me to fuck her. Much as I did want to, I told her sharply she'd get fucked when I decided she could, not because she was a horny slut who'd take the cock from anyone. She looked downcast, which pleased me. Awaiting my arrival, the table was nicely laid with a linen tablecloth, place settings for two with her best china and cutlery to impress me. I ordered her to stretch across the table's edge, feet apart on the floor and bottom raised. She obeyed without demur, only allowing a sharp intake of breath to show her fear as I doubled the belt taken from my trousers in my hand. 'This will hurt me more than you,' I said, unable to resist cracking the old joke, enjoying complete mastery over her.

I walloped her plump arse unmercifully until she was scarlet on both cheeks, sobbing for relief. In the dominating mood I'd now adopted as our future way of life together, I made her thank me for giving her what she deserved. Making her remain bent over the table, I fucked her before allowing dinner to be served. Still kept naked, without granting her permission to join me, I dined alone. All the time she gladly did as I ordered. Pleased that all had gone as planned by her daughter, I moved into her house the next day, certain I had a willing slave and was on to a very good thing as Marion's next husband.

With a tame wife, one who admitted that being submissive was what she liked, she came to believe regular spankings or canings made her appreciate what she had. I later borrowed some of her daughter's bondage equipment and put it to good use, with a home-made explicit videotape showing Marion undergoing the treatment during several of our CP and S&M sessions.

As for naughty little Shirley, she still succeeds in business as a professional Miss Whiplash, with a devoted clientele who pay her to get insulted, whipped, spanked and generally led a dog's life. She has the collars for that too, and leads and feeding bowls.

She has a regular boyfriend; one of her clients she can boss about and get her cleaning, ironing and housework done for free. He's not so hot at satisfying her sexually, it seems. What else can I think when she phones me at work, asking me to drop in at her place on my way home? I have to tell her mother I'll be late getting home as something came up. I'll leave you to guess what that something might be.

Charlie, Sunderland.

CHAPTER SIXTEEN
Sitting Down Sex

I was blissfully married to an ever-randy husband for twenty years, but Ted died two years ago and he's been sadly missed. We had a sex life second to none. One of his favourite things was eating me out. He'd lay on his back for me to 'queen' him, squatting over his face. He really got off (and me too) while I was grinding my cunt onto his nose and mouth, making him a prisoner below me, trapped between my thighs and hardly able to breathe. I'd order him to bring me off repeatedly by sucking hard on my cunt lips and clitty, as well as licking me clean and tongue-fucking me with his well trained snakelike tongue.

I must admit his warm breath on my juiced-up quim was a real turn-on. Best of all, I found, was the feeling of dominance I got perched over him until he begged to be allowed air. I never once spared mashing his face with my crotch, drenching him with my juices. Later we'd fuck like sex maniacs, so aroused by my sitting over his face routine. More often than not after 'queening' him, I'd insist on mounting him to show I was still the boss woman. I'd call him 'cunt licker' and 'feeble sex slave' while thrusting down, impaled on his prick, my boobs bouncing like wild things as I fucked him.

Being what I'm told by admirers as an attractive woman and at thirty-eight years in my prime, I have no trouble getting men for casual sex. Known as the 'Merry Widow' at our social club, chaps of all ages chat me up and hope to sleep with me - even the sixteen-year-old son of a neighbour, who has. Trouble is I can't get as highly sexually aroused before I fuck as I used to with my late husband, not unless I first squat on the fella's face, excited by the fact and ordering whoever's below me to lick out my cunt. This seems an unacceptable kink to many who boast of being a with it and anything goes type of stud. To me they aren't.

No sexual adventure in their souls at all, I think testily, telling them not to come back. My dear husband promised me I'd always be guaranteed a seat as long as he had a face. At the club I soon found that the women, once close friends, were keeping a tight grip on boyfriends and husbands, treating me as a danger to their relationships. Stuck for a partner to sit with one night, I had to settle for Robbie, a quiet single chap a year or two younger than me. He was a shelf-stacker in the local supermarket and still lived with his old mother.

He was generally considered a wimp, but my late hubby had told me Rob had an Oxford honours degree. He'd given up teaching at a famous private school for being too timid and fearful of the six-formers - and they were all girls! I think he was afraid they were going to seduce him, and I had no doubt he was still a virgin.

One night I asked him to walk me home as prowlers had been seen lurking in the dark. The third time he did I invited him in for a drink. Randy as ever with a man near, I sat on his lap and began kissing him. I pressed my boobs against him, wriggled my bum into his crotch, and thrust my tongue between his lifeless lips.

Wimp or no, I felt a hard cylinder of flesh rise and press through my dress against my bottom. With Robert still dazed, I led him upstairs to my bedroom. There he actually managed a few feeble protests as I began to undress him, while we continued the kissing and fondling. But to say that is not entirely correct. It was me having to be the aggressive male and make all the advances. I was doing all the kissing and fondling, pulling at his clothes, a job accompanied by me telling him sharply he must do as I ordered or I'd be very angry with him. That scared him. He acted like a timid virgin girl, muttering that his mother would be expecting him with his supper!

I told him I'd got something tastier for him to eat. 'You're not leaving until you've proved you're not the wimp and mummy's boy the women at the club say you are. They make fun and jeer at you behind your back,' I said. I had his trousers half down, and he was hopping around trying to pull them up when I lost patience and thrust him flat on the bed. He landed face down. With a good tug I had his pants around his ankles, revealing a neat milk-white arse, a tempting target too good to resist. As he attempted to rise I pushed him flat with my hand between his shoulder blades.

'You will lie there and not move!' I ordered sternly. Bare bum up, he quailed visibly, turning a very fearful face to me, no doubt the only other woman to see his backside since his mother changed his nappies. Intoxicated by the surge of power within me, wanting more, to have my victim sobbing and begging for mercy, I struck out at his unprotected buttocks with my hand, smacking the cheeks as hard as I could, uncaring that my palm stung as well as his bottom. Something else was discovered then; I'd always liked being dominant, such as squatting over men's faces, but now I knew just how good the feeling was to sadistically dish out physical punishment.

'Take that, and that, you male chauvinist pig!' I croaked, my breath laboured through spanking poor Robbie's arse as hard as I could. Hardly a male chauvinist pig, he screeched and clenched his cheeks, pleading to be spared as his backside turned bright red. 'Your mummy isn't here to save her baby boy, you big wimp,' I told him savagely. 'You've got me instead, so expect no mercy. Have you ever had a woman sit on your face?'

He squealed that he'd never heard of such a thing, begging me to stop spanking and let him go. My arm hurting from its exertions, I decided he was lucky. Next time I'd get a whip or cane, and there was going to be a next time, plenty of them, the way I felt.

46

I commanded him to turn over, and when he resisted I knew the reason why. So I made him obey with more hard smacks. He had a glorious erection, a rearing seven or eight inch prick that would have graced a porno video. He cringed when I said he had hidden talents. Gathering some tights and stockings from the top drawer of my bedside cabinet, while he cowered on the bed, I bound his wrists to the rails of my headboard. Asking if he was ashamed of himself, a dirty little boy unable to control his lust and showing off that disgusting penis, he nodded miserably. All the same, his dick remained hard, which told me he was extremely excited.

He whimpered apologies while I insulted him further, his agony of shame and humiliation adding to my pleasure in dominating the poor sucker. Stripping off before him, I rubbed the sodden crotch of my panties across his nose and mouth, getting him used to the strong scent of my aroused cunt before straddling his face. Once settled over him, with the point of his chin against the puckered ring of my arsehole, my parted cunt lips covering his mouth, I ordered him to lick.

I reached behind to prise open my bum cheeks and give him breathing space, and was rewarded by feeling a wet tongue lapping around the lips before probing inside.

It felt so damn good that I told him he'd licked out women before, dirty little cunt-licking sod. Even with his nose and mouth squashed by my quim, I heard him trying to mumble he'd never done such a thing. My stomach surged with the sensations of arousal and with it, despite the brave tongue-fucking I was loving, came the urge to have more than a tongue up me - such as a big engorged prick.

Sitting up over his face, simply by reaching back I found what I needed. Despite Rob's protests and whining, his dick pulsed iron-hard and stuck-up like a flagpole. It was made to measure, in the right place at the right time.

Shuffling backwards, I expertly guided his knob to my slot and thankfully impaled myself on the rigid stalk, squirming down on it until my bum nestled against his belly. Rob immediately began to jerk his hips and lift up to me, fucking me splendidly, his upward heaves matching my downward thrusts to ensure fullest penetration. 'Go on, fuck me, but don't you dare come yet,' I was urging him. 'What would your mother say about what her precious boy is doing? Fuck me until I tell you it's okay to come, but not before I've had plenty.' Riding him furiously as I was, while using dirty talk to increase our lust, made me aware it was hard for him to last out. I felt he did try, out of fear.

I came at least twice before he shot into me, and I said that for a first time that wasn't too bad. But if he didn't do better in future, I warned, his arse would be skinned.

So began our 'courtship', and I found the more I made Rob humble and pay for his supposed 'sins', the more I liked it, and so did he. He'd always been scared and dominated by his mother, so transferring that fear to a mistress was a natural progression.

When I did get to meet her, she advised me to be strict with her boy. Give him an inch and he'll take a yard, she said. I could have told her the kind of inches he was giving me, seven hard ones nightly, but I didn't.

So I got myself a trained slave, one that lets me squat on his face as well as cook and clean for me. Kept in line with the whip, cane or a good spanking across my knee, I couldn't ask more from a subservient male. Women at the social club joke about my relationship with Rob, claiming he's not my type. They should get one; under my domineering influence he is exactly my type! An obedient and loyal subject, ready to fulfil my every wish on pain of corrective discipline, I think every woman should have one.

Ms T. L. C., Norwich.

CHAPTER SEVENTEEN
Peeking Partners

All marriages become stale. Familiarity breeds contempt and boredom. While Harold and I weren't contemptuous or bored, after nine years we had begun to take each other and the sexual side of our marriage for granted. My husband regularly bought adult mags, and his main interest in them was reading the explicit letters printed. Unlike wives I know, I didn't at all object to Harold having his 'girlie' magazines in the house. He often read out the letters to me he considered of special interest.

It was obvious his favourites were the letters from men who wished to watch their wives undress and expose themselves to other men, and even want them to fuck with these men. He also took a great interest in letters, stories and pictures featured in mags specialising in bondage and correction practices. Though men were pictured being disciplined and bound up by masked females in rubber suits, it was mainly naked girls who were tied up and receiving bottom spankings, and worse. I always found these pictures and stories very erotic and arousing, fantasising such scenes with me as the victim, even when my husband was fucking me.

One evening Harold brought home a hard core video. We watched it together on the couch. It proved extremely erotic viewing and got us very horny. There were the usual big-breasted women and hugely hung men, but for once there was a story that turned us on. A Peeping Tom husband was outside a window watching his wife parading naked before several men. Aroused, he masturbated while she had a threesome with her visitors, being fucked in every orifice. When the men went, the husband entered the room where his wife had been left naked and exhausted on the floor with her hair, mouth, breasts and belly saturated with their thick come.

Not expecting him to return and catch her, she abjectly begged and pleaded forgiveness, clutching at his legs and crying in the most humiliating manner. He took off his belt and lashed her around the room. She was scrabbling about on her hands and knees and screeching as he thrashed her buttocks. I'd never seen anyone be so degraded and made to grovel, and yet it turned me on! When she was allowed to stop, ordered to remain on all fours, he made her suck his big cock to get hard enough to fuck her in the arse, the final act of disgracing her. Again, I found it highly arousing and wondered what it would be like to be humiliated and punished.

I had no idea why I felt that way, but I did. Considered a respectable and level headed deputy head teacher, it made me very excited fantasising about being dominated and sexually abused. The torrid video got both of us aroused. He wanted my clothes off, unheard of in our lounge in the early evening. We were both naked and doing more than usual in our foreplay; while he was tonguing my cunt I sucked his prick. He was rampant and about to mount me on the couch, so I thought, as we're so hot I can ask him to do something I've always wanted. 'Smack my bottom first, and then fuck me,' I said, and as I never use the 'F' word, that pleased him.

He turned me over his knee and began spanking me timidly. I said he could use more force and smack my bum really hard. I told him I deserved it. I reminded him I'd had an affair with the head of my previous school, something we tried never to mention, but I wanted to be spanked really hard. I added that when Harold fucked me I fantasised all sorts of dirty things, like being fucked in a classroom by sixth-form boys, as it was the only way I could get an orgasm with him. It was thrilling to say such things, let alone do it to make my husband smack my bottom hard enough to make me sob and beg forgiveness.

It proved a tremendous turn-on for him as well. His smacks became excruciatingly hard and painful. He called me a bitch, a slut, and said that he wouldn't be surprised if I had let my schoolboys fuck me. He then pushed me to the floor and onto my hands and knees on the carpet. Curling over my back, he announced, as I was such a bitch, that he would fuck me doggie-fashion, and up my bum as well as my cunt if he wanted to. I've said I never used the 'F' word, well, Harold was not into making crude remarks when we were making love either. It proved it excited us both. 'Go on then, fuck the arse off me, you bastard,' I screamed.

In turn, my hubby answered by saying he'd screw me like the horny slut I was, and fill my greedy cunt until the spunk was oozing down my legs. 'If that isn't enough, I'll bring in other men to fuck you while I watch,' he added, 'then thrash your arse with your old school cane until you crawl on your knees and call me master.'

I guess we'd both needed to say these things, but were too inhibited or proper to do so. We both fucked like sex mad teenagers until having shuddering climaxes. Harold praised me for giving him the most marvellous fuck of his life.

In our loving mood, between his sucking on my nipples while I played with his cock, we discussed letting our hair down as we had, saying we should have done it years before. It made sex very erotic and he teased me about wanting my bottom spanked, saying he'd enjoyed doing it and would do it again. I said I needed discipline, wanted to be submissive to him, and even other men. I asked him about his interest in the letters about men watching their wives with other men. He admitted it would be his fantasy come true to see me undress before other people, men and women, but he wasn't sure about me being fucked by them.

Thinking later about his wish to show me off naked as he took pride in my provocatively large breasts and buttocks, I said I'd please him and do it. Although I didn't fancy getting out of my clothes cold-bloodedly before others and then posing my naked charms, I did feel it might be quite exciting to be spied on. He agreed it would be fun, keeping us randy thinking others had seen me in the bare buff. At once we put our minds to how we were to safely achieve the effect. Once tried, we repeated it. Our secret vice keeps Harold happy and both of us randy. It also gives him good reasons to discipline me by caning or spanking, for often the private exhibition I give goes farther than Harold likes. Here is how we manage our peep show.

During the evening I'm informed by my husband what time he'll invite a friend home for a drink, usually someone from the pub or someone he's done business with as a motor dealer. They find me as if caught by surprise when arriving, excusing myself as I'm about to take a bath. Wearing just a bathrobe as I answer the door, my large bust allows more than a glimpse of rounded flesh and cleavage before I clutch the neck together. I scold Harold for not informing me he's bringing home a friend. I delay my bath long enough to make sandwiches and put out a tray of glasses for drinks, then say they must excuse me.

The robe is silky, one Harold bought me on a holiday in Hong Kong. It clings, allowing one to plainly watch the contours of my breasts and buttocks jiggle as I bustle around. Once I go up to the bathroom, my husband remarks on my well-developed body, leading on the visitor to agree. Harold then slyly suggests would his guest care to see more? The answer has always been an immediate and eager yes. So the pair tiptoe upstairs, and I know it's show-time, as they say.

We live in an old Victorian house with a loft reached by a stairway. It holds the family junk we've gathered for years. The planked wooden floor is covered by thick insulating carpet, which deadens footsteps. Once up there, several people at the same time can look down into the bathroom, given a fully unimpeded view through a steam ventilator fixed in the ceiling. So Harold and his friend can stare at me slipping off my bathrobe and standing naked as I run the bath water. I busy myself adjusting the hot and cold taps with my big tits swinging about with each movement.

The show continues with me slipping into the sudsy water and soaping my breasts, getting out to towel dry myself before dusting powder over my body. This gives the viewers plenty of me to look at, and when it began was what we decided was naughty enough. But knowing I was being seen naked made me very horny. I began to play with my breasts and nipples while in the bath, and then to finger myself. One night I masturbated while perched on the toilet seat, my legs outstretched and toes curling as I actually gave myself a great orgasm.

The gasps, moans and cries I made when coming so strongly, the spasms jolting my body, were not put on for my viewers pleasure as I was helpless to stop myself. After such a truly lewd exhibition, Harold said I'd gone too far. He said it was so horny that the man with him had offered money to fuck me, which excited Harold as much as me. Still, for my wanton behaviour, I was made to bend across my husband's knee for a spanking that left my bum stinging. I was then pinioned to the bed by cords, and fucked while helpless. The sex was so heightened for both of us that I knew my impromptu act had been a success.

The game continued with me secretly sending for a variety of sex toys like love balls and vibrators. I use them to great effect after a bath to bring myself off while being spied on. I fake nothing, my body undulating and jerking as I lay on the bathroom rug, my cries genuine as I fuck myself to a splendid orgasm with a dummy dick. When my husband and his viewing partner go downstairs again, I join them later to make coffee, tremendously tickled to imagine what the man is thinking. I smile at him, stare at his crotch as if innocently, making him embarrassed with the bulge in his trousers still noticeable.

Of course I'm made to pay for this once our guest has left, getting the belt across my backside while on all fours, caned while tied to a chair, or pulled across Harold's knee for a slippering or spanking. Whatever the punishment, we always end up fucking.

But during one particular evening performance in the bathroom, the biggest black latex dildo I owned being worked up my cunt was too much for my husband to stand. Leaving his friend watching, he came down from the loft and burst into the bathroom as I was recovering from a mighty climax. Taking a seat on the toilet and forcing me while still limp to go over his knee, he used the twelve-inch dildo as an object to thrash me on the bottom.

I was left sobbing and really humiliated that it was all seen by the watcher in the loft. That was one time I did not join the men afterwards. But Harold and I both get what turns us on. He is thrilled when exhibiting me to other men. I get to flaunt myself naked and masturbate before his friends, paying for it by being bound and punished for my wanton behaviour. Harold enjoys deciding how I'll be disciplined. I know it is my nature now to exhibit myself and then be humiliated by my dominant partner. We make wonderful love after each covert strip show, more frequently and more frenzied than we ever did before. It makes it all very worthwhile, we agree. Don't you? If not, why not? Too afraid of being open and honest with each other, perhaps?

Mary, Dorset.

CHAPTER EIGHTEEN
Teaching the Wife

More than a year had passed since my wife said her need for sex was gone. She claimed she just didn't want to fuck any more. Okay for her, maybe, losing interest - but what about me? It resulted in heated arguments. She moved into another bedroom. I waited out the months hoping things would change; her plump curves were so right for me. I was still keeping her in money; I'd always been a generous provider and good earner. But it made no difference. She'd gone right off me.

I thought she was having it off with another bloke, but that wasn't so. She said our sex just bored her.

One morning the early post brought a letter from her sister, so I took it through to her bedroom. She sat up to reach for it, and I noted she was still sleeping nude as we had when sharing a bed. Her big creamy boobs with the rose-pink nipples lifted over the duvet, having me instantly horny and stretching out to cop a feel of them.

She said, 'Leave me alone, Tom, you know I don't want to.'

Well, a man can only stand so much. I told her she was a cold bitch and I'd deserved more as a caring husband. Really aggrieved, as she drew up the duvet to stop me ogling her breasts, I tugged it away, leaving her naked.

'Don't you dare!' she squealed, rolling over to escape from the bed and make for the door. I was quicker, pinning her face down with my left hand gripping the back of her neck as she struggled to rise.

'Bitch,' I told her, 'you've asked for it!'

As if the most natural thing in the world to do, I began to use my free hand to chastise her soft bottom. It felt marvellous, a wonderful relief, spanking her bare arse while she kicked and screeched, threatened and protested. My strong right arm rose and fell vigorously, delivering a rapid flurry of stinging blows to her bum. How she wriggled and howled. I felt every slap was well deserved, the cow getting her comeuppance from a husband who'd always been too easy with her.

She yelped, cursed, and said it hurt, but I knew every bit as painful was the utter humiliation of being spanked like a naughty girl, and by a guy she thought was under her thumb. Much as my arm ached, I rained down smack after smack and loved every howl it brought.

She clenched her arse cheeks and drew them in tight, squirming and twisting to exchange each tender part getting the necessary correction. Unable to escape from the bed, she twisted her face to glare hatred at me. I saw tears brimming in her eyes, and seeing I had no intention of easing up, she finally began begging and pleading for me to stop.

I considered she'd been taught a valuable overdue lesson for stopping my ration of sex. And I'd learned a lesson myself; that it was highly satisfying and erotically arousing spanking a female's bare arse. The evidence for that was in my pants. I had an erection as hard as blue-steel and rearing up my belly. The fine sight of a pink, well-spanked bottom, cheeks parted and relaxed after the onslaught, proved too big a temptation for me with such a hard-on.

'No, don't you dare, Thomas!' she screamed, guessing my intention as she looked over her shoulder to see me unzipping my trousers, at the same time clenching her arse tightly.

I overcame the hindrance of having access to the goodies between those tight rear cheeks by landing another flurry of hard smacks on her tender bum.

Ordered to lie still or I'd tie her to the bed (which I decided I'd do next time), she obeyed and then lay sobbing quietly, awaiting my next move dutifully in case she got another walloping. The lovely pink buttocks relaxed for me as I entered a finger to the knuckle in her sex, finding it easy to penetrate, the inside soft and moist.

That's how the coupling was made, our first fuck together for many months. With my wife face down, back dipped and arse tilted, my belly curved around her ample backside as I eased my prick inside. The bulbous knob stretched her outer lips as I eased in more long thick inches.

Slowly and seductively working my stalk in moist inner flesh, withdrawing to slide up deep again while muttering in her ear what a nice tight cunt she had, I was rewarded with a low moan of grudging pleasure. My quickening thrusts had her jerking back to me. As I came, shooting a long volley of spurts up her, she went into a frenzy of humping her body into the mattress, coming violently.

Having recovered, she got off the bed to closely inspect her well-thrashed botty in the wardrobe mirror. Despite the fact she'd had a marvellous series of climaxes, she ordered me out of the room. In my new role as a dominant husband, I told her it was my house, bought and paid for before she came on the scene. Moreover, she was my woman and she'd better believe it. Leaving, I said I'd do what I liked. Any nonsense and I'd spank her arse again.

She had a special steak dinner ready for me when I came home that evening, but her stubborn pride wouldn't let on how she felt.

After eating, declining to help with the washing up as I usually did, I strolled down the garden and saw my neighbour's face grinning at me across the hedge. He gave me a thumbs-up. Walter was a wimp with an imperious wife - like I'd been, I guess. Asking why the stupid grin and thumbs-up, he beamed as he said he'd heard about what I'd done that morning. It seemed his wife had given a coffee morning that day. During the girl talk, discussing husbands, my wife Nancy had proudly admitted that hers had smacked her bum and she still had the reddened marks to prove it.

My neighbour had come home from work and was told about it by his missus, hence his going out into the garden to congratulate me. It was plain he wished he could do the same to his wife. As for me, armed with that information I went back indoors to have it out with my Nancy, asking what made her boast of being spanked like she was proud of the fact.

She'd finished washing up and was bending over a cupboard under the sink to put the cleaning liquid away. I slid my hand under her dress and found the gusset of her briefs. I was sure she'd widened her thighs to give me better access as I stroked her through the lacy material. It soon moistened, and she didn't move to prevent me fingering her.

'I didn't know you were the strong silent dominant type,' she said in a hoarse voice as the touching up got to her. She began moving against my hand. 'I prefer you that way. I've always thought men should be masterful with their women. I need a strong man...'

'You've got one now,' I told her. 'Any lip in future and it's the belt you'll get.

No argument, you'll do as I say.' When she murmured that's how it would be, I remembered she'd never been keen to suck my cock, resenting giving me the pleasure. 'For starters, suck on this,' I ordered, bringing it out of my trousers. She turned around on her knees and took it deep in her throat. Judging exactly that I was about to erupt by the way my legs trembled and my grip in her hair tightened, she let my cock slip from her lips.

'Please fuck me, Tom,' she begged. 'Make me come and come like you did this morning!'

I stood with my rearing cock glistening with her saliva, and she drew off her briefs and sat up on the edge of the sink. Her legs went up over my shoulders as I moved between her thighs, my cock aimed directly at the pouting cunt she offered up for me to poke. I told her she was a slut, a horny cow and a tart, which she agreed was right and urged me to talk dirty as I rammed my dick home.

There were no separate bedrooms for us that night as we continued our romp, with a little playful spanking to show her who was the dominant partner. It was a renewal of our marriage, a whole new relationship. We could even arouse each other by telling of our previous partners and sexual habits and fantasies.

She said one former boyfriend bossed her. Liking it, she had deliberately annoyed him, hoping he'd spank her or tie her up during their sexy sessions. She'd had to fantasise the bondage and spanking while masturbating, even imagining being his slave. She'd then met me and we married, settling down and thinking there was no place now for kinky sex games in a solid marriage.

Of course then she'd found it dull and I didn't have a clue what would have satisfied her. I'm glad now I know what makes us both incredibly randy. I'd never suggested it before as I thought she'd think me perverted.

Almost at the stage of divorcing when all that was needed was complete honesty between us, doesn't it just show that man and wife should have no secret desires without revealing them?

Tom P., Suffolk.

CHAPTER NINETEEN
Mandy's Birthday Present

I'm always being handcuffed or bound up and caned on my bare bottom prior to being fucked in my fantasy. I'm kidnapped by a group of men so that others, male and female, get to see me tied securely and watch me being thrashed and screwed. The blue movies my husband sometimes brings home always turn me on. If there are scenes of bondage and spanking, and a black man fucking a white woman, I get horny and demand sex right there and then before the television screen. So my husband makes sure he gets the right kind of videos to get me going.

Hubby Joe is a wife watcher who gets his kicks from seeing other men having sex with me. I wondered what I'd be getting for my birthday when he promised me something special. Joe's no cheapskate and gets whatever I ask. I have no secrets, and so he knew of my CP fantasy, saying I ought to experience it at least once. At home, expecting Joe to arrive from his carpet shop, I answered the doorbell, getting my birthday surprise.

I was faced by an extremely large and handsome black man, built like a gladiator. He said he was Joe's present to me. I had to do everything he said or be punished. Taking my elbow, he guided me into the kitchen.

'Relax and enjoy,' he said, introducing himself as Leo. Reaching out, he grasped my breasts, squeezing them painfully when I tried to stop him, so I had to let him continue cupping and fondling them. He said my husband was right; I had big tits he'd enjoy playing with, even more so when they were out of my bra. 'Do you like your nipples being sucked?' he asked. 'Or do you prefer getting your cunt licked?'

I suddenly realised this sort of thing was fun in a fantasy, but very different for real. The front of his jeans bulged obscenely, and I was very apprehensive. 'Please leave,' I asked feebly. 'I'll tell my husband you did all you came to do, and I'll pay you extra to what he promised.'

'Too late,' Leo said. 'I've seen you now and want to fuck you. Any resistance and I'll spank obedience into your white arse.' These were almost the very same words I'd imagined in my fantasy, and I wondered if my husband had told him.

I trembled when he ordered me to undress. He leaned against the edge of the kitchen table making crude remarks about my breasts and vagina as I stripped. Tits and cunt, he called them, saying he'd enjoy screwing me.

'Ever take a big black cock, woman?' he asked.

Standing naked before this stranger with my breasts and sex on show, I tried to order him to leave the house.

'In your dreams,' he laughed. 'I give the orders here. Didn't I tell you, no argument? Now you must pay.' From the inside pockets of his leather jacket he brought out a tiny whippy cane and some short lengths of soft curtain cord. This aggressive stranger seeing me in the nude was beginning to excite me, although I remained very apprehensive. Again I offered money for him to leave, but he refused.

'Turn,' he commanded, and I didn't dare disobey. A churning in my tummy and the moistening between my thighs were signs that I was becoming aroused, as well as being afraid. He fondled my buttocks, delving a hand between them to stroke my outer lips. He sniffed his fingers, saying I couldn't deny I was on heat, and as for my fine big arse, he hadn't decided whether to kiss it, spank it, or fuck it. More likely all three, he added, then drew my arms behind my back and bound my wrists together.

Made to face him again, as he unzipped his straining jeans and exposed his cock, I turned my face away. Stepping beside me, he brought down the cane with a swish and a crack as it striped my bottom, and I yelped in pain.

'Be silent, or you'll get worse,' he said. Ordered to kneel on the kitchen rug, I didn't dare disobey, seeing his weapon bobbing before my lips, and shocked by the enormous length and thickness of it. 'It's bad manners to speak with your mouth full.'

'Oh, God, I couldn't!' I groaned, understanding what he meant. 'It's too huge, I'd never get that in my mouth!' On my knees with my wrists pinioned behind my back, I was helpless as he placed a hand behind my head and drew my face forward until my lips brushed against the purplish bulbous knob of his monstrous prick.

'Open up,' he said menacingly. 'Kiss it, lick it, then give it a nice suck, baby.' I shook my head in refusal, fearful of choking on the size of it. To ensure that I obeyed, he leaned over my head and thwacked the cane downwards, directed with unerring aim to land in the crease of my buttocks.

As my lips opened to shriek, he grabbed a handful of hair and fed his prick deep into my mouth. I gagged and tried to accommodate the thick stalk between my tongue and palate as he thrust his hips at my face, fucking my stretched mouth. 'Suck, slut,' he ordered. 'I want you to take it in your mouth yourself next time I tell you to. Get my drift?' Withdrawing, his prick glistening with my saliva, he left it poised throbbing just an inch from my lips, expecting me to engulf the brutish thing in my mouth again. I'd fantasised such a situation often enough when masturbating, but the black knob, as big as a duck's egg and waiting to be taken into my mouth, was for real. I sobbed that it wouldn't go in, so he told me to open wide, giving me another cut of the cane to sting my backside.

Terrified of getting a further smack, I enclosed my lips over the huge knob and sucked gingerly. 'It won't bite you,' he snarled. 'Suck harder and bring my spunk up from my balls. So how do you like eating black snake, white woman?'

I could only gulp with a mouthful of throbbing cylindrical flesh, nodding to show I liked it in case of getting caned again. But as I sucked on the pulsating stalk of rampant cock, the thought of what I was being forced to do became unbelievably arousing. I began to like what he had caned me to do, beginning to suck avidly on his dick to make him lose control, as I was losing control.

It was then I saw that another black man was in the house - a big man like the one whose prick I was now greedily sucking.

'She loves it,' the newcomer observed. 'She loves chewing black cock. The dirty bitch is a natural. Fuck her face good, Leo. I'll bet she's sucked more pricks than just her husband's.'

Leo laughed, saying he was going to saturate my throat and would make sure I'd swallow every thick drop. 'Then you can have her till I'm ready to shag her, Troy. We'll bind her over the table and you can go to town on the bitch. She's loving all of it.'

Talking about me so lewdly was both humiliating and shameful, but at the same time strangely erotic. I was considered a slut, meat to be fucked or spanked, and it really made me suck the more gluttonously on Leo's weapon. I heard him grunting, felt the tremble in his knees, and was thrilled to think I was making this dominant hunk lose control. His grip tightened in my hair and his flanks shuddered, as he let fly long spurts of come into my throat. I gulped and swallowed, choking on the deluge.

My wrists untied, the one called Troy led me to the kitchen table. I was ordered to lie face up across the top with my legs over the edge. With Leo's help, although I did nothing to obstruct them, the pair of them bound my wrists and ankles to the four legs at each corner. Troy then knelt between my spread legs and went down on me, while Leo bent over to suck and pinch my nipples. It was then that Leo made me answer a series of humiliating questions as I was writhing in helpless ecstasy with a probing tongue up me.

'Yes, I love sucking a black cock,' I was made to admit, and any delay in answering Leo got my nipples painfully tweaked and pulled. My poor nipples were extended until I was ready to confess to anything. I told them of my fantasising and masturbating, and my strong desire to be punished and dominated. Worked up by revealing my lewdest secrets, as my climax surged with Troy's tongue buried deep inside me, I begged to be made to come and come... so he withdrew.

'Please fuck me then!' I begged, looking over the tips of my breasts to see Troy standing before me with his superb prick in his hand. I wanted that inside me urgently, every thick inch of it. He opened my sex and eased his big knob inside. His series of long and deep thrusts quickly had me coming violently, and disappointed when I sensed him shudder and have his own climax. But as he withdrew Leo took his place, and another big black root entered me. 'Yes, you fuck me too,' I croaked.

In my lustful frenzy, bound but able to work my pelvis to match Leo's mighty thrusts, I lost count of the climaxes I had. My naked body bathed in sweat, I felt myself untied after Leo had fucked me and deposited his load. He sat down on a kitchen chair and patted his knee in a signal to me. In my dazed state, lifted from the table by Troy, I unsteadily draped myself across Leo's lap. 'What a dirty bitch you are,' he accused. 'You, a married woman letting me and my brother fuck you without a thought for your husband. Don't you agree that kind of disloyalty deserves a good spanking?'

I had to agree, even though I knew what it would mean. A nod of my head and the first tingling smacks stung my bare bottom. It went on until I couldn't worry about how humbling it was to beg and plead for mercy. When Leo took pity and stopped, he stood up and I was sent tumbling to the floor. To add to my humiliation, the brothers laughed and chatted about what a greedy fuck I was, anybody's for the taking and a first class slut. I was too far gone to care.

Exhausted by such numerous sapping climaxes, my poor arse stinging, all I could do was lay unable to move. I sensed it was my husband standing over me, grinning as he used his camcorder to record my degradation.

'Happy birthday, love,' he laughed. 'How was it for you, living out your favourite fantasy for real? From where I was observing, you sure revelled in those boys giving you the treatment. They were the best I could hire from an escort agency, and I've recorded it all.'

The two black brothers stood nodding and grinning. 'Nice work if you can get it,' said Leo to my husband. 'It was a pleasure to fuck your wife. Nice arse on her for spanking, too.'

Sometimes now I close my eyes and imagine myself tied across that kitchen table with my legs straddled over the edge. Recalling what Leo and his brother did to me makes me respond in like fashion. If my husband is handy, I jump on him. If not, then I have to masturbate. I want the same birthday present next year. Meantime I get off watching the video I starred in, now labelled *Mandy's Birthday Treat*. I'm looking forward very much to making the sequel!

Mandy, Bristol.

CHAPTER TWENTY
Lesbian Leatherings

Marriage was a horrendous time for me. Not just my husband, but all men, were complete turn-offs as sexual partners. From my teens I'd known I had lesbian desires, but married to please my parents and perhaps to prove to myself I wasn't gay. My husband gave up on me and we divorced. I'd confessed to him that I preferred my own sex. He had a sister, Milly, and he told her I was a would-be lesbian if I could find a partner.

She then sought me out, although in the past she'd ignored me the few times we'd met. I was glad of a friend, as everyone was annoyed at me, especially my mother for not making her a granny. I thought Milly was being kind, but it soon proved her interest in me had an ulterior motive. She was a dominant butch lesbian who had been delighted to learn I was untried at female sex and intended to take me under her wing.

My experience of sex with girls was no more than holding hands and sweet kisses with school chums with a crush on each other. Milly, experienced and domineering, was very different. Within minutes of my first visit to her flat she was bullying me and had me in tears. She said I'd been ashamed of what I was, and had married to hide the fact. Told I was weak and had to be taught not to hide my true sexual nature, I was totally stunned when she produced a riding crop from a drawer. She said I deserved thrashing and made me kiss the tip of the crop, saying it would prove to be my friend.

Spanking, whipping and caning often figured in my fantasies when I masturbated. I'd imagine I'd been a naughty girl and given a caning by my headmistress. At other times I was the teacher and caned boys and girls, as well as fantasising about making them play with my breasts and vagina. Milly knew nothing of this until I was forced to confess it to her. I recognised that she was into dominating and punishing any weaker females who fell into her clutches - as I had. Sobbing before her after the interrogation, it was then that she'd produced the riding crop. I was too intimidated to refuse when ordered to step out of my panties.

She laughed at my fear, saying she'd do more for me than her brother, my ex-husband, had ever done. Ordering me to raise my skirt and bend over the seat of a chair, I cried real tears and she told me not to be such a baby. If I continued to act like one I'd be put in nappies and given her breasts to suckle, she said, or I could take my punishment like an adult. The first sharp crack of the crop made me scream as it stung my bottom, pleading for her not to hurt me.

But the whipping continued and I cried pitifully, all pride lost as I humbly begged Milly not to beat me, that I would do anything. My poor buttocks burned like they were on fire, making me writhe in a futile attempt to ease the sting. With the last strike, and I demeaned myself again by actually thanking her for stopping, she ordered me to stay still across the chair, quite out of breath from her exertions in flogging me. I waited for whatever was to happen next, and felt her palms dividing my inflamed cheeks.

To my shock and surprise she began running her wet tongue up and down the lips of my sex like a cat lapping up cream. The tip of her tongue ventured into my bottom hole, then lowered to probe inside my quim. The heat generated by the whipping of my bottom had seeped through to my sexual part to agitate it. With Milly's long tongue adding to my turmoil, the whole length of it flicking sensuously inside me and laving my clitoris, I couldn't help my sobs turning to low moans of pleasure and my bottom jerking in response as I was made extremely aroused. It was my first real involvement in lesbian loving, something I had long desired to experience, and Milly was an expert at seduction.

'Yes, go on, more please,' I whined, and shook in ecstatic bodily spasms as she brought me off on her tongue. She sat me up before I'd really recovered and slapped my face to make me pay attention. I was ordered to strip, and I stood shakily to pull off my clothes while she undressed without taking her eyes off me. She said I had a young girl's breasts and bottom, and a cunt hardly used, as she could tell while tonguing me. Her bosom was heavy and pendulous, with large rubbery nipples. I was told she had pleasured me, so now I could do the same for her.

She drew up a chair next to the one I'd been bent across, sat, and opened her thighs wide. 'Give me relief like I did you,' she ordered. 'Masturbate yourself at the same time.' It would be a first time for me to do such a thing, and I suppose it seemed to her as I hesitated that I was reluctant. 'You'll be taught to do anything I tell you from now on,' she said, and powerful woman that she was, she had no problem in dragging me across her knee.

'It'll be my hand this time,' she said, 'but it'll sting your pretty arse just as much.' Though I begged, said I was willing to lick her, wanted to lick her, I was given such a severe spanking that it was a relief to be placed on my knees between her thighs and ordered to use my mouth and tongue on her.

It was not unpleasant, and when she became agitated, nearing her orgasm, it was thrilling to know I was bringing her such strong sensations.

But excited though I'd been during that session with Milly, I was afraid of her dominant personality taking over my life. I deliberately avoided her, and soon after I met a nice young girl who enjoyed playing smacking and caning games with me. Like myself, she'd been undecided about her lesbianism. Alison allowed me to flog her pert little bottom with a swishy cane, and then she returned the favour by caning me. With both our girlish bums red and smarting but warmed up, we'd have sex. Kissing ardently, sucking on each other's nipples, fingering each other, we'd end with me lying on top of Alison like a man on his wife and rub our mounds and clitties together.

It gave us lovely orgasms, but what Milly later described as kid's stuff. By chance she spotted us at a gay club and immediately took command of us both. The music was slow and smoochy. While dancing with me she thrust her prominent crotch hard into mine. Her breasts flattened mine and she began kissing me lewdly with open wet lips and probing tongue, like the other women who were dancing there. She next danced with poor Alison and did the same to her.

We didn't have the courage to defy her when she ordered us to leave with her. The taxi took us to a house where lesbians met, and in the room we were taken to there were stocks and hooks hanging from the ceiling, and whips and canes on the walls. Alison and I quaked and huddled together, realising the women were not only gay, but into CP and S&M rituals. Alison sobbed, and I was laughed at for demanding to be allowed to leave.

'Nobody makes demands in here, but us,' Milly warned, while the others congratulated her for finding such fresh and sweet meat.

We were in a den of sadists, some of the women dressed in all kinds of revealing leather uniforms and carrying whips or old-fashioned birches made of twigs. All wanted to fondle and kiss Alison and me, pulling off our clothes until we both were naked, getting slaps for trying to stop them and finally studied by them and hearing remarks about our breasts and bottoms. A large buxom blonde woman said she couldn't wait to fuck us both. She wore a shiny black latex bra with holes cut for her nipples to protrude, but most alarming to us was the tight black latex panties she was squeezed into which had a frighteningly large and realistic dildo thrusting upward from it.

Because I'd demanded to leave, I was bound hand and foot, with my wrists attached to a chain fixed to the ceiling. I was told I had to learn my place as a lowly newcomer; a 'passive' as they jeered I was. I couldn't steady myself and spun around on the chain as I was flogged by a woman with a birch. While I screeched in pain, every time my bottom spun to face her, she thrashed me. But it was also the stuff of my fantasies, strung up naked while another woman birched me with others encouraging her. I felt myself becoming aroused, and on each turn around I saw quiet little Alison on a nearby settee being mounted and penetrated by the buxom blonde dyke who wore the latex panties with the big replica prick attached.

There was no doubt Alison was responding, for she curled her legs around the woman's back, bucking her body to get depth into her while her mouth was glued to the female on top. She tore her mouth away to scream out she wanted to come, then that she was coming, and from her undulating body there was no doubt she was. I'd thought of Alison as my lover. To see her writhing on the end of another woman's dildo made me shout out that she was a deceitful bitch, begging that my bonds be freed so I could go for her.

The women thought that enough reason to untie me. Going to Alison, I swore at her, and pulled her hair as she rallied and we began to wrestle on the carpet. Pulled apart, Alison was then strapped onto a tilted bench, her head high at one end and her feet on the floor with her bottom raised in the middle. Milly handed me a whip with nine dangling tails, asking if I really was a true butch dyke that dominated and enjoyed flogging lesser mortals. Incensed as I was, I quickly showed her by making Alison sob and beg for mercy as I whipped her little arse until it was a mass of angry red weals. For my zeal in thrashing Alison I was congratulated, and realised they had in their own way initiated me into their circle.

On future visits to the club I was sometimes a 'passive', and sometimes considered butch enough to start an apprenticeship and help with the bondage and correction of submissive types, both male and female, for at times gay men were admitted to serve us and do housework.

Game nights were held; charades in which special roles were enacted. In one I was a schoolgirl caught kissing another girl and sentenced to ten strokes of the cane with others.

Dressed as schoolgirls, we'd line up outside the headmistress's office and were ordered to strip off our knickers to be flogged. In time I played the headmistress and administered the punishment.

I began to sleep with club members I fancied. On other nights I was sent out to lesbian bars and clubs to find new naïve girls to entertain us, just as I'd been recruited by Milly. For those who may wonder, take it from me that such clubs do exist.

So the life of a dedicated lesbian is the one I have chosen for myself. I won't pretend what I'm not any more. The ritual punishments I'm giving to new members of our society are something I've learned as natural to me.

Sex is never better than after a caning delivered to a submissive, just to show who's in command. I can be a truly severe mistress and I have my admirers, Alison included, whom I number among my lovers and willing slaves.

At club meeting nights or at our favourite bar, you'll know me now as the dyke who wears men's clothes and has an eye for the girls.

Harriet (Harry), Manchester.

CHAPTER TWENTY ONE
Family Fantasy

Exactly what first started me needing to be punished and humiliated for sexual satisfaction? It was undoubtedly a mixture of the incidents and experiences I'll relate here. Being severely dominated, physically corrected and made to suffer utter ignominy at the hands of others, male or female, is what I find more erotic and sexually arousing than anything else. As an outwardly respectable and normal thirty-six-year-old wife and mum, being humiliated and disciplined remains a secret desire, one I only realise in my favourite fantasies.

I masturbate at least every day while imagining myself being used and abused, spanked or whipped, forced into committing way-out sexual acts. This always results in my climaxing, often several orgasms coming together. You may ask, if my need to bring myself off is so frequent, what kind of husband do I have? Well, we do have sex at least twice a week, always in bed at night, and I do have strong orgasms if I fantasise about being spanked or caned while Arthur is fucking me. I do not tell him the reason I have such frenzied climaxes. He thinks he's a great lover, but he has little idea what pleases a woman, even though I've tried to put him on the right track. No imagination, poor Arthur.

Not long after we married, over twelve years ago, lying naked together on the bed after making love, I rolled across his lap as he lay face up and cocked up my bottom to him. During our engagement I'd had an affair with his sister's husband and Arthur had forgiven me. I reminded him of this and said I'd need a strong hand to keep me in check. Of course, I was angling to get my bottom smacked, which I longed to happen. I said Arthur should warm my backside with a hard spanking to make me a dutiful wife. He didn't take the hint, and thought I was being frivolous. He said I had learned my lesson, and how could a pretty little wife like me annoy him?

He kissed the bare bottom I presented, which did not satisfy me. In desperation I said he should spank me just to see how it feels, in case he ever needed to correct me. He might like doing it, and it might make me extra randy, I suggested, knowing well that I knew it would. To satisfy me, he gave my bum a few friendly pats, which I hardly felt. I was really frustrated, but the kind idiot just cuddled me and said I was never to think of my affair with our brother-in-law - that was in the past. He thought that was why I cried.

I knew then I'd fulfil my wish only by fantasising. Faithful wife though I wanted to be, I wouldn't turn down an affair with a macho domineering male who would rule me as my master. Afternoon is the time when thoughts of being put across a knee and given a smacked botty comes to mind and arouses me. I know I'll stop my hoovering, dusting, baking or preparing dinner to go up to my bedroom. There I strip in front of a long mirror to caress my breasts and sex lips, getting in the mood. I pretend I'm being forced to admit to my lover (never my husband), that I'm being unfaithful with another man.

It can be the neighbour who's a policeman, or even his son who is still at grammar school. I've confessed to having it off with the local vicar, our milkman, my husband's brother, and even his father! At times it's another woman I confess to, one who uses a dildo on me. I'm tied with my wrists behind my back, pushed face down on the bed and my fantasy master or mistress stands over me with a whip. Such is my arousal and the power of the fantasy, I smack my own bottom loudly or use the back of my hairbrush to thrash my cheeks, bringing on a violent orgasm without touching my sexual parts.

A very probable cause of my strong desire to be punished is not a guilt complex as many so-called sex experts claim. My affair was merely for physical satisfaction, and nothing serious. More likely, I got the desire for correction when I was sixteen, and quite a well-developed girl already having randy thoughts. I had a stepsister who was also sixteen. Once, for staying out late and being seen kissing a boy, her mother, my stepmother, said she must be taught a lesson. I was present when she was ordered to roll up her frock for punishment. I guess my being there to witness it was to warn me not to step out of line.

Stepmother had a cane that hung on a hook in the cupboard under the stairs. Dorothy, my stepsister, was then ordered to bend across a chair seat and had her knickers drawn down. She cried out before her mother began to strike her slim milk-white buttocks with the cane. I'm sure more force could have been used, but it left Dorothy howling with a red striped bottom. Watching, I felt a most strange feeling churning in the pit of my stomach and down to my virgin sex. It felt moist and seemed to throb, a sensation I knew from when I aroused myself with secret dirty thoughts and played with myself. It was arousal all right, but somehow stronger than I'd ever experienced.

I'd go directly to my room and finger myself to a climax, as classmates of mine all admitted they did when in bed at night. But this could be any time of day, and though masturbating always produced a strange and nice feeling in my virgin pussy, I was always more highly aroused after witnessing Dorothy being caned. Thinking of her pale buttocks being striped, wishing it were me revealingly bare my bottom to be humiliatingly thrashed, I scared myself by having my first real orgasm. Left numb across my bed gasping for breath, body still twitching in the dying spasms of a mighty climax, I knew I'd achieved the real thing. Caused, I knew, by the thought of being stripped, caned, dominated and humbled.

I had a stepbrother too; Dorothy's brother, Richard. A randy boy of eighteen, he was forever trying to lure me into the garden shed to kiss me, feel my growing breasts and get his hands in my knickers. Discussing Dorothy's caning with him, I shyly admitted I found it exciting and it made me feel 'funny' inside. You mean horny, Richard said, adding if I felt that way why not try the real thing?

'Let's go to the shed and I'll cane you if you want to know how it feels,' he offered. He said if I did, he'd be glad to lend me his girlie mags, some of which had pictures of girls being tied up and spanked. I followed him when he led the way into the garden, my stomach churning with arousal.

There was an old chair in the shed and he sat down, pulling me across his knees. He said I needed spanking anyway, being such a goodie-goodie and daddy's pet. I told him not to take off my kickers and don't hurt me. Left hand on my neck pinning me down, he used his right to fold up my dress and then pull down my knickers to reveal my bare bum. When I complained that he wasn't supposed to see all that, he told me sternly to shut up or he'd really hurt me, giving my bottom a really hard smack and stinging me painfully. He was in reach of the potting table and found a short cane among the litter on top.

'Stay still!' he ordered, as I struggled. To warn me to be obedient, he swished down the cane with force, my bum on fire as I screeched for him to stop. But he continued, and my pleas became quiet sobs as I realised he was mastering me. Caning me had given him a really hard erection; I could feel the stiff stalk pressed against my tummy, making me feel randy as the heat in my thrashed bum percolated through to my pussy. When the bamboo cane broke, Richard reverted to using his hand to spank me. Jerking his hips, he thrust his rampant cock into my belly as I lay across his lap. I was spared further spanking by his arousal making him explore between my cheeks and fingering my pussy. I gave a loud cry as he brought me off, Richard and I both shaking as we came together, his Y-fronts and jeans soaked by his deluge. Shocked by what I'd allowed, I jumped up from his lap, pulling up my knickers and fleeing to my bedroom.

But next day, thinking how thrilled I'd been by Richard actually spanking me and fingering me, I hung about in the garden until he appeared. From then on, when the chance arose, we lost no time in continuing our spanking and caning sessions.

But Richard insisted we did other things if I wanted him to carry on with our secret meetings. He was a bossy boy and strong, for which I secretly admired him, even if he twisted my wrist when I dared to oppose his bullying. I even enjoyed being ordered to do things he demanded, like letting him play with my breasts and suck my nipples. It progressed until I was made to rub his cock until it got hard and he shot his sperm in my hand. When I complained some of it had stained my dress, he said if I sucked him off when he was about to come, there'd be no mess as it would go down my throat. I was then told to kneel and take his cock in my mouth.

Finally, buying condoms to use on me, in my bedroom when we were the only ones in the house, he made me roll one on his cock and let him screw me, taking my virginity.

I complied with all this because I found it arousing to do things supposedly against my will. I always protested I didn't want to do what he forced me to accept, having to be smacked or caned into submission. He added a leather belt as an extra to beat me with, and began to tie me up, knowing it increased both our pleasures greatly when he fucked me.

In time Richard got his girlfriend pregnant and had to marry her, going to live with her family, ending four years of fun between us. I resented his wife for having him, and after the wedding reception I went home tipsy and envious of the honeymoon couple. I had to masturbate to take my mind off being left alone.

My powers of imagination have developed over the years with the need to arouse myself. Visiting Richard and his wife's family is a favourite scenario. I picture Richard, his wife, her mother, father and sister waiting to welcome me to their home. Right away the women strip me naked while the men leer.

I'm handcuffed, and any show of reluctance or resistance is punished by the women. For not pleasing them I'm given the belt. I actually flick a leather strap at my bottom to add realism when I act out this scene.

After having made me give them all oral sex, I'm tied hand and foot, bending over a stool, and the father fucks me in the back passage, the thought of which gets me highly excited as I'm lost in my fantasy. Richard's wife straps on a dildo to fuck me, his sister brings me off with a vibrator, and the mother squats over my face.

Whatever they do, I'm made to thank them. I'm glad that no one can see me as I fuck myself useless with a courgette, my hips a blur as the most gloriously sapping climaxes wrack my body. All this I do in lieu of having actual correctional and bondage sex. My husband won't do it, so in the privacy of my mind and my bedroom, who's to say I shouldn't? Glad to write and get this in the open, even if I remain anonymous and change names.

Anonymous wife, South Coast.

CHAPTER TWENTY TWO
Keep Talking

It's good to talk, so went a popular television advert to entice us to use the telephone. My wife Jo and I discovered this was so on holiday in Spain one year. Finding it accepted to go topless around the hotel pool and on the beach, she took to it like one always awaiting the chance to flaunt her voluptuous goodies. Not bettered by any female in the hotel, her splendid tits measure a firm thirty-six, she's really in her prime. Add to such great boobs a curvy figure and broad rounded arse, seen to best advantage in the bikini briefs she wore. From the rear, this, the sole garment she wore most of the day, was a mere thong separating the plump cheeks of her buttocks.

She admitted to being thrilled by showing her body off on the beach or poolside, where horny males of all ages were hanging around, walking past continually to eyeball her terrific tits as she sunbathed. I was pleased for her, and proud too. It reflected on my good taste in women, and I liked her to be admired. Also, it made her horny to be ogled so, and I was kept busy fucking her in our hotel room during the day as well as at night.

While I teased her and she confessed she'd always had a secret kink to exhibit herself, she said she knew what my favourite turn-on was. Right away she told me she was well aware of my hidden stash of bondage and correction videos secreted in our garage. Spanking videos, she actually called them, and said it was my turn-on. Wasn't I always patting her bottom and giving it a friendly smack in passing?

Apparently this proved I'd just love to place her over my knee for a good spanking. I had to admit that this was so. We should have no secrets, she said, but should talk of our desires. That's what was wrong with most marriages. She slyly added she'd watched the videos, finding them such a turn-on she had rubbed her clitty and brought herself off. This was the first time she'd admitted to me that she masturbated. She suggested we watch them together, and learn how it's done.

We'd wined and dined and had a tremendous bonk, so in the mood of the moment I divulged that I'd paid submissive prostitutes to let me spank their bottoms. She laughed, saying I should have paid her the money for doing the same, the idea of earning money as a pro exciting her.

I said never mind paying her, often when she'd annoyed me I could have pulled her across my lap, tore off her knickers, and given her arse a well-deserved smack.

She said that she'd respect a man who did that, keeping his woman obedient, and I should have put my foot down years ago. She then said I didn't know half of what she'd got up to as my wife. I was looking down on and fondling her naked breasts and getting erect again when she stopped me in my tracks. By confessing that at our daughter's wedding reception in the posh hotel that had cost me a bomb to hire, my kid brother Ed had enticed her into a bedroom and fucked her. Well, my erection was gone in an instant!

'I was tipsy,' Jo claimed. 'I told him no, but he upended me and then spanked my bottom until I let him.'

To my questioning, she admitted he'd made her orgasm several times, what with his hard young prick, and the unexpected thrills of being spanked like a naughty girl.

Unable to contain myself, I grabbed her and rolled her over face down on the bed. Right there under my nose was her superb bottom. She laughed at me, but not for long as I brought my palm down hard on the pliant flesh. I smacked her arse with all my force, and found it most gratifying - bloody marvellous, in fact.

With her pleading for mercy I at last relented, mainly because my hand stung and my arm ached. 'Any more dark secrets,' I asked, 'for trying it on behind my back will get you the severest bout of disciplining you could ever imagine.'

She slid off the bed, crossing to the dressing table mirror to gingerly examine the bright pink handprints on her buttocks. She said she'd deserved to be spanked, but goodness, hadn't I left her bum stinging. Then thick old me realised she'd set me up for the session by enticing me with the story about my brother - and I'd loved it.

It had also revived my erection, eyed with appreciation by my Jo. 'Don't think of wasting that, Bill,' she said. 'Fuck me.'

Such was our heightened arousal that we missed the dance that night.

So through open talk Jo and I discovered what turned us on, and got routine marital sex out of the usual rut. In my wife's case it was showing off her body, and mine was being dominant and giving corrective punishment for her misdemeanours. Mail order firms supplied handcuffs, weighty nipple clamps, open crotch rubber panties and matching bras, bondage aids like confining straps with buckles and locks, plus a good varied selection of sex aids.

For my last birthday, Jo's present was a gift-wrapped leather whip with knotted tails, handed to me as she leant forward over the table and hoisted her skirt to reveal she wore no panties. She then said my brother Ed had fucked her regularly throughout our marriage, even as a teenager. Well, I no longer needed to be inspired to redden her arse and then fuck it right afterwards.

Jo also told me she had fantasised about being in another woman's power. So, an advert in a specialist magazine brought an answer from a married couple like us.

We exchanged visits, and I had the pleasure of spanking the young wife's bum prior to fucking her while her hubby did the same with Jo on the bed beside us. The girls also gave us a treat with a sensuous show of lesbian sex.

Through meetings with these two, and once trusted, we were introduced to others, exchanging visits and even going on holidays in a group. I've now had the pleasure of spanking almost a dozen other females, and fucking them too, with or without their husbands present.

Jo plays her part by having both men and women spank or whip her, as well as having sex with the other men and women of our circle. It's all done without harming ourselves, and behind closed doors. If you don't indulge, don't be critical.

Wm., Bath.

CHAPTER TWENTY THREE
Taming Teresa

Too late to change her mind, looking apprehensive as she was led into the so-called correction room, my wife Teresa gave me a pleading wide-eyed appeal to cancel the proceedings. But she'd admitted she'd been bitchy, and so very hard to live with. She deserved to be taught otherwise by Martin and his friends in their private club. They were dedicated to bringing shame and humility where it was proved to be required. Thinking it was all a joke and a fun thing, Teresa had volunteered.

But the cold steel shackles put on her were real, allowing just enough movement to shuffle into the correction room with the clank of metal chains. Fear and humiliation showed in her face as she saw the audience assembled to witness her ordeal, many of the women present her closest friends. She begged to be released. As I wavered Martin shook his head at me, signalling a threat that I could soon find myself suffering the same indignity before an unsympathetic group.

Martin then announced to my wife that as it was her first official ordeal, she was required to truthfully answer all his questions. That way he would know her punishment was deserved and any hesitation or avoiding the truth would add to her being disciplined even more severely. She refused to admit that other men had fucked her. I did want to believe her; nagging wife she might be at times, but not unfaithful. But men standing before the little stage shouted that she lied.

Martin became insistent, interrogating and warning she'd be shown no mercy if she didn't co-operate. He reminded her that her husband had given his permission to allow anything necessary in a treatment to make her a better wife. She quivered as he casually ripped off the light white cotton robe she'd been dressed in for the inquisition, exposing her bare breasts. Trying to cover them in her modesty got her thighs smacked with the light cane Martin carried. Others grasped her wrists and drew her forward, making her breasts jiggle.

Vulnerable and shamed by the crude remarks passed about her, she tried to resist as Martin swivelled her around and swiftly bent her over a purpose-designed wooden whipping horse.

Aided by two women from the audience, it was a moment's work for Martin to expertly lock her in place, wrists clamped and feet forced wide apart and buttocks uplifted. Bare except for her skimpy briefs, these were now ripped from her. The heartfelt sobs of humiliation I heard were real, and yet I was beginning to revel in my uppity wife being put through the ordeal.

As she began to complain that they had no right at all to do this to her, she got a noisy spanking on her bottom for her resistance. The loud cracks as Martin's palm struck her clenched buttocks served as a warning of worse to come if she didn't behave.

Her initial defiance was soon vanquished. Invited onto the stage, her best friend began swishing a thin cane with unerring accuracy onto Teresa's fleshy moons. She yelped and squealed, accusing her friend of being a sadist. As her hubby, I perhaps should have been outraged by the treatment she received, but it was the most erotic sight I'd ever witnessed, to see my naked wife writhing and her lovely bottom being thrashed as she cried out for mercy, saying whatever they wanted she would do.

'Go on!' I shouted to the girl caning her. 'Give it to the arrogant bitch. Make her confess her adultery and admit to being an unfaithful slut of a wife.'

Nodding agreement, Martin took the cane from the tiring girl and offered it to me. I accepted it and increased the strength of the strokes. Teresa's blonde hair flew wildly as she tossed her head, crying out as each stinging blow landed. Fair-skinned as she was, she striped beautifully in a criss-cross pattern reaching well around the curve of her bottom.

Now she called out that she'd tell everything truthfully if only the caning would stop. Her frame shook with sobs and her backside clenched and flinched at each fresh strike. Yes, she had been with other men, women too, even the girl who had caned her.

I heard her admit she'd taken it in the mouth, between her tits, even in her behind. I told Martin he could do what he liked with the dirty bitch. Best of all, I knew that from then on I held the threat of a spanking or caning over her, and wouldn't hesitate to do it. She looked at me, and silently begged me to forgive her.

Naked, she docilely let herself be strapped into a specially shaped X-frame bolted to the wall. Her back to the frame, arms and legs spread-eagled, a thick leather belt was buckled around her waist and her wrists and ankles made secure. She was completely immobilised by the contraption, spread out like a pinned butterfly. At once another woman came before her wielding a soft leather strap, the ends of which were divided into finger-length tails.

'No, please no!' Teresa pleaded, fastened as she was and not able to do anything more than protest about another of her gentle sex whipping her breasts. Although the tails didn't strike her at all hard, the sensitivity of the tender targets wrung cries of hurt and shame from Teresa's lips as she was tit-whipped. Left red and swollen, the nipples tight, clamps were fixed to stretch each bub. 'No more, have pity,' she moaned.

Then to her astonishment (and mine), Martin spun the X-frame to which she was bound. It turned like a wheel with a push of his hand, stopping with her long blonde tresses brushing the floor. He then turned to the woman wielding the leather strap with the tails, indicating that she continue whipping. With Teresa in the upside-down position with legs and ankles fastened wide apart, it meant her hairy mound was now head-high to the woman with the strap.

At first light flicks between my wife's open thighs brought squeals of protest. Harder strikes on the fleshy outer lips of her sex made her protests turn to cries of agony and abject pleading for mercy.

It was a sobbing and humbled wife who was eventually released and fell gratefully into my arms. Laid on a couch still shaking, the older woman who had whipped her then soothed her, taking her breasts from her blouse and feeding a big nipple for my wife to suckle, saying, 'Comfort yourself on that, my dear, your ordeal is over and you did well.'

Accepted then by Martin's CP group, my wife and I are now regular attendees of their meetings. I've since watched Teresa do the strapping and caning of deserving cases, both male and female. She's a different woman, and far more interesting to have as a wife. And much sexier.

Gordon, Brighton.

CHAPTER TWENTY FOUR
Teacher's Pests

Eight 'A' levels meant I could study at a prestigious university, but being the daughter of a single mum meant that financially it was out of the question. Jobs in offices or shops paid peanuts, so I had to come up with something better. That's how I came to work for a woman I'll call Madam Thong, a strapping Miss Whiplash type who was coining in money chaining up, beating and generally torturing her masochistic male customers.

At first I was employed as a receptionist in her spacious flat. It meant answering the phone, taking appointments, and acting scornfully while ushering in her clients when they called to be 'corrected', as their treatment was known. Generous tips and pay far above average made it a good position. And as one interested in all unusual human behaviour, intending to qualify as a teacher of psychology, I found it fascinating to study the types who came for Madam Thong's therapy.

All kinds turned up, most of them regulars who arrived weekly to be bound, thrashed and walked on with high heels. Others were 'babied' and kept in nappies, fed from bottles and spanked if they were naughty. All were generally made to grovel and beg, to obey and be humiliated. Allowed a peek into the 'treatment' rooms where they were taken, I saw canes, whips, manacles, stocks, whipping stools, frames for confining wrists and ankles; in fact, everything for the bondage and punishment of the willing victims.

My employer's working garb was a black leather bra and black leather leggings with open crotch, completed by matching high heeled shoes which kneeling slaves were forced to kiss. She looked the part, with creamy breasts overflowing the low cups of the bra and arse cheeks almost bare; handy for queening some lowlife client to the point of suffocation. Her arrogant pose and the thonged whip dangling from her wrist made an awesome sight for her submissive worshippers.

I soon saw why they went in fear and dread of such a super-bitch. All too often I found myself getting all hot and turned on at the mere thought of dressing like that, and even more so by imagining men crawling before me, cringing at the swish of my cane or whip. My sex throbbed and my panties grew sodden with the juice of arousal.

One day, as if reading my mind, my boss asked if I'd learn to service the customers. Her clientele was getting too big for one dominatrix to handle. She'd apparently watched the way I'd treated them, with cold contempt, and decided I was the right stuff.

She said the rewards were fantastic; easily enough to pay university fees and rent a nice apartment. As I would be a teacher, she suggested I act as a strict headmistress. This would appeal to the punters who fantasised about being naughty boys and were punished in the appropriate way. This included being bent across the desk for a bare bottom caning, or an over teacher's knee spanking with shorts pulled down, and then being ordered to stand in a corner. I could envisage the screams as I swished the cane, and the pleading for Miss to show mercy.

To let me see how she operated, promising I wouldn't spare the rod, I was allowed to discipline some cringing clients, and took to it in the manner born. I had one who fancied he was a circus horse (no kidding!) and I slapped a saddle on him and rode him around while lashing his arse with a riding crop. He whinnied and neighed at my command, sat up to do tricks when whipped, and all with a massive erection to prove he got turned on being ill treated. For that too, having the insolence to get an erection without permission, he got whipped and left tied-up in a small cupboard.

I was accepted, and given a room as a classroom with a blackboard and some desks. I chose lacy black bra, briefs, suspender belt, and black fishnet stockings with knee boots as my working garb, this all worn under a dark cloak and a mortar-board on my head. The equipment deemed necessary for teaching and disciplining unruly 'boys' included canes, whips, handcuffs to chain them to their desks, and a penis clamp for those caught masturbating.

For my very first pupils I had four middle-aged 'scholars', who were visibly nervous as I entered the class swishing my cane. It was great to think I was to make their lives a misery. No doubt that's what they wanted, but I determined to be the terror that would make them wet themselves in fear. Right away I insisted on a school uniform, blazers and shorts, although in the case of one who confessed to cross-dressing, I allowed him to come dressed as a girl. For the least misbehaviour I thrashed them all mercilessly, trousers down and either across the desk or over my knee. Without fail they soon had bursting erections.

Swishing down the cane with all my force on trembling pale and fleshy buttocks, it gave me added pleasure to note my other pupils flinch and cringe in fright, waiting their turn. I was to discover that having absolute power over males was a never-failing natural aphrodisiac, making me hornier than I'd ever been before.

It meant serious sessions of self-relief upon returning to my flat after work as a dominatrix. I depended on a realistic latex dildo for repeated climaxes, penetrating myself and working the ridged stalk up my cunt to the cervix, then the clever dummy prick did the rest. Switched on, its head rotated and swivelled, even thrust and shunted back and forth to bring me off in helpless spasms.

And while my plastic penis pal stretches my cunt and fucks me, I pluck and twist my nipples for an added sensation. I position a mirror to watch myself coming.

Although assured of certain multiple climaxes, however, such a regular routine, like any other, becomes familiar and loses its impact. I began to long for a real flesh and blood prick to satisfy me. But I was too busy with studying at university and working every spare moment as a dominatrix to have a boyfriend. As a last resort, sleeping as I always did with my huge life-size Teddy Bear beside me to cuddle, poor Ted was ravaged when I fixed a strap-on dildo around his loins and rode him until I orgasmed in the woman superior position.

Of course I had a ready-made selection of real pricks in the class I dominated. On one occasion, announcing it was medical inspection day, I had them strip off and stand beside their desks. Using my cane to tap the knobs presented, using words gauged to arouse and bring on erections, I judged how hard and stiff they got for my purpose of using them to satisfy my lust. I chose a supposedly gay actor, as his handsome prick reared level with his slight belly and temptingly thick.

Cowering before me, I called him a slut and a filthy beast for flaunting that disgusting thing in front of me.

Slashing the cane across his bare arse, I drove him into a side room where instruments of torture were kept. I slammed the door shut and he cowered before me, his eyes on the fearsome cane while I was licking my lips at the sight of his magnificent cock. I fought an irresistible urge to get it in my mouth, to suction that nice fat stalk until it had to jerk and quiver on my tongue and erupted down my greedy throat. My cunt opposed this by throbbing to show who had first claim.

Binding his wrists behind his back to a metal ring set in the wall, I told him his behaviour and poor class work had earned him special punishment. When I took his rampant tool in my hand he sobbed it was only other gays who did that, he was not that kind of man.

'You are now, wimp!' I told him forcibly, smacking his face to silence further protest and rubbing his cock, uncapping the shiny pink bulbous head as the outer skin slid up and down as I massaged the stalk. Gay he might have been, his moans agonised, but his cock throbbed and twitched in my hand like any other I'd toyed with.

'No, please, Mistress,' he whined, in a frenzy at having a female handling his dick. 'You shouldn't, you mustn't,' he pleaded pitifully. 'No, you can't, not in your mouth.'

Too late was the cry, as they say. Stooped before him, I sucked the delicious stalk between my lips. Without knowing how many of his kind had blown him, I determined to prove what a girl could do. The way his knees buckled, and from his moans of pleasure, I knew I'd won, more so when his pelvis jerked to fuck my face as a sign that he couldn't control his lust.

This was all too evident when he shook and jetted spurt after long spurt of thick spunk down my throat. When his spasms had subsided and I released him, he pleaded that he hadn't meant to insult me by losing control in such a disgusting way. I agreed he deserved strict disciplining for his arrogance, patting my knee as I sat and glared at him, not to be defied. He obeyed meekly and accepted a spanking. In other sessions alone in that room I got him to fuck me, with me always mounted on him, as was proper for his dominant mistress.

We became friends after business hours. He'd visit my flat where he was free to dress as a girl, and I'd help with his choice of clothes, his wigs and face make-up.

We'd sleep together when we went out dining, always making it a fun bondage and spanking session before I sat over him, impaled on his cock. In time I had sex with several of the more fanciable 'pupils' in my class, and even the wife of a businessman who'd asked my permission to view her husband being beaten. I offered her the whip and she flogged her hubby's backside mercilessly. Then in the private room he was tied securely to a chair and made to watch me strap on a dildo and fuck his wife.

Later in our acquaintance, staying at their country home or in their villa in France, she paid me to let her see her husband fuck me after she'd caned his arse and got him erect. His wife claimed their previously stale marriage had never been happier or more eventful. She now dominates him, and confines him to a spare bedroom as a punishment if he forgets who is his mistress as well as his wife.

Dominating people has now become a way of life for me, one in which I'm richly rewarded in every way; physically and financially. I have men who grovel at my feet. Lovers of both sexes. And invites to the best homes in Britain,

France, Spain and the Caribbean.
  What more could a dominant girl want?

Andrea, Westminster.

CHAPTER TWENTY FIVE
Toy Boy Torment

When I worked in East Africa as a United Nations doctor, a German couple lived in the next bungalow. Hans and Gerda Buhle were doctors too; medical missionaries. They told me that in his boarding school holidays their sixteen-year-old son Kurt would be coming out from Berlin to stay with them. I had a swimming pool in my garden. Surrounded by high trees it was completely private. I said when Kurt arrived he was welcome to use the pool.

  Waking one morning I heard loud splashing outside my bedroom window. My house-girl, Nkutu, came in with coffee and said that the German family was using the pool. The way the young African girl giggled made me wonder what was so funny. Opening the curtain to look out on the garden and pool, I saw all three Buhles were in the absolute starkers. As a doctor I was not shocked by nudity, but had to giggle with my servant at the sight of fat Hans with his pot-belly. His wife Gerda was a big woman too, with pendulous breasts bouncing about. Young Kurt was worthy of admiration, though, so splendidly clean-limbed and athletic. Well-developed for his age, the boy had inherited from his dad a very large penis and balls.

  I had been celibate for over a year since my divorce. Seeing how very handsomely built the teenage Kurt was made my vaginal juices run. My inner sex throbbed as if desperate for penetration by a rampantly stiff prick. His lovely firm bum looked adorably sweet to me. It was a strange desire I felt, a powerful craving to fondle those ivory-smooth buttocks, to kiss them and, strangest of all, to spank them! As the sight of his beautiful penis was so arousing, I blushed deeply, imagining sucking on such tasty flesh and feeling it growing rigid in my mouth. The shame I then felt getting so incredibly lustful over a youth young enough to be my son, did not prevent me giving in easily to an irresistible urge to flaunt my body before him.

  I stripped to join the Buhles at the pool, my sole objective to let young Kurt see me naked, a thought that sent erotic shivers up my spine and tightened my breasts and nipples. Trembling as I went to join them, I was unable to keep my eyes of him to judge how he would see me. As a desirable woman, I hoped. He was a cool one, no callow youth it seemed, the way he eyed me up and down and nodded with a secret little smile, as if liking what he saw and well aware of what I'd intended. Then he leapt quickly into the pool, which I guessed was to hide a growing erection. At least, I liked to think so.

  With Kurt still on holiday his parents asked if I'd look after him for a few days. They'd been ordered to the Sudan to help at a refugee camp until a relief medical staff appeared. My stomach did triple somersaults at the chance of having him all to myself. But my conscience made me promise to be strong, that it would be very wrong to seduce the youth, no doubt a virgin. But then I saw him crossing the garden, blond hair shining and with that scrubbed look on his boyish face. In the heat of the African day he wore shorts and flip-flops, and was coming for a swim. My guilt suppressed by the sensations surging through me, I slipped off my dress, bra and panties. Passing the bathroom, I grabbed a towel to cover my naked state. He called my name to announce his arrival and I went through to the lounge wrapped in the towel.

I was going to say he'd caught me about to shower, but the boy wasn't wasting time on games that may or may not lead to sex. He caught hold of the hem of my towel, tugging it away from me as he said wasn't this what I intended? Never dreaming he would be so forward, I turned and ran into my bedroom. As Kurt followed, I faced him, nervous and unsure. I felt at a loss between my desire for him and the boy's obvious wish to have me. I stuttered that what we were thinking was not right. I was old enough to be his mother. He merely said I had good breasts and cupped them in his hands, making my stomach turn over and my vagina palpitate.

He was so confident I knew he'd been with women before, his fingers pinching my nipples and announcing they were very stiff. While I stood dumbly, his other hand began probing beyond my moistened outer lips and fingering my sex, flicking my clitoris. I wanted to moan that he should fuck me, but deep shame made me push him away. The beast in him was aroused and I felt fear, despite being the older head. Down came his shorts to reveal a really startling erection, rearing up against his belly. I tried to dash past him, but he grabbed me and threw me face down across the bed. 'I know the word,' he said savagely. 'I don't like prick-teasers! Now I fuck you good...'

'Don't you dare, you wicked boy!' I screeched, trying to get up, but held down by a strong hand on the back of my neck. Ordered to behave, to stop struggling, I recalled how once I'd fantasised about spanking his tight young buttocks. Now I felt a stinging strike land on *my* bottom as he used one of his rubber flip-flops to flay the unprotected cheeks. My howls of pain were intermingled with squeals for mercy, and my backside burned a fiery red. As the thrashing ceased I lay sobbing, feeling the boy parting my cheeks and fingering my cunt. His touches on my clitoris reminded me how aroused I'd been, and soon brought me to the brink of a climax despite wanting to deny the young brute the pleasure of knowing he'd excited me. Then he was taunting me that my bottom was jerking, my cunt squeezing his fingers, that I was losing control.

The heat from my thrashed bottom and the titillation of my cunt had me trembling. 'Please,' I begged, my entire being needing his prick. 'You shouldn't. You mustn't, Kurt. You're making me too worked up and excited. I - I'll come. You'll make me...'

'That's what you want, isn't it, English lady?' he laughed, adding that he was going to fuck me.

A glance over my shoulder showed he wasn't bluffing. Next moment I gasped as his stiff young prick thrust into me, to the hilt. Already on the brink, now uncaring as the thick stalk skewered me, I came violently as he fucked me savagely from the rear. My bottom clashed with his belly as we jerked in unison, his teenage cock remaining firm with the virility of youth long after he cried out he was coming, filling me with his hot cream. I had climax after climax before we rolled apart, soaked with sweat.

At once he began gloating how he had spanked me and fucked me, and now he intended to thrash me any time I resisted his advances or refused him sex. He would sleep with me until his parents came back and I was his woman, his property. It was a tribute to his dominant personality, no doubt, that I, an older woman, in the days following docilely placed myself across his lap to be spanked like a naughty child. I knew I liked him doing it. Another favourite order he gave me was to suck his prick. 'Eat it, English slut,' was how he commanded I do it.

Once I got the taste of it, I loved to drain every thick drop from him. One morning, still in bed together, I was sucking his prick to milk its contents with such mounting lust that I wasn't aware his parents had returned and were in the bedroom.

'What are you doing to my boy?' Gerda Buhle screamed as her son's prick slipped out of my mouth. 'Get something to beat her with, Hans,' she told her man as I tried to leap off the bed and escape. Held down, seeing her glare of hatred and knowing I was for it - that it wouldn't be a fun spanking - I saw her husband return from the lounge with a thin bamboo cane, normally used to hold my tropical plants upright. Kurt, I noted, had fled.

'Turn her over and hold her down for me to thrash,' she said vindictively. Testing the cane, she made it swish through the air. I cowered and clenched my bum cheeks as the cane hissed, while Hans pulled a cushion under my thighs to raise my bottom higher. With his large hand pressing and making my back dip, my buttocks presented a very fine target. I begged to be spared, my tears real, saying I was sorry.

'You will be,' Gerda swore, reminding me I'd promised to look after her precious boy - not seduce him. If only she knew! Too old to be made an example of by a severe caning, I let myself go with howling and screaming that she was a German cow as the cane cut the air to sting my ravaged bottom. This only incensed her further as I squirmed and thrashed about. Her arm tiring, she passed the cane to her husband, whose fresh energy inflicted further agony.

When finished, he stuck the cane in the cleft of my bottom. No doubt they consoled the poor boy, while I knew the young lout had spanked me and fucked me at will.

I was left sobbing with my buttocks striped red and purple, a souvenir of my toy boy torment. A further humiliation was that my house-girl came into the bedroom as I lay blubbering with a thrashed behind. Kurt had been a busy boy while his parents were away. My servant showed all the signs of being pregnant within a few weeks of Kurt returning to Berlin. She admitted to me that while

I'd been at work in the local hospital, the randy young German had been fucking her too. And I got the beating! Well, that's life, I suppose.

Doctor S, ex-Kenya.

CHAPTER TWENTY SIX
Coming Attractions

Reading a sex manual by a so-called sexologist, I was surprised and envious to see stated that: *If a woman who is normally capable of experiencing an orgasm is properly stimulated immediately after her first climax, she can in many instances be capable of having a second, third, fourth or more strong orgasms before she is fully satiated. Indeed, in clinical tests (who does these tests?) females have been observed reaching full climaxes more times than this, even twenty and above within an hour.*

It went on to state that this was accomplished by foreplay of the woman's choice, be it dirty talk, oral sex, spanking and dominance, whatever the woman found erotically arousing.

How d'you think I felt reading that? I'm twenty-eight, perhaps a little embarrassed about sexual matters, but I've had lovers and even a husband, yet never had an orgasm. Not one, never mind the twenty or more mentioned by the sexologist, so no wonder I felt I was missing out. Not even one brought on by masturbation, you may ask? Convent educated, taught by nuns, as a girl I was too scared to masturbate. When I'd grown out of the fear of hell and damnation and thought about fingering myself, I guess the old shame and guilt still lingered, so I didn't try.

But I did embarrass myself by fantasising about screwing around, using crude words about being fucked, sucked, whatever - even being taken across my boss's knee and having my bare bottom smacked. A lesbian girlfriend, who I once slept with to see if that would do the necessary, used to joke that every time she came, her cunt fainted! So I decided to get help, writing to the sexologist whose book I'd read, pleading never mind the twenty climaxes, I'd settle for one real goodie. To my surprise he replied to my letter, sympathising but assuring me such multiple orgasms were possible.

Giving me the phone number of a professional masseuse who'd helped in researching the sex manual, I called the number. A very pleasant woman called Helen answered, who realising I was shy and embarrassed, gently coaxed me to admit I was eager to be 'fully satiated', as the book claimed. She confirmed she'd had successes in bringing women to climax through various methods.

So, I drove some fifty miles to a neat cottage outside a village, wondering if my journey was worthwhile, yet excited enough to be moist between my thighs. A tall man of late middle-age let me in, saying he was Charles, husband of Helen. In their cosy lounge I was faced with a pleasantly plump lady of fifty, or so. She wore a starched white overall like doctors wear. I was brought a cup of coffee, and then put under scrutiny.

The questions were very personal. How often did I desire sex and in what positions? Did I suck penises or lick women? What did I think of CP and S&M games? Had I ever made love to another woman with a dildo, or been the one receiving the dummy cock? In that respect, when alone did I fantasise about being dominated and then masturbate using vibrators?

I thought my unease and blushes made them settle on domination and bondage disciplining as what excited me most. But talking openly about anal sex, sucking men off and other sexual practices with Charles present made my embarrassment obvious, and his wife said it proved what deep-seated inhibitions I had to overcome or I'd never know the joy of a powerful orgasm. 'Sex without guilt or shame,' she said, 'is what we demand. Accept our therapy and treatment or leave,' I was told sharply.

But the questions became even more personal. I began to cry and refuse to answer. At a nod from Helen, her husband asked again if I wished to leave or accept their therapy? 'I want to stay,' I sobbed, and found myself being pulled across Charles's knee. It was Helen who drew down my panties, saying I had to learn the hard way now I'd agreed to stay. I cringed, thinking my naked rear was just below a virtual stranger's nose, then forgot that as the spanking began, each smack ringing out as I howled in pain and agreed I'd co-operate with whatever they considered necessary for my treatment.

The beating stopped, but I was kept across his lap. 'Talk or be spanked for your obstinacy,' Helen told me commandingly, advising that it was obvious being obedient was right for my nature.

So I talked, which increased my arousal; draped across the man's knee. I heard myself relating how I'd let a girlfriend's father, a West Indian doctor, fuck me in his car when driving me home from his daughter's seventeenth birthday party. I'd also had a lesbian affair with a fellow schoolteacher at the school where we taught. On a school trip abroad to improve the pupils' French, at a ramble in the woods when left alone with a sixteen-year-old boy whom I was aware had a crush on me, I allowed fondles and kisses. Not on the pill at the time, I stopped short of letting him penetrate me, although I desired it, but prevented by the fear of an excited boy making me pregnant. Greatly aroused by the thought of what this boy was doing with his teacher, I rubbed his cock and he drenched my hand when he came. He fingered me and I was near to an orgasm, but afraid of others discovering us.

I suspected Helen and Charles were aroused, hearing of my sexual history. My briefs were sodden and my sex was throbbing. If bold enough I'd have finger-fucked myself, and through being watched I'm sure I would have had my first orgasm. I also knew they'd deliberately set out to lower my resistance, saying I was ready to undergo more treatment.

'You have proved yourself worthy by having sex as a teenager with a black lover, father of your friend,' Helen said. 'Also by lesbian experimenting, as well as the naughty encounter with a boy pupil.'

So I was led into a spotless tiled room with a padded massage table, which had loose straps with buckles at the four corners. Ordered to strip, I obeyed and was told to lie face up on the table. My breasts and body were quivering in my excited state.

'Her breasts are firm, swollen, and note how her nipples are thickened and erect,' Helen said, as she and Charles stood either side of the table. 'She's very aroused, ready for our special treatment.'

I felt my wrists and ankles being confined in the straps, binding me to the table. Then Helen lifted a leather strap with the end split into fingers. She began lightly whipping my breasts, stomach and between my parted thighs, until I was writhing with arousal, the tormenting flicks agitating my already excited sex. Then Helen stopped to tell Charles to 'test' me.

'She's really excited,' he announced, feeling inside me. 'Let's try the vibrators, Helen.'

Craning my neck to see what they were doing, I saw Helen between my spread legs and holding the cylindrical stalk of a long and very thick vibrator. She said I would love its size, and in the same instant, slid it deep inside me. The whole girth and length went in easily, oiled as I was with my juices. It was switched on, and incredible sensations were powered inside me. The realistic bulbous head turned and twisted, boring deep into my passage. I began to buck my hips helplessly as if electric shocks coursed through me. My cries came from deep in my lungs, and the first jolting spasms of continuing orgasms wracked my whole body.

There was no doubt that my interested audience were delighted to see me thrashing about on the massage table, the persistent vibrations pulsing through my cunt sending me into convulsions as climax after climax shook me rigid.

If I'd never come before, I was making up for it now. Gasping as I remained in the throes, I begged them to stop the sweet torture and withdraw the vibrator. I dimly heard Helen say she'd counted well over a dozen strong climaxes. As the big sex toy was withdrawn I still heaved from continuing orgasms, as it seemed the unremitting vibrations continued. In my delirious state I was a whimpering shell of a woman.

'Comfort yourself on this, my dear,' I heard Helen say, looming mistily over me as she fed her husband's cock to my face. 'Suck on it like a baby,' she advised, and gratefully I accepted Harold's real and rigid flesh into my mouth, sucking on it greedily, wanting its emission to quench the dryness in my throat.

I was helped into the shower, still dazed as Helen soaped me under the refreshing spray. My bottom wet and sudsy, Helen gave it several resounding whacks with her hand to wake me up. She said it was obvious my 'thing' was being dominated and spanked or caned to get aroused enough to have orgasms. She advised I find a strong partner, male or female, to obey and find fulfilment in my sexual life. That's what I've done since. Offered to stay that night after dinner, I slept between Helen and Charles. She then insisted that I let her husband fuck me to prove I had gone all the way to lose my inhibitions. Just to make sure I agreed, however, a spanking was administered across Helen's knee to warm me up for her husband's pleasure, and to ensure I climaxed. Which I did, and I've had no trouble doing so since.

Ms Dorothy, Suffolk.

CHAPTER TWENTY SEVEN
Spanking for L-Driver

I never thought I was into kinky sex, spanking games and bondage, but one never knows. I'd failed my driving test five times through being timid and nervous, fear of failing because of a sneering husband's reaction. I decided to take extra lessons, not telling my husband of the secret driving tuition, hopefully to pass my test and flourish the licence under his nose.

Then I fell for my driving instructor. He wasn't all that good looking, but his personality was strong and he was big and very manly. He was the opposite of my dentist husband. I became close to Edward and fantasised about having a sexual relationship with him. Feeling like I did, a very love-struck woman infatuated with a younger man, I wrote him a letter confessing how I felt about him, opening my heart.

After I'd posted it I was sorry, and went for my next driving lesson afraid and ashamed to face him. I'd told him I'd do things for him I wouldn't do for my husband. Things like sucking his penis and letting him tit-ride my breasts. I wrote these things because I knew men liked doing them to women - all in the cause of pleasing him. Writing that he could do as he liked with me, I signed off with a P.S. that I'd always be obedient to his wishes.

When I got into his car he patted my knee and kept his hand there, fondling higher under my skirt. I took that to mean he'd taken note of my brazen letter. But he never suggested we drive somewhere to make love or said nice things to me. He told me very sternly that I'd better try harder to pass my test. 'We'll start the lesson,' he snapped. 'Any bloody silly mistakes or lack of concentration will mean you get in the back of the car for me to spank your bottom. Being severe with you is the only way.'

I could hardly believe he wanted to get me in the back of his car and smack my bottom for doing wrong things during the lessons. Changing gear too late, not signalling, he marked as two faults to go on the spanking list. He seemed deadly serious. Soon I was more nervous than ever and making errors repeatedly, yet I found that my trembling was as much from excitement at the thought of being spanked, and knew it was mounting arousal.

'Will I be made to drop my knickers for that?' I joked timidly, as I forgot to indicate once more.

'No other way to spank a bare bottom properly,' he said bluntly.

And I knew then that he meant it. The thought of lifting my buttocks to be smacked like a naughty schoolgirl made a tight knot of nervous apprehension form in the pit of my stomach. A few more careless mistakes had him frowning and ordering me to drive to a deserted lane. Getting into the back seat, he slapped his knee and sternly ordered me to join him.

Shaking, I protested, but meekly got into the rear of the car and was told to remove my panties, or else he'd do it. I was shamed to note the crotch was quite sodden and the enclosed air in the car reeked of my juice. Humiliated to think he'd noticed, and trying to avoid a spanking, I said tremulously that he could fuck me if he cared to. That I, a married woman with a good husband and two children, should be saying that another man could fuck me, was quite beyond belief.

I thought Edward might welcome the chance; I'm curvy, and have nice breasts and a rounded bottom. Men look at me, and I do still get chatted up. But he was not amused. I wasn't to know that he was strongly into CP as his sexual preference. He coldly demanded my panties, which I handed to him in real fear, then at his command I stretched across his knee. I shuddered as he rolled up my dress, looking closely down on my bared buttocks as I trembled at what he was seeing.

I had my crotch firmly pressed to his right thigh, my left leg on the seat and the right with my foot on the car floor. In this position my bum cheeks were separated, allowing him to view my sex lips and the tight brown pucker of my anus. I groaned in mortification and tried to clench my cheeks tightly to cover my undying shame and utter humiliation. Edward immediately gave my poor unprotected cheeks a couple of vicious smacks, making me howl and kick.

'Don't struggle or clench your arse cheeks to pretend you're shy,' he said crudely. 'How rich coming from a married woman who's just said I could fuck her. What would your husband think if he knew that? You knew you would get spanked for driving mistakes. Now it's evident you need punishing for being such a loose woman and wife. Do you agree?'

Tears were hot on my cheeks and I'd never been spoken to like that in my life. I now knew he was a sadist and I was in his power, being humiliated over his knee. A vicious warning smack made me answer as I knew he wished to hear.

'I - I am a bad wife,' I sobbed. 'And you're scaring me. I thought you wanted to fuck me, Edward. That's the only reason I said it...'

'But you said it, and meant it, you randy slut,' he said, to further degrade me. 'So accept what you deserve. I do this on behalf of your husband, the poor bastard.'

Whack, whack, whack went the stinging smacks on my flesh while I screamed and my bum turned to fire. With each blow he recounted driving mistakes I'd made, then went on smacking my smarting backside for being such an untrustworthy wife. Reduced to sobs, I knew he was my master.

That in itself was strangely erotic. The heat in my well-spanked bottom was spreading its glow to my sexual source and was becoming exceedingly pleasant, making my cunt pulsate wantonly. It was a new and thrilling experience after years of routine married sex. The mounting sensations were quite deliciously lewd. Once again I begged him to take me. I didn't care - I just wanted to be screwed!

It brought more spanks for my impudence, then a disdainful push of his hand to send me tumbling between the car seats. I was crouched before him, snivelling. I was told it was he who said what would happen. Ordered to unzip him as I knelt awkwardly between his legs, I was told to suck him to a full erection and then suck him dry. I obediently did as he ordered, until my mouth filled with his seed and, swallowing urgently to stop choking, I rubbed my cunt and had the most shattering climax.

Later, while preparing tea for my family, I felt continual arousal thinking back on the afternoon. I had been spanked like a kid, made to fellate a demanding man, and then masturbated while crouched between his knees. I was hooked, an addict on spanking and being dominated by a masterful man. And I still take lessons, even though I've passed the test.

Pamela L., West Midlands.

CHAPTER TWENTY EIGHT
Spanks for the Memory

Once I fell head-over-heels in love with a neighbour, but he wasn't interested no matter what I did. I was just seventeen and I suppose the man in question was a handsome hunk of forty. In a bid to male him aware of me, I sunbathed in the garden in the tiniest bikini that barely covered my boobs and pussy. I ignored boys of my own age to fantasise about my mature chap undressing and making love to me.

In a bid to get him really going and leave no doubt about how I felt, I began to go around my bedroom naked, standing at the window when he was in the garden below. I even began to cup and fondle my tits, and stroke my pussy lips, certain that would get him going. But he always turned away when he saw me, ignoring the curvy young figure I displayed for him.

What kind of a man ignored such a blatant offer? I was determined to get him. He had a wife, or at least, he lived with a woman called Jane.

One day I met him in the street and he smiled and said hello. My parents were out that evening so I told him if he called the door would be unlocked. I'd be up in my bedroom waiting for him, which showed how desperate I was.

He nodded and later, waiting in my room, lying on top of the bed in the buff, I was so aroused I played with myself. When the door was pushed open I almost had a fit. His wife had come to make trouble for my throwing myself at him. The first thing she did was call me a dirty little slut for flaunting myself. Sitting down on the edge of my bed as I reached for some clothes, she was big and strong enough to drag me across her knee and hold me there. Ordered to lie still, her severe voice made me obey. Jane then smacked my bare bum really hard with the palm of her hand until I was crying, both with humiliation and pain.

It continued until my bottom was on fire and I begged her to stop. I said I wouldn't flirt in front of her husband again. She was laughing at me when she said he was merely her lodger, and I'd been wasting my time anyway, as he was gay. I'd been spanked like a child, and all over a gay! That made me feel even worse. Added shame was that he must have told her I'd be waiting.

'If he means nothing to you,' I blubbered, 'why did you come here to spank me?'

'Because parading naked makes you a disgrace to the female sex,' she scolded me. 'A pretty girl with such a nice figure mustn't lower herself for any man - they're not worth it.' Made to feel shameful, I cried bitterly. 'There, there, little girl,' she consoled me, taking me into her arms and holding me against her comfortable bosom to soothe me. I lifted my face gratefully and she kissed the tears from my eyes, then unexpectedly clamped her full lips to mine.

It became a passionate series of kisses, with her tongue seeking mine, our open mouths rolling over each other's. It was nice, and it was easy to respond. As our kisses grew in intensity, I realised Jane was fondling my breasts, cupping them, plucking and pinching my nipples, and then lowering her head to suck on each in turn. She was seducing me...

Although nice, I'd never thought of having it off with my own sex. But now one had spanked me, which although stinging my bottom, I found undeniably sexy. Being treated severely had been surprisingly pleasant, because my parents never cared what I did. Her kisses were like those of a randy boyfriend, and I was told how lovely I was, and not to waste myself on men. Then she rolled me off her lap until I'd been positioned on my back with my legs hanging over the edge of the bed.

In a swift movement she was on her knees, between my thighs, the palms of her hands prising my knees apart and her breath directly on my teenage pussy. Her mouth clamped over my outer lips and her tongue probed, lapping in the moist inner flesh, circling my sensitive clitty until I grabbed her head and bucked against her face. As she sucked me greedily I felt a sense of guilt at allowing another woman, one old enough to be my mother, to arouse me in such a way to the brink of a strong climax. I suddenly screamed that she was a disgusting old weirdo, a filthy lesbo, and thrust her head away.

She at once flipped me over on my tummy, angrily warning me not to ever call her names again. 'It is you, young madam, who are the disgusting one, flaunting your naked body to a man.' One strong hand held me down as, arming herself with one of my bedroom slippers, she used it with a will to thrash my already spanked bottom. I screeched both in pain and humiliation as she plied the thin leather sole, and had me begging and pleading I'd never call her names again, that I was a shameless trollop.

She stormed out, leaving me whimpering and sprawled across the bed. As I calmed, I got thinking of how aroused I'd been to be smacked by a stern mistress, and how her kisses had thrilled me. Moreover, as my fingers traced a line over my moist pussy lips, I admitted that I now wished I'd let her continue to tongue me. So what if we were of the same sex? Her kisses and her mouth between my legs had been more exciting than anything I had known. I became furious at being so stupid as to send her away.

The following day I went to her house intending to say how I was sorry, and hoping she'd resume making love to me. The man I'd had a crush on answered the door and ushered me in to meet Jane. Before I had the chance to apologise, he said, 'If I were her father I'd teach her a lesson that young girls should not be such lewd and forward hussies.'

'Well then, you teach her a lesson,' Jane said. 'Warm her hot little tush for her. Cane her arse for being so shameless.' I looked at her for mercy, but got none. She asked if I deserved a thrashing.

'I've been bad, I should be punished,' I agreed, words I thought I'd never say. Jane rose to guide me to a large chair, forcing me to bend forward over the seat. Going behind the back of the chair, she fastened my wrists with a soft cord. Walking to the front again, she rolled up my dress and pulled down my briefs to my ankles. I shuddered, thinking the man was seeing my bare bum, before remembering he was gay.

Jane handed him a cane and told him not to spare me. 'Make her remember this visit,' she said.

The swish through the air told me the bamboo was descending. Even before it landed I was squealing, then had a good reason to as my bottom stung and the caning continued relentlessly. When it eventually ceased I was left weak and whimpering, but the heat generated had spread through to my pussy and set it throbbing. An appealing look at the woman told her what I needed, and I let her lead me upstairs to a bedroom, willing to let her do as she wished with me.

I was ordered to bend forward over her bed, and she applied cream to my burning cheeks. Soothing as that was as she caressed my flesh, it was even more delightful as her greased fingers delved into the valley of my bottom and played with my swollen sex lips before slipping inside. Slippery as her fingers were, my juices added to the ease with which several entered me and very expertly titillated all the most sensitive areas, including my clitoris. She teased me as my bottom wriggled and thrust back to her hand as the first climax hit me. Little slut, horny minx, randy trollop, were just a few of the choice names she called me as I had several shattering climaxes as she went on touching me up.

Then she stripped off and joined me on the bed, our lips fusing in passionate kisses, which went on until I was laid back with her face between my thighs. I was told I was now hers, her property, and to forget or be unfaithful would mean the severest correction.

We met almost daily. Apart from spankings, I was often bound helpless to be licked or dildoed, the pleasure increased for both of us if I was helpless. Many were the strict orders I had to obey over the next year with Jane as my mistress.

On a Greek holiday, fancied by a young waiter who took Jane to be my mother, she had me tied to the bed to stop me keeping a date with him. We argued on that holiday, and it was the beginning of the end of our time together.

I went with men as well as women over the next year but, not shy to mention I liked to be dominated and spanked, not one of my lovers took the hint. No one took me seriously, though I longed to be under the complete control of a strict and dominant master or mistress.

Better still, I've been thinking, if I could find a married couple who'd be strict with me and use me as they wished. There'll be such a couple out there, no doubt, but I haven't found them yet. As I write this I've already enlisted in the Army and passed my medical and intelligence test, and I'm just waiting to be called up. Maybe my luck will change there!

Susan, Humberside.

CHAPTER TWENTY NINE
Rule of the Whip

I'd known Vicky since school. A bossy girl, always taking charge of things, I thought she resented me having boyfriends. I got married and we met again when we were invited to Vicky's housewarming some years later. It was warm in the crowded house and I told my husband I was going out for air, but he was too busy at the bar to come with me. The night air was sultry and I stood by the swimming pool thinking how refreshing it would be to jump in. The same thought must have occurred to Vicky, for she came out and said it would be fun to take a dip.

The pool area was deserted, and urged on by Vicky, I took off all my clothes, including bra and panties. She did the same. Giggling like schoolgirls we clasped hands and leapt into the water. It was colder than we thought and we climbed out shivering. In the pool's pump-house a selection of towels hung from a line. Vicky grabbed one and towelled me all over, especially my breasts and between my thighs. I'd had a few drinks and was feeling light-headed. I found, when she dropped the towel and went on fondling me, that I became aroused.

I'd known she'd had a schoolgirl crush on me, and had an idea she might be bisexual or lesbian. We were soon exchanging long passionate kisses, the open mouth and deep tongue kind, with our breasts flattened together as our naked bodies clung in a really torrid embrace. First experience of female love or not, I was horny for more as her left hand cupped my tits in turn, her mouth lowering to nip and suck at my nipples. Vicky's other hand was between my thighs, gliding sensuously over my moistened lips.

I parted my legs to give her access to invade and titillate my inner sex. Then I sensed someone else was present, unseen and no more than a shadow nearby. I'd been responding to her with a fervour that matched hers, now I wanted to pull away, thinking we'd been providing entertainment for a sneaky watcher. Shaking with lust, I said it wasn't right, that I was a married woman and no lesbian.

'You are aroused and don't deny it,' Vicky said, and I got a hard slap on my face and told I must be obedient to her. 'You know you want it,' she said fiercely, pulling me down to a cushioned lounger. She draped her naked figure over me and rubbed a stiff nipple to my mouth.

Ordering me to suck, she spitefully smacked my upper leg to make me comply. I felt frightened of her sudden power over me and dutifully sucked each breast as the nipple was fed to my lips. As if satisfied with that, she slid forward over me with her opened thighs over my face and her pouting sex an inch above my mouth. She ordered me to suck her, and I knew I must. In what faint light there was I could see her thickened sex lips parted, like a mouth begging to be kissed. Humiliated and angry at myself for submitting so willingly, I also acknowledged a new desire to be dominated by her. When ordered to get on with it and lick her, I decided to do all I could to make her come.

Her clitoris was erect and enlarged, big enough for my lips to suck on. Writhing and squirming she groaned, until she was convulsing in the throes of a hectic climax. Sitting up, she reached back to find my sex and finger it. The excitement of sucking off another woman and making her come so strongly spread like wildfire through my body until I erupted in the most shattering climax I'd ever experienced. The prolonged intensity of the orgasm was so great, so weakening, I could only lie in the arms of Vicky and murmur that I didn't know how it could be so wonderful with her. She said we would have other times just as sensual, and that I was now her lover, her slave.

Later, back in the house, Vicky danced with my husband, Ray. The room was crowded, and soon I noticed they were missing. I determined to find them, going into the hallway leading to bedrooms and bathrooms. The first door I pushed open revealed a neighbour of mine, a young woman I thought the perfect wife and mother. She was naked, busy bending over her seated husband and sucking his cock. At the same time a man I knew to be her father-in-law was thrusting his prick into her from the rear. I beat a hasty retreat, suddenly realising the party arranged by Vicky was really an orgy for willing participants.

In another bedroom I found an interested group watching a couple fucking lustfully, and saw my husband's flanks thrusting as he pistoned into Vicky. Furious that they were doing it before an audience, I screamed for everyone to leave and then threw myself at Vicky, blaming her for seducing Ray and branding her a cheating slut. Ray shouted how could I complain? He'd been the shadow I'd seen earlier and knew I'd had sex with Vicky. Turning to leave in humiliation, I heard Vicky say I should be made to pay for my outburst. While Ray held me from behind, and despite all my struggles, my clothes were torn off me by Vicky, my wrists tied behind my back, and I was held down across her knee.

With my naked cheeks exposed, my rear was smacked extremely hard and painfully, yet another humiliation as the watching men and woman urged Vicky to spank me harder. I was then spread-eagled on the bed with my wrists and ankles fettered to the bedposts. As I sobbed that Ray was a bastard for going with such a slut, he reminded me again that I'd done exactly the same, as well as having an affair with a neighbour that he knew about. He told me to grow up, and asked how I thought Vicky could afford to buy such a grand house. 'She earns it as a dominatrix,' he told me. 'Whipping clients and charging them enormous fees for being humbled in the meanest possible ways.'

'And I want you to come into the business with me,' Vicky said, as her hand lightly trailed across my breasts. 'Think about it and say yes, if only for the money,' she added, laughing. 'Never mind for the fun we'll have together. Fun like this,' and then she was lightly kissing and sucking my nipples before sliding down my belly until stopping at the fork of my thighs. Her breath was warm on my quim as she whispered I was the sexiest woman she had ever desired. As Vicky's tongue flicked and lapped inside my wet channel, Ray kneeled up on the bed and fed his cock to my mouth. I wanted them both, I decided. I wanted the best of both worlds.

I became Vicky's partner in the domination business, being as dominant with my clients as I am submissive with her as the 'wife' in our mistress and slave relationship. I'm rather good in both roles: lording it over those who get their kicks from my being strict, or being subservient to all my mistress's wishes and commands - even to sharing my husband with her. To see her in black tight-fitting leather with knee boots and a whip is an impressive sight. She's not above disciplining me severely if she thinks I've been too lax with my clients, so I know who is the dominant partner. Especially when ordered to her bed at night when she awaits me with her cane and strap-on.

Ray's wife, Blackpool.

CHAPTER THIRTY
Hots for Chum's Mum

I'm a seventeen-year-old girl and I fancy my boyfriend's mother. I've known her for three years and really love her. I worship and adore her, and would do anything to make her love me. It's different with her son Robbie. We were an item in a kid's way at school, then stayed friends after leaving. I was considered his girlfriend, but as it meant visiting his house and being near his mother, I let people think that. I never allowed more than kisses or a fumble at my breasts. In fact, I remained a virgin.

My strong desire for his mother made me wonder if my sexual preference was only for my own sex. I considered her son quite immature and still a mummy's boy. She was very strict with him, making him be in at a certain time of night. He complied even if we were at a disco or the cinema, and I suspected she still used a ruler to punish him if he came home late, as I'd overheard her mention it. I'd have liked her to be strict with me; my parents not caring when I stayed out late.

So I thought Rob's mother was lovely. Called Moira, she was in her forties with a beautiful full figure. When she and Rob went on holiday to Spain I was invited to join them. We went topless on the beach like most women and girls, and I was embarrassed as she soon noticed I couldn't keep my eyes off her gorgeous breasts. I longed to hold and kiss them, to suck on her thick nipples. My love and desire for her intensified. Seeing her naked, except for bikini briefs, made me ache to make love to her, want to sleep with her naked beside me.

Much admired around the hotel pool and on the beach by the men for her splendidly statuesque figure, I noted with pleasure she gave them no encouragement. I knew her husband had left her, that her friends were all female, and I hoped beyond hope she was a lesbian, or at least bisexual. That encouraged me to get her alone and tell her I loved her, thought her beautiful, and wanted her to do as she liked with me.

We were in the double hotel room that we shared. It was after dinner and she'd undressed to shower before we went with Rob to a disco. Wearing just a light robe that showed the curved contours of her shapely breasts and the protruding nipples, even the dark outline of her pubic mound, I had to pour my heart out to her. She answered sympathetically, saying I was very young, that my love for her was a passing infatuation.

I protested it was real, and she let me hold her hand and squeeze it before letting go. I saw her face was flushed like she was excited, or sexually aroused. Asking her if that was so, she said my expression of love had made her feel strange, because it had been unexpected. I plucked up my courage and kissed her, and slipped a hand into her bathrobe to cup one luscious breast. For a moment she responded, our lips fusing and even our tongues touching. Then she pushed me from her, saying she hadn't allowed me to do that.

At the disco I was very depressed through being rejected. In a mad moment, as if to get revenge, I offered to go outside with her son Rob and let him do what he'd always wanted - have sex with me. Against a wall I let him get my boobs out and feel them, and suck on the nipples. He took my hand and I discovered he had his prick out of his jeans. It felt hard and warm in my palm, and he told me to rub it. Then he whispered hoarsely would I suck it? I knew men loved that, although I'd never done it.

Bending over, I covered his stiff cock with my lips, and was sucking it when he began to push his thighs against me, just like he was fucking my mouth. Then he said he wanted to put it between my legs. He peeled down my knickers and pushed me up against the wall, and after feeling my pussy, guided his cock inside me. I was wet and he went right in as far as he could go, moving to push it in and out of me. Then, before we knew what was happening, his mother was confronting us, pulling him away from me.

Rob turned and ran like a scalded cat, leaving me cowering against the wall. His mother shook her head sorrowfully as she regarded me. 'How could you, Janine, you naughty little minx?' she said, her voice more sad than angry. 'I'll deal with Robbie. You go back to the hotel, and don't you dare leave our room until I return to deal with you.' I promised I would wait, was sorry she had caught us, loved her, and would do anything for her. I was told how could that be so when she'd seen what I was doing with her boy? I burst into tears and ran sobbing to the hotel.

Waiting in our bedroom seemed forever, trembling in fear of her anger, and even more afraid she'd want nothing more to do with me. She told me later that she'd sought out Rob and boxed his ears in the disco, ordering him back to his room and humiliating him before a crowd of dancers. Keeping me waiting had been part of her plan to increase my agitation, making me a nervous wreck. I trembled before her as she bustled in, holding up my knickers that she'd retrieved in the street. How dominant she seemed.

Even in my shame and fear of her, I loved her, worshipped her, and got down on my knees to beg forgiveness. She said all my big talk about loving her was nonsense; I'd proved myself to be a horny little slut. I pleaded what had happened with Rob was only because I was miserable, thinking she didn't want me. I didn't like boys or what they did to girls. I knew I was different, and all I wanted was to be with her, not her son.

'You acted like a trollop, so now you must be punished like one,' Moira said quietly, but with menace in her voice. Sitting in a chair, she pointed a finger at her lap. Without a word, knowing very well what she meant, I laid myself over her knee. I felt mounting excitement too, a definite sexual surge of sensations pulsing through my pussy as she lifted the hem of my dress. 'Just as well you've got no panties on for what I'm going to do,' she said grimly.

My dress was carefully folded up to the small of my back and all was revealed of my bare bottom. Scared now of feeling pain, I begged to be spared. Flinching and clenching my bum cheeks in anticipation of a very hard smacking, I blubbered like a baby. 'I'm sure I'll scream,' I blurted. 'If you hurt me, they'll hear me all over the hotel...'

'Oh, I intend to hurt you, Jan,' she assured me, but you won't be heard.' At that, as I opened my mouth to further protest, she pushed my knickers between my lips and effectively gagged me.

The first smarting smack to my wriggling buttocks made me realise this was no pretence or token punishment, but for real.

Tears blurred my eyes as each blow increased the tenderness of my chastised behind. But even the humiliation of being spanked was proving, as it always would in my future relationships with dominant women, to be erotically arousing.

The heat in my smacked bottom had seeped through to my sex, increasing its demanding throb. Released from Moira's lap, I drew my knickers from my mouth and sank down across the bed as Moira laughed at my plight. This was not how I'd imagined any loving relationship with her.

'You're horrible,' I sobbed, my bottom on fire as I gingerly felt its raised surface. 'You've no right to spank me, I'm not a child...'

'I'll do as I like with you,' Moira said, 'if you claim that you love me and want me to love you. That's my terms, and if you want to play with the big girls, you must first learn your place.' I glared at her from the bed as she came and sat beside me. Her hands folded up my dress again and gentle fingers lightly soothed my thrashed cheeks. 'You have such a pretty bottom, Jan,' she told me.

'It makes me want to do other things with it as well as spank it. Kiss it, for instance,' she said. 'Kiss it better.'

'You enjoyed beating me,' I wailed. 'You smacked me because you like doing it. Do you get pleasure from smacking girls on their bare bottoms?' I sneered.

'Men's too, let's not be sexist about this,' Moira teased. 'Oh yes, even grown men like to have their arses whipped. And usually when they're tied up securely, helpless to stop dominant mistresses using and abusing them. One day you'll enjoy doing it to men as much as I do. But how could I resist punishing such a sweet girlish bottom as yours?'

She leaned over me to kiss each cheek, then prised them apart to delve her wet tongue between them. With fingers and thumbs splaying my cheeks wide, it gave full access for her to lap and lick at my private places.

The probing of her snakelike tongue on my swollen sex lips, and her mouth sucking on my sensitive clitty, made me gasp and jerk in the spasms of a wonderful climax. When, still dazed, I looked up as I rolled over, she stood beside the bed and shed her clothes. She was magnificent.

'You have so much to learn, Jan,' she told me. 'I shall take great pleasure in teaching a randy little minx like you all there is to know of domination and correction.'

'Even if you have to take me across your knee and spank true obedience into me?' I asked, hopefully. 'Or tie me down to have your way with me?' I drew off my dress and bra to be naked too.

'Of course,' Moira said, drawing me into bed with her and taking me in her arms. Automatically, I nuzzled my face into her comfortably ample bosom, kissing the softly rounded flesh and finding the hard nub of a nipple to suck on. 'Yes, I like it, do that for a start, my love,' Moira said, her hand stroking between my thighs. 'There are so many nice things we can do to each other.'

Which we did, sleeping together for the rest of the holiday, and making love during the day with secret trips back to our room. I didn't need the son once I had the mother.

Janine, Southampton.

CHAPTER THIRTY ONE
Pick of the Crop

My wife Gloria had become a law unto herself. When I moaned about this to her mother, who is also my mum-in-law, of course, she simply said it was about time I showed Gloria who was boss. My wife was staying out all night and no doubt sleeping with men, using the excuse she was staying overnight at her ma's house. As I was staying there some of the times she claimed, I knew she was lying.

You might say who am I to complain about Gloria playing away when I was having it off with her mother? The fact is mum-in-law Sheila had been my lover and I was her toy boy long before marrying her daughter. It was one of those things, with me a teenage apprentice and Sheila a brassy blonde with big tits who seduced lucky me at work in our lunch hour. Later she introduced me to Gloria and we soon were engaged. Then, when my wife began screwing around, I turned to Sheila for guidance about her girl's behaviour. As an ever-randy widow, she lured me back into her bed.

For all that, she really wanted Gloria and me to remain married. She said that even while mounted over me, having first sucked my cock and then straddled my thighs to fully impale herself on it. With her breasts swinging over my face and her nipples brushing my lips, it seemed hardly the time to discuss her daughter's future as my wife. But as she ground down on my cock, she insisted I try harder to save the marriage. Once she had climaxed and we were relaxing, she went on about what I should do, and what I should have done, blaming me for Gloria's wild ways.

Claiming I'd been at fault because as a single girl my wife had always been ruled with a rod of iron by her late father, a very strict disciplinarian, who had dominated Sheila too, I had been weak and allowed Gloria too much freedom. 'We ladies need a real man with a strong hand to keep us from going astray,' my mum-in-law stressed. 'Even if it means beating us regularly to keep us happy and respectful, and aware who our master is.'

I couldn't believe punishment would keep a wife happy and in line, having the utmost contempt for wife-beaters.

'Not wife-beaters, Ray,' Sheila corrected me. 'They punch their women in fits of temper or drunken rages. They're beasts. I'm talking of dominant husbands who administer necessary correction to wayward women in a fitting manner. I mean spanking when put across a knee like the naughty girl she is, or caned when bound and bent over a chair or on a bed.'

She assured me that protest and screech like they would, the errant females would admire and adore such men because it shows the wife being corrected is loved and it's for her good. I wasn't too sure Gloria would feel that way about me being heavy-handed over her sleeping around.

'Her late father spanked her, as he did me when we displeased him,' Sheila revealed. 'We both thought the world of him, even if he did administer corporal punishment and make us obey his every whim. Your wife has lost his steadying influence through marrying a weakling like you.'

Encouraging me to dominate Gloria to save our marriage, she related how it had been for her as a submissive wife. Anything he thought deserved it got Sheila grounded, spanked, whipped, tied to the bed until begging forgiveness and made to perform sex acts to show she loved and wanted to please him. She said she was never happier than when under the thumb of a strong man.

I wondered if I was up to it.

Sheila rolled off the bed and flaunted her fine arse by waggling the cheeky moons before my face. Automatic in my response, I reached out to trail fingers over the ivory-smooth curves. She tilted it brazenly, prised apart the lovely globes, and taunted me to respond. I gave her backside a light pat for her wanton behaviour, hardly a smack, and no more than a token gesture for her being rather naughty.

'You can do better than that,' my mother-in-law scoffed. As I sat up and swung my legs out of bed, she draped herself across my lap. She said patting her bum had been a natural response, an expression of wanting to smack it. 'It makes men feel powerful. Wallop obedience into your wife and learn to enjoy doing it,' she advised. 'Practice on me, Ray, and don't spare me. Warm my backside well...'

My first smacks brought derision and an order to use much more force. Doing so, I began finding it increasingly pleasurable to rain slaps on the rounded cheeks under my nose, watching them glow rosy-red. My arm ached and my palm stung; small inconveniences compared to the thrill of spanking Sheila's buttocks until she cried and begged for mercy. I reluctantly let her go, and struggling stiffly to her feet, she inspected her blotchy bum in the mirror.

When I returned home that evening I found my wife just out of the bath, drying herself in our bedroom and ignoring me as she dropped the towel and posed naked, dusting her nice neat tits with talc. As if in defiance as I admired her beauty, she stuck out her tongue lewdly while cupping her breasts.

'Lie on the bed,' I ordered, trying to make my voice harsh. 'You heard me. Lie down and spread your legs for your lord and master.' She looked amazed, and then laughed in my face.

Giving her a hard push, she toppled back across the bed, sprawled gloriously naked. Complaining she wanted to dress as she was going out, I told her she wasn't, and that was definite. She tried to rise, but I rolled her over. With a hand on the nape of her neck burying her face in the duvet cover, I felt the pliant curves of her bum and delved between her thighs. It was satisfying, after being fucked about by her for months, to hear her muffled protests, demanding I let her go because she had a date.

'Not any more you don't, unfaithful cow!' I retorted, giving her fleshy bum a hearty smack. That didn't hurt, I discerned her saying scornfully into the duvet, and I was to release her at once or else.

'This will hurt,' I promised as I struck her again with a smack that even hurt my palm. She howled, so I continued with a flurry of heavy slaps. Her yells and the angry red marks on her flesh told me she was hurting now.

More powerful smacks and she began sobbing and pleading for mercy, a different girl after her show of defiance. It seemed her mother was right; putting women in their place suited them, and made them more obedient and respectful of their men. As she lay whimpering and moaning that her bottom was stinging, I drew apart the scolded cheeks and found her cunt was wet to my touch. A finger slipped inside proved how drenched she was, and squelched noisily in her juices. I said the spanking had made her randy, and she began working her hips as I fingered her. 'Go on,' she urged, 'make me come... please.'

The way her arse gyrated showed she was on the brink of a major eruption. I had an urge to use more than my finger as I widened her cheeks and went in face first. With my tongue exploring her, flicking her clit and lapping in every nook, she bucked and writhed in a multiple orgasm. 'You're killing me, Ray!' she squealed in ecstasy, convulsing in the mother of all climaxes. Then, while she was still having spasms, I mounted her from the rear and fucked her to even more orgasms.

I reported my success next day to mum-in-law, and she told me to keep up the dominant attitude. Going to a drawer she said I could choose a momento of her marriage to keep Gloria faithful. I saw an array of canes, whips, straps and manacles for wrists and ankles in a wide selection of CP and S&M equipment. I chose a riding crop, thinking how I'd enjoy striping her arse with it. After fucking Sheila as a thank you, I went home and found my wife had remained in, just as I'd ordered. She'd gone to bed to await my arrival, and drew back the duvet to show she was naked, just as I'd ordered her to be.

A few light cracks of the crop had her begging me to fuck her. She swore she'd never be unfaithful again, and if she annoyed me she deserved to be punished in any way I thought fit. 'Right now though, Ray,' she pleaded, 'I really could do with my husband's hard cock fucking my pussy.' Positioned between her welcoming thighs, my knob slid along the ridge of her cunt lips and forced the entrance, her back arching as she heaved up to take my full length. I considered I owed my mother-in-law a vote of thanks for putting me straight about her darling daughter.

After our fuck Gloria picked up the riding crop and smiled, saying she recognised an old friend, as her father had used it to keep her obedient. I said I'd now carry on the tradition, and wouldn't hesitate to use it if she displeased me again. And that's how it has been ever since.

Raymond, Sheffield.

CHAPTER THIRTY TWO
Bound to Please

I've replied to your CP survey earlier, telling how I got to be a 'professional submissive' to pay my college fees. To me, someone who considers herself a truly natural born masochist who can give herself freely to whoever is my strict master or mistress, it is the ideal way to make a good living. Who gets hurt? (Well, apart from my spanked bottom!). I mean, I enjoy yielding to my clients' demands, and they enjoy and pay well to dominate me.

Normally I have difficulty in reaching a satisfactory climax during sex without suffering domination and humiliation. If occasionally I'm in a relationship with a boyfriend who is not into corporal punishment, he always has to stimulate me with his tongue or his fingers after he's had his climax. While he's titillating me thus I have to fantasise about being beaten and degraded to achieve my orgasm. I imagine myself being soundly whipped, offered to endure sexual perversions from other women, or being sold as a slave to a cruel master or mistress who keeps me in bondage.

If I fantasise these scenes vividly I ensure having multiple orgasms of the strongest kind. So, out with my professional work as a submissive, I prefer boyfriends who dominate me in every way as well as our sexual life. I never want to get my own way, even if it's about what to wear to a party or club, or where to eat when we go out to dine. And I will never refuse his most way-out sexual demands. Or if I do protest, it's done to get me spanked or caned to bring me into line.

My ideal master was Craig, a married man I had a torrid and punishing affair with and hoped to marry, even though he already had a wife. He was a natural sadist, the masterful macho male who was the right type for a girl like me with submissive desires. I was to discover his whole family were of the same mind, no doubt being the reason for Craig's dominant personality. Even his wife was the kind of cruel bitch one rarely gets to meet.

Soon after meeting him, he ably demonstrated his sadistic tendency by showing me up at a party with friends. He spanked me across his knee, panties drawn down, in the kitchen of my flat while others were there pouring drinks or getting food from the buffet supper laid out there. This was to show everyone the hold he had over me. Then with everyone knowing what he intended, he led me through to the bedroom and screwed me. I had a tremendous series of orgasms, showing I found his arrogance erotic and very sexually arousing.

Sure I was his and obedient in every way as a slave should be to his master, Craig decided it was time he took me home to meet his family. I agreed, not sure of what they'd be like, but on arrival found I was to be the star attraction in an orgy of sex and sadomasochism. He, his brother, his wife, and even his father, watched while I was ordered to undress. Naked, I was forced to serve them drinks while they openly discussed me, all of them copping feels and painful pinches at my breasts and buttocks. Craig warned me I would have to do everything they asked.

I was a captive in that house, but a willing one. We all have inner desires, but most people are afraid to try them out. Though apprehensive, even scared, I obeyed when ordered to suck off all three men in turn. Any complaints about my ability to give a satisfactory blow-job and I duly had my bottom smacked. When I had drained the men it was Craig's wife's turn to want pleasuring. I was made to kneel between her parted thighs, and directed to suck her until she quivered and came against my mouth. It was heaven for us both.

Yet my thanks for providing these entertaining services was to be tied on my back to a low coffee table, my wrists and ankles bound to the four legs. Totally helpless, I was fondled by all. Craig's father, squatting over my tummy, fed his cock into my cleavage and moulded by breasts around it. He then began to rock his hips back and forth. I had the brother's cock in my mouth, and Craig's wife knelt at the foot of the low table between my thighs to suck me.

Almost delirious with ecstasy, I begged to be fucked by all or any of them. Before they had finished with me, my hair, face, breasts and belly were splattered with the men's thick semen. I was sent on my way with a last caning by the vindictive wife, but I looked forward to each time I was invited to Craig's home for a family party.

His wife took to beating me at every chance, I'm sure because Craig was obviously finding more pleasure in fucking me than her. Jealousy made her by far the most sadistic of the family. Her sessions with me included my being clamped in wrist manacles and hoisted on tiptoe to an overhead beam in the cellar. She'd flay my bare back and buttocks with a tailed whip and then leave me hanging for what seemed like hours. On her return, when released, I'd collapse on the floor. At other times, as if to compete with her husband's frequent use of me, she'd strap on a realistic double-dildo, half of which went into her, and she'd fuck me with the other half. It was their increasing feuding over me that made me break off this very odd relationship.

I continued with my work as a paid submissive. One day Craig's father came to the house of correction, asking for me. He said he was there to be punished by a dominant woman, and that I deserved to be the one to flog him for what he'd done to me. Although not really my scene, for the kind of money he offered I took him into a punishment room. I have to admit this very arrogant man was the one person I'd have picked to punish. It was a great pleasure to bind him so hard the cord cut into his flesh. Flogging his back and arse with all my strength was all the more enjoyable for his pitiful cries and pleadings for mercy. I then beat him all the harder.

Left whimpering and on his knees, he was then ordered to lick and tongue my cunt. I told him spitefully that if I thought his performance was poor, he'd be severely flogged again. He called me mistress, and although I enjoyed the session, being dominant with other men has failed to excite me. It was no doubt because I held Craig's father in such contempt. So I'm content with my life as a servile female. Being a wife to a dominant husband would be my ideal; someone like Craig, whom I still have feelings for.

Alison, Leicester.

CHAPTER THIRTY THREE
My Slave Next Door

'The mother's friendly enough,' I heard our newly arrived next-door neighbour say. I was eavesdropping, my ear against the fence separating our gardens.

'But the daughter, Chloe, isn't.' I knew that was the wimpish son, George, bad-mouthing me. A gawky teenager of my own age, I guessed he'd run a mile at the sight of a girl's fanny. 'She's an awful tomboy and a horror. Her parents should have spanked that cocky arrogance out of her.'

I had to stifle a laugh of pure wickedness, finding it very complimentary being described as an arrogant tomboy horror. As for George, he sounded more like my father. *Spanked* indeed. For that remark I fully intended to spank *him*, and hard enough to make him sob for mercy. George, I said to myself evilly, you don't know it yet, but you are mine. I was in the mood to dominate.

Looking over the garden fence next day, I saw him with a girl I knew called Rose. She always attracted boys with her big tits and loose reputation. She'd boasted to me that she'd taken two cocks at once, one in her minge and one in her mouth. He left her to go into the garden potting shed, hurrying as if to avoid her company. Seeing me, she shrugged as if to say what a girl's blouse George was. Intrigued, I climbed over the fence to join her. She said George's parents were out, so she'd called by hoping he'd try his hand with her.

'Let's teach him a lesson,' I said, and we found him skulking in the shed as if afraid of us girls. I saw a bundle of bamboo canes used for tying up plants and chose one. Swishing it under his nose made George tremble and go deadly pale. I liked that, and looking back I've decided that's when I first discovered the power conferred by dominating a weaker type.

'Kiss our shoes and then drop your jeans,' I ordered. 'Let's see what you've got in there.'

George couldn't move, so I cracked the cane across his knuckles. Howling, he tried to bolt, but the stronger Rose grabbed him and bent him over the rough table used when potting cuttings. Bottom tilted high, firmly held though squirming, his protests became louder as I yanked down his jeans and Y-fronts. 'Please, don't,' he squealed, delighting me.

He had narrow hips and a lovely boyish bum; even then obvious to me it would be a joy to chastise. I was slow off the mark, for Rose clearly thought the same and armed herself with a cane. Following her first strike at his gyrating arse, I cracked down a sizzler to make his defenceless cheeks sting. George was screeching like a stuck pig, which was music to our ears.

Standing on either side of George's arse, Rose and I cut the air with the ferocity of our caning. This already had his cheeks criss-crossed with angry red stripes, all the more prominent because of the whiteness of the unmarked parts.

'Turn, wretch!' I ordered sharply, and he obeyed, head lowered and in a cringing attitude, sobbing at the indignity. Real tears, I was delighted to note, as much for the painful smarting of his caned posterior as for the great embarrassment of two girls thrashing him.

He began to beg pitifully, which only increased our sadistic pleasure. I used my cane to knock away his hands, used to cover up his dick. Rose and I exchanged pleased looks. Despite the beating, or because of it, George's dick stood bolt upright, looking painfully stiff in its rampant state. We girls immediately taunted him, accusing the humiliated boy of loving to have his bottom caned, that punishment turned him on. Tears streaming down his cheeks, he tried to deny this as our teasing increased. But he couldn't dispute the brute of an erection he had standing before us.

'Dirty, dirty little boy,' Rose scolded him. She took off the tie he wore, even on a hot summer's day, and handed it to me. 'Tie his balls up, Chloe,' she said.

I felt his nuts twitch as I tied a knot around them, then gave the end of the tie a sharp tug to make him howl. He begged abjectly, whining to be spared, but from the continuing rigid thickness of his throbbing root, I suspected he was secretly excited by our tormenting and turned on by being dominated. Of course he would never admit to that, unless perhaps made to by a good caning.

'I'm going to milk him,' I announced, holding his prick in my fist, my own arousal making my panties damp.

'Yeah, empty his balls,' Rose agreed, her own excitement evident in her lustful expression. Moving behind me, her hands went around my waist and cupped my boobs tightly. With her crotch now placed firmly against my bottom, randy and desperate to come, she began to grind and swivel her groin against me, to bring herself off.

Then her right hand dropped from my tit and went under my skirt, rubbing my wet lips through the squelching crotch of my knickers. I heard her gasps as she contorted in her climax while thrusting against my bottom, and then my body was jerking as I came violently while pumping George's cock. Crying out, his thick cream spurted in an arc over my wrist, and we were three youngsters in a huddle together, having a united orgasm that left us all breathless.

On future occasions George was hauled into the potting shed to be strung up to the roof joists or tied across the potting table, and often left there until Rose and I decided to return. He was regularly chastised and milked. He always acted like it was against his will, but I know different.

One day, invited to tea by my mother, he and I were in the garden, just out of sight of the kitchen window where my mother was baking. He sneered that without Rose to help me, I couldn't boss him around. So we began to wrestle as I grabbed him to prove he was wrong. I managed to get on top, straddling him, exhilarated by pinning him down. 'Beg me to stop!' I ordered fiercely. 'In future you'll have to answer to your new name of Georgina.'

As he protested, I crushed down harder. 'I'm your mistress, and you'll do as I say from now on, Georgina.'

As usual, the wimp began to beg. Suddenly, my parted thighs settled over his crotch. Added to the strong feeling of arousal I always got by dominating him, I felt the cylinder of hard flesh in his jeans rubbing against me. As our struggling continued, I wanted more. I wanted that hardness inside me. But I also wanted total domination.

'Shall I sit on your face, Georgina?' I asked, shifting my bum until my thighs enclosed his head. I leaned back, pressing my sodden cotton-covered mound against George's mouth. This was the ultimate humiliation, taunting him cruelly as I gazed down at his forehead, just visible between my strong thighs. As I drew back I saw a pale face streaked with tears. 'Did you like that, my dear Georgina?' I jeered. 'Shall I sit on your ugly face some more? I will unless you tell me what your new name is, and who your mistress is.' He sobbed that his name was Georgina, and that I was his mistress. Further told what I wanted to hear, he dutifully repeated that he was a weak little girl who loved being beaten by the strong girl from next door.

I said I'd give him a pair of my knickers that he must wear when we met, but as I went back to straddle his crotch I felt his hardness pressed to me again, and made little shoves against it, growing more desperate to have it inside me. Thankful that I'd gone on the pill, I unzipped him, and as he whined that I mustn't, I pulled out his stiff cock. Drawing aside the leg of my knickers, I guided him home. Once stabled in my tight pussy, I bore down, getting his full length sliding up into my juicy inner channel.

'Go on, fuck me,' I urged him, keeping my voice low so my mother wouldn't be alerted to what we were doing. 'Do it right or I'll whip your arse for you.' His flanks worked, thrusting into me beautifully as I ground my pelvis back to his upward heaves. His prick felt snug and tight as I revelled in every inch of it. I was quickly brought to the brink of a glorious climax. Below me, from the gasps issuing from his throat and the quickening stabs he made at me with his hips, he was almost there too.

From the kitchen I heard a call from my mother. 'Chloe! Where have you got to with George? Your tea is ready. Are you coming?'

Lying impaled on George, spasms wracking my body, I felt his body jerk as he pumped his jism into me. I tried to maintain a normal voice as I heard my mother repeat her question, asking if we were coming.

'Yes, mummy, I'm coming,' I managed to call. 'And so is George...'

Anonymous.

CHAPTER THIRTY FOUR
Housewife Needs Correction

I'm what's regarded as a happily married woman, loyal and respectable. I'm tied to my marriage contract, but not tied as in bondage games, which I found began to feature increasingly in my daytime fantasies. Through boredom, these were lewdly imagined in the afternoons, but masturbating also gave my sexually frustrated body much needed relief. My vibrator guaranteed a strong climax. I'm Barbara, thirty-six, and husband Roger is forty-eight. We have three children, two teenage girls and a boy.

I'm one of the lucky people, my partner being a businessman and earning enough to keep us all in luxury. When I told him I was not happy with our married life, he was shocked, asking why. I said his work was his main interest, and I wished we made love (I actually said fuck, as I was angry with him) more than we do. 'Why can't we do fun things like fuck in the kitchen or bath, or on the rug before the fire?' I suggested. 'Why not screw while watching a dirty movie?'

I was to astound him even more.

'Wouldn't you like to put me across your knee and give me a good spanking?' I asked, daring to bring up what I desired to happen for real, not just in a fantasy. 'Or how about tying me up and ravishing me while helpless, being masterful and making me do sexy things men want women to do?'

But he merely accused me of being over-sexed, and of having perverted ideas. 'Get out more now the children are at boarding school,' he advised bitterly. 'Take up charity work, or something.'

We live in an accessible suburb, so I began to go into London for day trips. At first it was to shop, visit an art gallery, go to a cinema or theatre, and eat lunch at a restaurant or pub. My husband didn't mind my excursions.

Back at home I still secretly masturbated, thinking it would be erotic to do it before Roger, or do it together. I grew tired of visiting the West End, and found myself gravitating to pubs and clubs in less fashionable areas. I knew deep down that I wanted to be accosted, picked up.

Just considering it excited me. It was not a regular lover I sought, just someone for a discreet and illicit encounter.

Then one warm afternoon I was approached in a Soho bar by a boy with dreadlocks, a handsome black youth of West Indian origin. He introduced himself as Alvin, an actor between jobs. He was fun to talk with, and after several drinks he suggested we go on to his place. Apprehensive, even scared, I nevertheless determined to see my adventure through, going with him to a tiny but clean, if untidy, flat.

There he undressed me without asking to, which I liked, as it showed he was masterful. It was nice to be held by a younger man and told I had a lovely body. He said when he first saw me he told a friend, that woman has a great pair of tits to play with. Then he sucked my nipples, laid me across his bed, and licked my aching sex. When he stood to undress, I was left so aroused by what he'd done that I fingered myself. He had an ebony body and a big brute of an erection, as thick as my wrist and longer than my husband's penis by many inches. He ordered me to suck it, making sure I would by grabbing a handful of my hair and pulling me up to a kneeling position, to feed his monster into my stretched mouth.

It seemed to swell and grow stiffer as I sucked, then he pushed me under him and we fucked energetically on his creaky single bed. He'd moved his dressing table so we could watch as we writhed together. It looked wonderfully erotic with his black body against my white skin. Also arousing was the thought of a stranger fucking me, a respectable married woman taking a big black prick and loving it. With his cock and his tongue, I was brought to numerous shattering climaxes that afternoon. We lay with our naked bodies sticky with sweat, kissing and fondling. I'd never known anything like it sexually. But reluctantly I said at last that I had a train to catch, and would like to dress.

He laughed and said he'd consider it, and asked if I was a married woman. I said yes, and then he taunted me, saying didn't my husband ever screw me?

'Naughty lady,' he said. 'If you like to be screwed, I can arrange to get you all the cock you want. From me and my friends. You'd be on to a good thing, all the prick a randy bitch could take, and paid for enjoying it.'

I told him I wasn't a whore, at which he laughed scornfully. I felt shamed, yet for some strange reason it was also quite exciting to be compared to a prostitute.

He offered me the use of his shower, and I didn't want to return home without having one. It was an afternoon to remember, I felt, but a one and only. Alvin, it seemed, didn't think the same. I got in the shower and closed the screen door in his face, showing him he'd been allowed enough liberties. He'd done well enough, surely, having his way with a merchant banker's wife.

With cooling water streaming down my still sensitive breasts and soaping myself, I was annoyed when he slid open the frosted screen and joined me. His cock was erect again and rearing a goodly nine inches, making it obvious he intended to fuck me in the shower.

'I've a train to catch, I told you,' I said sharply in my most haughty voice, showing I wasn't just there only to please him. In answer he slapped me across my breasts, and as I turned away to protect myself, he gave my wet buttocks a series of loud smacks that made me squeal in surprise and pain. 'Please, I don't want any more sex, Alvin,' I said, inwardly furious he'd slapped me, but afraid of making him angry. He snarled that I was keen enough for his black meat before. 'My husband will be waiting,' I insisted, but he laughed, jeering that he was going to fuck his wife for him, and would do so whenever he wanted.

I was scared as he roughly forced me against the shower wall, my forehead pressed to the tiles. He stood behind me, raising my arms. Looking up, I saw a pair of opened handcuffs hanging from where the water pipes were fixed to the wall. He must have done this before! Both my wrists were clicked into the steel manacles, and tethered securely I had to stretch up on tiptoe. I pleaded to be freed, but got my sudsy bottom loudly and soundly spanked, stinging me painfully and each slap sounding like a pistol shot. I howled and sobbed in humiliation that this boy was doing as he wished with me.

He then soaped my shoulders and the slope of my back until warm sudsy water cascaded down my spine to find a natural channel between the cheeks of my buttocks. I felt breath on my neck as he slid his engorged monster into the slippery cleavage of my bum, the bulbous knob nestling snugly, surrounded by my ample moons. I felt a strange mix of resentment, fear and excitement at being at his mercy, handcuffed and helpless, my beaten bottom throbbing, wondering what to expect next. I determined not to help him, but wondered if that was because I wanted him to use me.

'Don't expect my co-operation,' I said, trembling. But the plum-shaped knob nuzzling the moist lips of my quim set me on fire. Alvin panted into my ear that I should lift my feet up onto the edge of the shower tray, put his arm around my waist, pulled my hips back towards him, and thrust his length up into me with one aggressive lunge. With his big hands cupping my breasts to steady me, and his stiff manhood embedded up to the balls, I could not be entirely indifferent to being penetrated so deeply. 'Bastard!' I swore at him, feeling the surge of excitement that would lose me any control. 'Go on, then,' I said, as if bitter. 'Fuck me if you insist, you beast. Fuck me all you want.'

'With pleasure,' he said scornfully, adding to my ignominious treatment. I knew in future he'd insult me, call me names, say I was *his*, and own me and my body - if I didn't escape his clutches.

He withdrew his cock, the stalk making an embarrassing sucking sound as it pulled out of me. Showing not a shred of compassion, he then thrust back into me and I got a smacked bottom as he used my suspended body. The forbidden pleasure too much to resist, I angled my bum and worked my hips to get more of that black length in me, uncaring that he was mocking me as I shuddered in my orgasm.

The spasms continuing, I kept on grinding my rear to his shunting belly, my eagerness to take more of his cock so wanton that my wild gyrations made his prick slip from me. Or so I thought as I squealed at him to thrust it back in. But he had other ideas.

Adjusting his position slightly, he pressed his huge knob between my buttocks and against the tight ring of my bottom. It was well soaped, and a stab of his hips forced an entrance and I squealed with shock as I took a cock up my back passage for the very first time. My gasps and protests only made him slap at my hips while he buggered me. Appealing to him that he'd gone in the wrong hole only made him laugh. 'Doesn't your husband have you this way?' he sneered, saying I was so tight that my Roger was missing out.

Then the rhythmic motion began to work its magic. I felt deliciously full up there. His prick, big as it was, slid up and down as if contained in a tube of velvety flesh. My moans turned to sighs of pleasure, I whimpered and became aroused as never before, thrilled by the salacious thought that this black youth, whom I'd not long met, was fucking me in the arse. My penetrated buttocks worked back to buffet his belly. I screamed for him to fuck my arse, feeling rude and crude as I came violently, shouting my delight.

My handcuffed wrists hurt as I tugged and jerked, my whole body in a frenzy, threatening to tear the pipes from the wall. To add to the insult of being so degraded, he said I was a natural for taking it up the rear, and would get it there again, often.

At last he freed me. Exhausted by the sapping power of the climaxes he'd given me, I slumped to the shower floor. While I weakly tried to recover, he boastfully announced that I'd been fucked both ways to a frazzle, a testament to the power of his black cock.

On the short train journey back home, my sex and bottom throbbed in unison. I felt a real woman for once, but cringed as well as the thoughts of what I'd been put through by the cocky younger man shamed me. Just as disturbing was the thought that although humiliated, I'd also loved the feeling of being powerless, the used and abused half of the afternoon's partnership, the submissive woman in a torrid sexual session. With my gentle husband it was as if I was fragile when we screwed. I was secretly thrilled to think I could be so roughly treated, spanked and insulted, made to come often in such absolutely mind-blowing ways.

Later that evening, sitting at dinner with Roger and our children, the conversation around the table fell on deaf ears as I revelled in recalling my afternoon's romp with a black youth; particularly being bound helpless while he greedily screwed my bottom. Sitting with my family, I should have thought of myself as a disgraceful wife and mother, but if only they knew I was gloating over having such a secret.

But my mind was also made up that it would be wrong and very dangerous to meet the youth again. Let him be grateful he'd enjoyed a woman above the usual class of female he most likely had, I decided, while somewhat ruefully admitting to myself that I'd miss being treated like that again. When rising to leave the table, it was fortunate I was nearest the telephone as it rang. Upon hearing a familiar voice I froze. It was the husky tones of Alvin, reminding me I was on call as required. He said he had a whole list of men wanting to meet me, and there would be money in it.

'Impossible,' I said, trying to control the tremble in my voice. 'I'm not available at any time in future, thank you.'

As if reading my thoughts as to how he got my home number, he coldly informed me that while I was slumped on the shower floor, he'd gone through my handbag.

I was told he knew all the relevant things to know about me: my married name, home address, golf club, and to make sure I'd submit to him, he'd kept my gold credit card and driving licence.

'You'll be called on to come up to town, and you'll come,' he said menacingly. 'We wouldn't want your city gent hubby to know his wife's a black stud's bitch and a submissive whore.'

As I replaced the phone, trying to compose myself, Roger asked who had called. 'What did you mean, you weren't available any more?' he asked. I made up a story that I had been helping in a charity shop, as he'd suggested, but felt it was time others did a share of the work.

I lay restless for hours before sleeping fitfully that night, pondering my future as a sex slave to Alvin. No doubt I would be forced to perform every type of sexual act for the men he'd arrange. As my pimp, and me the prostitute under his power, he'd no doubt keep all the money earned. The prospect was both frightening and exciting. Of course, I could have woken my husband and confessed all about that afternoon's escapade. But I didn't.

What eventually did happen does merit another letter on the subject of CP and S&M practices, and those who indulge, both by dominating and being subjugated. It's quite a story, and worth telling. Called 'Housewife's Choice' perhaps?

Barbara, Wimbledon.

CHAPTER THIRTY FIVE
Wears Wife's Clothes

For birthdays and Christmas I always bought my wife Suzanne sexy underwear, like lacy bras, matching briefs, suspender belts and sheer stockings. Little did she know I got my kicks wearing them when she went out.

I'm not really mad on sex unless made to do it by a partner, and my biggest thrill is making love when dressed as a woman. Before marrying, I visited a mature lady prostitute who specialised in satisfying clients like me. She'd dress me in feminine attire, apply make-up to my face, provide a wide selection of wigs, and then act as a dominant man and arouse me to erection for sex. She would always be on top.

If I didn't do all she asked, I'd get beaten, usually by bending over her knee or a chair to be very painfully smacked or hit with a leather strop. I miss going there, but I've never been unfaithful to my wife. I'm not attached to men, I just love the feel of wearing sensual female clothes. It's an urge I've had since my youth. I'm mainly into exotic underwear, and with a padded bra, slinky briefs and stockings, with my favourite blonde wig, eye shadow and lipstick, I flounce about the house and arouse myself, fantasising as I masturbate.

My favourite fantasy is always about me being caught wearing women's clothes in public, jeered at and taken into a house to be spanked across a strong woman's knee. With my fancy briefs pulled down and my bottom bared, I'm further insulted by several women present for the rearing erection I get. Filthy cross-dressing pervert, I'm called, among other humiliating insults, crying as my bottom is thrashed, but actually revelling in the shame and degradation heaped on me. Being a timid woman, dominated by stronger men and women, I considered would be my idea of heaven.

When younger I used to sneak into my sister or my mother's bedrooms and dress up in their clothes. My big sister Mary had lots of make-up, which I used to beautify my girlish face. I'd never needed to shave and knew I'd have made a very pretty girl. With mum and Mary out, I was admiring myself in a frock one day when discovered. Mother screamed in disbelief and Mary smacked my face and ordered me to take off her dress. I was sixteen at the time, and sobbed as my shameful secret was revealed, mainly because it meant it might stop me dressing up again.

Ordered to strip off the clothes that offended them, I did so with trembling fingers, as I knew it was all I had on. I also knew the mix of excitement and fear I felt was sexual. More shock befell them as I obeyed and stood with a hard-on, my unruly dick quite painfully stiff.

'Thrash the dirty little beast,' Mary advised my mother. 'Whip this kinky obsession out of him.' She pushed me forward over the arm of the couch, handing mother one of her flat shoes. 'Use that to warm up his backside,' she said, sounding really vicious.

Thwack, thwack, thwack went the hard leather sole against my flesh as mum flayed my bottom. But she wasn't using enough venom in her strokes, Mary complained, taking the shoe from her, and I squealed as she mercilessly struck at my already stinging bottom with such obvious pleasure that my mother begged her to stop. To make sure I got properly punished, the sadistic Mary flogged me out of the room and upstairs to my bedroom. Though I sobbed and pleaded for mercy, pushed forward over my bed as the beating was continued, the thought of me showing my bare bum and dangling balls was erotically stimulating. Mary saw how my tool reared and said I'd be locked in my bedroom until I could behave myself. No doubt some of that humiliation and thrashing formed the basis of my favourite fantasy.

It's not so unusual for men to dress as women now, but it made me an outcast in my own home. It also showed a dark side of my sister. I'd always thought her mannish, butch is the term, and most of her close friends were women, but now I was to learn of the cruel streak in her nature.

Knowing now that I had a thing about dressing as a woman, the sadistic bitch would lay out her smartest clothes and underwear on her bed, tempting me. It was always a trap, for she'd return to catch me, often with a girlfriend or two to ridicule me.

With mother out at her regular bingo night, Mary would interrogate me and reduce me to tears, making me confess about all the times I'd worn her clothes, and even more embarrassing, about masturbating while I wore them.

She'd flog me on the least excuse. To show me up before her friends I'd even be put across her knee for a spanking. I dreaded it as well as looked forward to it, and I know she was into being dominant and giving corporal punishment.

She beat me until I left home to get married, but Suzanne and I were not exactly compatible and the marriage soon became stale. Four years went by with sex almost non-existent. To satisfy myself I began cross-dressing again, using Sue's wardrobe, the exotic flimsy female wear I'd bought for her myself. I resumed wanking while in her clothes, fantasising about being spanked and dominated as before.

Sue began to go out more, hardly ever in each evening. I began to think she was with men, not minding because it left me at home to dress up. It thrilled me to think other men would be fucking her. But all the phone calls that came for her on our answering machine were from other women. It struck me she was in the local gay scene, making it with lesbians.

I didn't mind that either, as it explained why she'd never been worried about the lack of sex with me. Then she told me she'd met my sister at a club and they'd become friends, but in all this I was sure she had no idea I dressed as a woman or liked being disciplined and dominated.

One evening I was in Suzanne's best frock, dolled up in wig and make-up and enjoying a glass of wine, when I heard voices in the hall and my heart pounded. The lounge door opened and my wife stood there, looking puzzled. With her was my sadistic sister, Mary, who was delighted to point out it was me in drag.

'It's Ronnie,' she laughed. 'So he's still at it, getting a thrill dressing up as a girl. Didn't you know, Sue?'

Not amused, my wife ordered me to get out of her clothes, but Mary interrupted. 'Not so fast,' she advised. 'Let's look on the good side. You've got yourself a 'she-male' to be your slave and fulfil your every demand.'

My wife agreed, liking the idea, saying, 'He'd better toe the line or the town will learn what a poor excuse for a husband I've got.' She walked around me arrogantly, inspecting my looks as a woman, finally bursting into humbling laughter and making me cringe in shame. 'Now I can do what I like,' she said, 'and have my friends home without caring what he thinks.'

I was ordered to remain dressed as a woman and make sandwiches and drinks, to have to watch them grow tipsy and when tired of insulting me, begin to maul each other. Long kisses and roaming hands soon got too much for them. Still cuddling, they went upstairs. With my interest aroused enough to risk their anger, I followed.

Looking into the bedroom I saw them hastily discarding their clothes, lying naked on the bed together to continue kissing and fondling, my wife and my sister lost in a lustful embrace. They were fully aware I was watching, and this no doubt heightened their wanton behaviour.

Later I was blamed for spying on them. My sister, telling my wife how I should be dealt with, even to arming her with a belt, had me bent over with my dress raised and briefs lowered. After I was thrashed and sent to the spare room until morning, the two women went back to bed.

Next day, I wondered how my wife would accept that I dressed in her clothes. 'You do your thing and I'll do mine,' was how she put it, adding that some female friends from a gay bar were coming for drinks that evening. I was told I could dress up and I'd be serving the guests as a maid.

Mary arrived early and she and Suzanne had fun in making me up especially tarty with too much make-up, and then dressing me in a mini-skirted dress. Six female guests arrived, all gay women who danced and smooched all evening while I served drinks. They said how lucky my wife was to have a slave, making fun of my appearance, even crudely sticking their hands up my skirt to squeeze my prick. Enough of this got me erect, of course, a fact greeted with jeers of derision that I couldn't control myself.

From then on I was no longer husband and master in my own house, and known as a cross-dressing wimp who surrendered all dignity to be a slave. 'You wanted to dress as a woman, and so you shall as long as we require you to do so,' my wife ordered, but it was not out of kindness or consideration for me. Now I became an object to entertain her circle of lesbian cronies, whose greatest pleasure is to mock and demean anyone of the male sex.

For all that some were not above making me lick them. Others, no doubt bisexual, even mounted me and impaled themselves on my prick after getting me erect. Performing that party piece, with my wife sometimes the one on top, got me loaned out to other lesbian orgies. I was even kitted out in a scanty French maid outfit.

But caning me, spanking me, even whipping me, is without a doubt the favourite entertainment at these evenings. This is so popular and in demand that I have an almost permanently bruised and striped backside. My ambition now is to become a real woman. I am undergoing hormone treatment that has given me breasts I will enhance with silicone implants. Being fair, I never really had much facial hair and now I have none. I look like a woman and am getting the soft curves of one.

I've been promised that the lesbian group will pay the fee for the final operation to remove the last vestiges of my maleness. My reward for the entertainment I provide, and for being such a willing and submissive slave, I like to think.

Ronald, Bristol.

CHAPTER THIRTY SIX
Double the Pleasure

During my time in the Royal Navy, whenever sex was mentioned someone would always say 'subject normal', and in truth it was the major topic of conversation. I well remember one happy rating returning from leave and boasting he'd 'completed the double', and we all knew what that meant. It was the navy term for fucking a girl and her mother. In his case he'd shagged his mother-in-law at a boozy birthday party. Apparently she'd come on strong after the wife had been put to bed too tiddly to stay awake. One cannot ignore such fortuitous chances, especially when shown a picture of the mother sunning herself topless on a beach. Good looking and curvy, it must have been well worth throwing a sneaky fuck in her direction.

Never one to 'black cat' someone's story, I stayed silent as I remembered my 'double' episode. I'd just discovered my teenage neighbour had blossomed into a lovely girl with nice tits. The same age myself, I'd always ignored her. But now I visited Sara's house as if she was an old chum to do our homework together. All I wanted was to get at those tits, of course, and maybe into her knickers. Up in her bedroom playing records (put on to fool her mother that all was innocent) we smooched and petted until I knew I was getting there.

Little did I know she was as keen as me, waiting for me to get cracking, delighted when I unbuttoned her blouse. She actually went on to unhook her bra for me. I was in heaven with those gorgeous tits bared for me. Sighing as I fondled them, her nipples stiffly erect, she whispered, 'Suck them, Tom. Suck on my nipples.'

While I eagerly did that she unzipped me and took out my swollen cock. She rubbed it nicely, expressing her delight when I fell back and shot my load into some tissues she had. Her delight in seeing a boy ejaculating was obvious, and I was to be wanked off every chance she got - especially in the cinema.

So Sara wasn't the innocent I'd supposed, surprising me on a wet night in a near-empty local picture house by bending over in the dark and sucking me off very nicely. I discovered that a girlfriend of hers was lending her porno magazines, 'borrowed' from her brother's secret collection. She got her horny ideas from reading them, including wanting me to kiss her pussy. One evening we were petting and I'd taken off her knickers to feel her when she whispered, 'Lick me. Go on, Tom, lick my cunt.' It was my first experience of the art of muff-diving, and I loved it. I loved the taste, the soft interior my tongue probed, and loved the reaction of Sara as she stifled her groans and squirmed like a puppet as she came strongly. In return she let me spank her bare bum, an American CP magazine spread of several pages depicting a girl getting an over the knee spanking appealing to me, and making me want to experience the exhilaration of warming her butt until she squealed for mercy. Like licking her cunt, I took to it and never tired of paddling her bum until rosy red and she was begging me to stop. A spanking session always got us both randy.

A little time later she finally overcame her dread of me making her pregnant. She lolled back and raised her knees, showing her plump cleft and tangle of fuzzy hair. When I mounted her our bellies smacked together, and forgetting her fear of pregnancy, she clung to me and urged me on to fuck her harder. I had my mind set on joining the navy and fucking many women of different nations, not being married with a kid and a factory job. So I pulled out at the last moment and shot my sperm all over her belly and tits.

I used a condom after that, not trusting the little minx to release the grip of her arms and legs when I was about to come. A summer of screwing took place in her bedroom, to the accompaniment of pop records drowning her shrieks. So it carried on, my visits to her room when her mother was out or working. Our imaginations soared as we thought up new positions and bondage games to add to our sex play. I'd always thought I'd need to marry a sex maniac to satisfy my lustful appetite, and in the eager Sara I'd found one, knowing one day I couldn't do better when seeking to settle down. She'd encouraged me to tie her to the bedposts, and while helpless be made to do anything I demanded.

So it was one stormy afternoon when I had Sara spread-eagled on her bed, face down and bound by the wrists and ankles. We were both naked, and with her mother absent we felt safe to indulge in our fun and games. I had lightly spanked her bum, and was in the process of fucking her from the rear. The door suddenly opened and Sara's mother was there, eyeing the torrid scene before her with a look that could have turned us both to stone. I rolled off her daughter, my glistening prick waving in the air as she advanced to wreak her fury on us. It had been a fair cop.

'You horny little trollop!' she screamed at her daughter. Then it was my turn to be severely reprimanded. In her book I was a perverted lout and a sex maniac. She raised her hand and swept it down across her girl's defenceless bottom. I'd heard Sara howl before, but the swipe her mother delivered brought forth a scream of pain and humiliation. Her mother continued until Sara sobbed and humbly begged forgiveness. I stood terrified, waiting my turn. I was thrust face down beside the blubbering Sara and clenched my buttocks as the irate mum struck at me. Let it be said I couldn't sit down for days, such was the force of the beating I received for supposedly corrupting her darling daughter. I'd lost my erection when she'd burst into the room, but strangely enough, having been punished and ordered to rise and dress and leave, I was sporting another one.

There was no doubt it was through having been beaten by a strict and angry woman.

'Dirty beast,' she scolded me. 'How dare you stand there with that gross thing on display?' But I got a sneaky impression she was not only angry, but also very impressed by the sight of my dong.

I'd always thought her a looker, though twenty years older than me. Divorced for years, a busy self-employed florist and mum, she was no doubt frustrated too, at times.

Sara went on a school trip to Greece soon after that, and I'd passed my test and was driving my dad's car in town when I saw her mother. Pissing with rain, Ruth was drenched and laden with carrier bags full of shopping. I'd laid low for a month or two, but stopped beside her as she hurried to a bus stop. Opening the car door, she climbed in beside me and thanked me without any warmth in her voice. I asked if she'd heard from Sara, and by the time we'd reached her house the ice was somewhat broken. I carried in the shopping and she asked if I'd have a coffee once she'd dried herself and changed. Waiting downstairs, I was surprised when she called for me to go up.

On entering her bedroom, I saw her standing beside the bed, gloriously naked. While I stood taking in the unexpected scene, she closed up to me with her perfume strong in my nostrils and her magnificent breasts almost against my chest. Unzipping me, she slipped her hand into my jeans and asked what have we in there? Shaking with arousal, I told her she knew, having already seen it fully erect. She then drew it out and bent over to kiss it, drawing her tongue up the shaft and covering the knob with her lips to give it some gentle sucks.

When she stood to face me, my stiff dong still in her hand, I asked if it had tempted her when she'd first seen it. The devious bitch said she was doing this because she didn't want me hanging around her girl like a randy hound. 'If you have to have it, fuck me instead,' she said.

I began to fumble at her tits and touch her cunt, desperate to fuck this choice woman. 'Don't spoil it by rushing things, Kevin,' she said, holding me off. 'Tie me up like you did my Sara. Do the things to me you were doing to her. Spank me if you think I deserve it.'

So Sara's mum was into bondage and spanking, I discovered, only too pleased to oblige her whims. Using stockings and her dressing gown cord, I tied her wrists and ankles, so she was spread out helplessly on the bed, warning that she was now to expect no mercy. I sucked her tits and then moved on down to lick and tongue her dark-haired pussy, finding it moist and pungent. I got out of my clothes and positioned myself between her thighs, thrusting my prick in up to my balls as I began to fuck her. She screamed she was being raped as we both heaved into each other. 'Raped, you horny cow?' I scoffed. 'You've taken plenty of big cocks in your time!'

She raised her arse even more to give me better access, our pubic hairs mashing. The randy bitch cried, moaned and grunted, demanding I fuck her harder, asking if she was a better ride than her daughter. Then her cry became a strangled groan as she began to convulse, her cunt contracting and pulsing as the sensations jolted her body and she came.

It was obvious she was mine after that. Resigned to her fate, she sucked me off before we fucked again. Later I made her confess to being a slut, and for her sins I had her across my knee to smack that fine mature arse.

From then on when her daughter was out of the way, we played our domination and correction games and fucked regularly. I had certainly qualified as 'completing the double', for when Ruth was busy in her shop, I was back to fucking and spanking Sara as well. My leaves when I joined the Navy were fun-filled as I took turns to screw them both. Enjoying the bondage and CP scene added to the pleasure for us all. I'd love to be able to say I had them both together, tied up side by side on the bed, but this was never so. Certainly I often fucked both on the same day, but never together. Both of them suspicious, I was often questioned whether I was screwing the other, but always denied it. Still, who's complaining? It was still twice the fun.

Kevin, Fareham.

CHAPTER THIRTY SEVEN
My Big Baby Boy

Other people's babies were my business since I was eighteen and qualified as a nanny. Looking back now in my forties, I could write a book about my experiences. I'd looked after their kids, but often the parents expected other duties. One rich American couple also paid me for 'extras', but neither knew the other was having sex with me. In the wife's case, it was with a selection of vibrators and strap-on dildos, and she was better at making me come than her husband. He liked his arse tanned with a leather strap he provided himself.

I was twenty-eight and a curvy wench. When the man pulled down his pants and instructed me to whip him, I didn't mind. It made him erect and he'd fuck me, even if it was a quickie that didn't really satisfy me. But the roll of banknotes left on my bedside table as he went out was a welcome addition to my building society account.

Later, when I got the confidence of his wife, she told me her hubby couldn't get a hard-on and never fucked her. It was obvious she was dropping a hint that she found satisfaction in other ways, and one day she showed me her selection of sex toys.

We were soon sleeping together when her husband was off on business. Again I got paid for my trouble, only it wasn't trouble, as I discovered I was bi-sexual.

Meantime, the husband was getting more confident of being spanked and whipped by me, often when bound hand and foot. He'd get it up enough to fuck me, always coming before I got very aroused. But when he'd zipped up and left me frustrated, there was always his wife's mouth or strap-on to give me satisfaction. It was a great job that paid well and took me around the world to exotic places.

I must admit I don't masturbate or fantasise if the real thing is available from either a male or female. In later nanny posts I lapsed on occasion with the big brothers of the kids I was looking after. Home for the half-term hols from their posh private schools, randy as only teenagers can be, the sods invariably chanced their arm with me. In one noble household, two brothers happened to try it on when I was feeling particularly randy, and they got what they wanted. And they didn't mind me spanking their arses when I claimed they'd been wicked in taking advantage of me. It also convinced me that I enjoyed punishing the male sex on behalf of us women, and from the erections produced by the boys when punished, it seemed it turned them on too.

Having got used to regular and paid sex with my clients, finding myself out of work I obtained temporary work in a massage parlour where my firm bust made me popular as a topless masseuse. I earned extra wages giving hand relief, blow-jobs or being fucked on the massage table or in the shower. Another good earner was for several of us massage girls to be taken to private parties in country houses to perform lesbian acts or to be fucked by the guests. Once, during a lesbian exhibition, I put the other girl across my knee and spanked her. This was unrehearsed. I did it because I had a sudden desire to give the girl's nice bottom a good smacking. It proved popular and was repeated at other performances. But an advert I spotted in a specialist magazine intrigued me, so I applied for the post. The advert was worded:

Lonely, solvent, middle-aged professional gentleman requires help of understanding lady, such as experienced nanny. He wishes to retrace his early childhood in every way. Caring but strict motherly nurse, interested in regression and the necessary training and discipline, would be ideal for this well-paid post.

It ended with a box number for applications.

It seemed too good a challenge to miss. A letter and CV got me interviewed at what is probably London's most expensive hotel. Not wishing to be taken in by a nutter (but I didn't object to a rich nutter), I bribed the chap at the reception desk to tell what he knew about my prospective employer. Satisfied he was well heeled, I attended the interview and found a man of around fifty and a little overweight waiting to interview me. From his words when vetting me, I knew he was into being an adult baby, and whoever got the job would have to act as his mother, nurse and nanny, and perhaps his lover, if he became aroused by the treatment he was willing to pay through the nose for. I was offered the job, and was happy to think I'd soon dominate him, even though he was a rich and powerful businessman. What makes such a successful person want to be disciplined and treated like a baby? Who knows what makes anyone tick?

When reporting to his office for the first time to confirm I would take the job, I decided to be firm and stand no nonsense from day one. Thinking that was why he was paying me such a fabulous salary, I deliberately ignored what he was trying to instruct me about his requirements. I could guess nappy wearing, breast feeding, botty smacking if I thought him wilful and naughty, being sent to bed when I decided, and ruling him with a rod of iron.

Silencing him, I warned him by producing my sternest look. 'From now on you'll obey me and do as I say, you nasty little boy.' When I saw him nod eagerly, I knew I'd got off on the right foot and made his day.

But to doubly ensure he knew his place, I ordered him to lower his trousers and underpants and lie across my knee. He went bright red, no doubt enjoying the humiliation, but said thank you for the kind offer, Nursey, but never in office hours. Our nanny and baby fantasy would be conducted in the privacy of his mansion or when alone on holiday. 'It begins right now, and will take place whenever and wherever I decide,' I rapped out. I then instructed him to inform his secretary he was not to be disturbed and went behind his desk. Ordering him to stand up, I sat in his padded swivel chair, patting my knee to show what I expected. Trembling visibly, he drew down his trousers and underwear, laid across my lap, and began whimpering that he would obey.

I was determined to give him a good spanking. My arm flew up and down in a blur as I smacked his very white fleshy buttocks until my hand stung. He began blubbering and begging forgiveness (for what, some fantasy misdeed?), pleading he would be a good little boy for me in the future.

'I'll soon make sure you will, and stop this blubbering like a big baby,' I threatened. My palm smarting as much as his reddened cheeks, I pulled off one of the slip-on shoes I wore and walloped his backside with that until his screams were for real. I could imagine the fleshy cheeks would be bruised black and blue once the red marks had faded. Ordering him to stand before me at last, I was not surprised to see his penis rearing up from under his shirt. He asked me nervously if he was allowed to use it, seeing that he couldn't always get it so hard and erect. Much as I was feeling turned-on too, I called him a dirty little wretch for having dirty thoughts about Nanny, and made him lower his head in shame.

A chauffeured limo took me to my flat to collect my things, and then to my new home. A butler showed me the room I was to use.

I soon discovered that Cyril, my employer, had never had a real childhood, with a cold father and an unloving mother. He could throw a tantrum if I withheld sex from him if he thought he was due it. It was a deliberate ploy on my part, knowing how excited he got when denied anything. I'd make sure he'd be smacked and sent to sulk in a corner until he could behave. Really, his biggest thrill was in having me using my power to dominate him. He loved nothing so much as being put across my knee for a good spanking and then being sent to bed.

If he was good I'd allow him a treat, and bath time meant drying and powdering him, dressing him in a nappy and night-dress, then putting him to the breast instead of a bottle. Nestled in the crook of my arm, he'd suckle happily on my nipples and make little contended sighs. This invariably made him horny.

He claimed once in a serious talk we had that his high-powered business life and decision making would be too much for him without my nursing and scolding, relieving all his stress by spanking his bottom, and relieving all his frustration by the sex we had. Visits to the most expensive psychiatrists had done nothing to help. If I was grossly overpaid, so had they been.

To show his kink or fetish is not unique but indeed quite widespread, on a recent business trip to America we attended a convention in a Los Angeles hotel for men whose 'thing' it is to be treated as a baby. All seemed intelligent business types with money. My employer was the envy of others at a private party when I said he'd been ignoring me and smacked his bottom before the men present. I then sent him off to bed to lie there humbled and wondering what I'd be up to. At once the men left in the room offered me employment as a strict nursemaid, telling me to name my salary. For trying to make me disloyal to my boss, I made the ones offering me work line up and bend over to receive punishment in the form of a caning on their bare backsides.

At the convention there was also on sale a large range of equipment for babying purposes. There were extra-large nappies, feeding bottles and bibs, as well as a selection of whips, canes and belts for punishing naughty ones who disobeyed Nanny. I do not find it a problem being strict with a middle-aged baby. The pay and conditions are great, and even the sex can be terrific.

Rhoda, London.

CHAPTER THIRTY EIGHT
Convent Girl Confesses

No girl could have led a more sheltered existence. After my parents separated and took new partners, I was sent to a boarding school run by nuns. The education was good except for preparing us for life beyond the convent. Any mention of sex was taboo and the discipline was harsh, thrashings and canings meted out for the least show of disobedience.

Of course, being blossoming teenage girls, our sexual feelings became so strong they could not be ignored. More so because of our ignorance. We had strange sensations that disturbed us, it was all such a mystery, and we were not allowed near boys when our hormones urged us to satisfy the frustration we felt.

Warned by the nuns and our priest of the mortal sin of playing with ourselves, we nevertheless resorted to masturbating when the urge became overpowering. Although ashamed, it did not stop me despite the resultant feelings of guilt. I enjoyed doing it, and to add to the naughty pleasure I even fantasised rude things as my fingers worked their magic to give me that ecstatic feeling. I pictured myself naked with men and women doing things that excited and thrilled me, even caning me for my sins and telling me what a dirty little creature I was.

I was relieved to find I wasn't the only pupil there who masturbated. In time I was approached by and included in a group of teenagers who kissed and fondled each other. Although full of guilt about this, we couldn't help ourselves indulging. One girl called May became sweet on me and we shyly whispered we loved each other. Of course it was all innocent petting, but urges take over. Our kissing gradually became more and more passionate, with us rubbing our bodies together.

One dark night in the dorm I was woken by May slipping into my bed. She drew off my nightie and held her naked body to mine. I discovered the thrill of having my nipples sucked, and how nice it felt when she lay on top of me and we worked our tight virgin quims together.

Another time, when May and I were out on a country ramble shepherded by nuns, we sneaked away into a copse and lay on the soft grass. Soon we were kissing and May's hand was exploring inside my knickers. I did as she asked always, never making the first move like she did; the passive half of our relationship.

Finding my slit all hot and moist, her fingers stroked and tickled, pinched my clitty (although we knew nothing about that in those days except that it was highly responsive to touch). I writhed in pleasure as she finger-fucked me (we did call it that even then, naughty girls!), and I was given such a strong orgasm that my back arched and I screamed out. It was our undoing. Heard by Sister Teresa, a feared nun (and no doubt a very frustrated woman), we were marched back to the school in utter shame and disgrace.

May was ordered to her dormitory and to speak to no one of the affair. I was told to strip in the nun's bedroom, which was called a cell. Why I'd been selected as the guilty one I was to learn; Sister Teresa didn't fancy May, or rather, she *did* fancy me. I was ordered to bend over and present my bare bottom to the woman. She was randy, I'm sure now in light of what happened, and no wonder leading the celibate life of a nun. I was shocked when she remarked that my breasts were lovely, moving behind me and reaching down to cup them in her cold hands, plucking at the tightening nipples.

Her touch lingered and made my breasts swell, delicious sensations pulsing through them, while my nipples stuck out twice their normal size and felt as hard as flint. I realised too that I was highly aroused being naked before another person. It didn't matter whether male or female, I was getting a tremendous thrill from exhibiting my body. It is obvious now that seeing me naked had got poor Sister Teresa very excited too. She trembled visibly.

The whole of that sparse little cell became electrically charged with a strong atmosphere of lustful desire. Sister Teresa's face coloured and her voice became unsteady. 'Evil creature, you wicked temptress,' she berated me, blaming me for her own failings. The devil's plaything, she called me, when she really wanted me for her own plaything. To make sure I knew I was wicked, she then produced a leather strap.

Saying I'd been caught committing shameful acts, she made me bend further over and slowly drew the strap across my vulnerable buttocks. This made me shiver, both in fear and anticipation, as a strange sensation churned in my stomach and sex, a throb of arousal as I clenched my cheeks and thighs together. I was ordered sharply to relax my bottom, the nun using the toe of her shoe to nudge my feet apart.

I was crying as she proclaimed I'd been indulging in disgusting and perverted practices with one of my own sex, no doubt seducing May for my own evil ends. Such wickedness must be beaten out of me. Although naïve about such things, I suspected she would receive pleasure from whipping me. Sadistic pleasure, maybe, but sexual pleasure too. It affected me too; I sensed we were going to share a sexual experience, the nun and her pupil. I trembled with excitement too. Sister Teresa said this was to be our secret. She was doing it because if I'd been taken before Mother Superior, I'd be expelled in disgrace. Anxiously awaiting the first slash of the strap, I became unbearably aroused.

She then cracked the leather down sharply across my bottom. It did hurt, and knowing it would please her (and I wanted to) I squealed and blubbered, begging her to stop and show mercy. I found a curiously delicious elation in being so servile, and it was a true sexual uplift for I was quickly on the verge of a climax. I was ordered to confess everything between the crack of the belt on my unprotected cheeks. 'Just what did you and May do?' she insisted, emphasising the interrogation by walloping my backside ever harder. Then she put words in my mouth, saying what she hoped we had done, no doubt, and wanting me to own up to such abnormal practices.

I tearfully admitted that May and I had kissed, fondled each other's breasts, experimented by sucking on our nipples, and in the woods I'd been brought to an orgasm by May fingering me. As the strap stung my bum, I admitted such innocent things had happened, but Sister Teresa had other more erotic and sophisticated sexual practices she wanted to make me aware of. Did we girls ever kiss and lick each other's sexual parts? I'd never dreamed that such a thing actually occurred, and was immediately intrigued.

Amazingly, she asked if we'd used such objects as bananas or carrots to penetrate ourselves and fantasise about having sexual intercourse with a male. Again, Sister Teresa asking me such things only gave me rude thoughts. She kept on about the various possible practices used by frustrated girls, keeping up the belting of my bottom until I began to confess to everything she wanted to hear, even enjoying being thought so wickedly wanton. In the end it seemed that I was anybody's, had done all she suggested, even to fantasising about being fucked in the garden shed by the delivery boy while watched by the old gardener. He too got in on the act and was sucked off later. I got quite an education while bent over being flogged.

The cell reeked of sexuality. I'm sure Sister Teresa was in turmoil. For myself, as each vicious thwack landed I tensed my buttocks and thighs, squeezing my pulsing sex until I could barely fend off the resultant orgasm. Afraid she might stop the suggestive talk and the leathering of my heated bottom before I'd come, I begged her to keep beating me. Then it was impossible to hold out any longer. My knees buckled and I almost collapsed as I shuddered in the convulsive spasms of my orgasm, loudly acclaiming my glorious relief.

Clearly understanding fully what she'd brought about, the nun seized me and clasped my nakedness to her. Her hug was so tight that our bodies moulded together. She'd been brought to a shattering climax herself, her crotch grinding against my thigh as she swooned.

As she began to recover I was told breathlessly that if I sinned in future it would mean further punishment to save me from the fires of hell. I was to confess all to her and not to the priest, otherwise I'd be expelled. I was sent away, hardly believing she'd been so tempted that she'd used me to gain relief from her frustration.

The things she'd charged that May and I were doing together soon became reality once I'd passed on the knowledge.

We discovered the thrill of spanking each other to warm ourselves up.

We brought each other to shattering climaxes by tonguing and licking our eager pussies.

We both lost our virginity to the same vaselined banana. We were often caught sleeping together by Sister Teresa, and I was always the one who got the thrashing. This could be with her hand while being spanked over her knee, or by a variety of things ranging from a school cane to birch twigs bound together.

Being called to her cell for confession and a beating invariably resulted in us both having an orgasm, even several.

I know I'd have been expelled but for the pleasure she gained from my visits to her cell for supposed punishment. It gave me a lasting taste for being dominated and made to confess my sexual misdeeds. And I never complained - I wouldn't dare!

Jill, County Wexford.

CHAPTER THIRTY NINE
Spanking Good Time

Sex meant little to me at seventeen, until a family friends' eighteen-year-old daughter moved in temporarily. Her parents were working abroad on a short-term contract and so Amy came to stay. She'd been exposed to the usual initiations and frustrations of an all girls boarding school and was a first class bitch. She boasted openly that she'd been the terror of fellow pupils and sadistically carried on being a domineering type with me. Worse even, for she treated males with contempt, so an intellectual submissive wimp like myself was fair game and Amy sharpened her skills on me at night when the house was quiet.

It meant, with my father and mother fast asleep along the landing, when she crept into my room to make me suffer for being a despised boy, I had to remain silent despite the canings and spankings the callous teenage bitch inflicted. Older, bigger and stronger, she'd pinion my arms above my head despite my muffled protests and struggles. I'd invariably end up tied spread-eagled on the bed, trussed up helplessly while she had her way with me. She even had cords cut to length for these bondage sessions. Try as I might to resist, I found it excited me to be at her mercy, to plead and beg forgiveness for whatever she accused me of doing or being.

But also during our tussles, having bodily contact with the well-developed girl, I found it difficult not to get an erection. For this inexcusable lapse she'd taunt and insult me as being dirty, dragging off my pyjama trousers to reveal the offending object. She'd play with it, warning me not to shoot off, gently caressing and stroking the engorged stalk to deliberately make me lose control, even at times putting her tongue tip in the eye, or sucking the knob itself until I had to urgently announce I was coming. No matter how I strained to contain the eruption, and how the cruel bitch enjoyed watching me struggle, I'd shoot off onto my belly.

For this disgusting lapse I'd be made to wipe myself clean with my handkerchief while apologising for not being strong enough to resist disgracing myself. Untied, I'd be made to turn over and present my bottom to her for punishment. This could be a severe caning made more unbearable as I dare not cry out with my parents near. As a precaution, Amy slipped off her knickers to stuff them in my mouth. Other times when hard, she'd lay on top of me and rub her quim against my prick. From that time on until she joined her parents in Kenya for a holiday, we had 'pretend' sex or I was bound, spanked and humiliated every visit. Of course my schoolwork suffered, but by then I eagerly awaited her tiptoeing into my room each night.

On her return she came to stay again, and we had full penetrative sex for the first time. She mounted me and guided my prick into her cunt by her own hand, but what bliss it was fucking that tight female passage as she bobbed up and down over me. It was the first of many, and we advanced to have oral sex to completion, with her sucking me off and getting a mouthful to swallow, while she got repeated climaxes with my tongue probing her slit.

It was not just night-time sessions by then. The summerhouse in the garden, hidden by bushes, became the venue for me to be summoned to have sex with her - and then be punished for daring to ravage her!

She'd taken my virginity, but I hadn't taken hers. One day in the summerhouse after a lovely fuck following an over-the-knee spanking of my bum, both blissfully exhausted, I dared boast how my cock brought her off so strongly. Adding that she'd remember me as the one who'd first fucked her, she laughed in my face, saying to shame me, that I was a poor second. During her stay in Kenya, it seemed her parents' Kikuyu houseboy was fucking her on a daily basis. It turned out that the African lad was on to a good thing in that house.

Amy returned home after a shopping trip to Nairobi one afternoon, hearing sounds coming from her parents' bedroom, noises she knew were the sounds of a woman enjoying a screw. Moans, gasps, loud cries and appeals to be fucked harder made her surprised to think her rather reserved and aloof mummy could be so responsive to a good rogering.

She thought her father, another stuck-up imperious snob, was showing surprising sexual prowess in there, hearing her mother in evident ecstasy. But Daddy was not the cause, when May dared peep around the door. The athletic servant was working like a piston as he rammed her mother's quim. And the way she humped showed how much she was loving it. When she came with a strangled cry, May saw the houseboy's buttocks quiver and knew he was coming inside her. May then stole a further look and watched her mother roll over and present her arse to the boy, saying she must be punished for what she allowed when Bwana was away from the house.

The boy knew what to do, finding a belt in the wardrobe and using it to flog the woman's arse until the white flesh was an angry red and she was sobbing, either in pain or remorse. The way they had fucked so lustfully, and when told to flog her, how the black lad knew where the belt was kept, suggested to May the pair had been at it before.

I suggested then that like her mother, she might enjoy a punishment for allowing the same boy to fuck her. Intrigued, I think, she lay across my lap and said I could spank her. Using all the strength in my arm, I smacked her cheeky arse until she was begging me to stop, as I so often had done with her.

I attended May's wedding several years later, and couldn't help looking at the groom and thinking he was just the type she had to marry; a weak chinless wonder.

As the newlyweds then lived quite near, it was handy for us to meet and continue our secret get-togethers. When I married I made sure my wife, Sarah, was the meek and submissive type. She was introduced to me by May, who had generally dominated her at boarding school.

With that recommendation, I married the girl, and soon we were having regular threesome sessions to make our lives interesting. At Christmas my presents to the two girls included a selection of the best bondage equipment available. We now intend to advertise and find new recruits to join us.

Don, Bath.

CHAPTER FORTY
Bitch With a Switch

I'm a solvent, hardworking executive type. Divorced and in my thirties, I should be in my prime sexually. Sadly, I can't make love unless a woman mistreats me first. I meet lovely women who go to bed with me, but to my shame I can't operate. Some are sympathetic and settle for me making them come with my fingers or tongue. Now it's got so I don't ask women out because I know I'll fail them unless I'm chastised. I turned to prostitutes, but even then I stayed embarrassingly limp.

It's not that there's anything wrong with me physically. I get a real stiffy when beating my meat, my lurid imagination running wild as I fantasise about another sort of beating; I'm on my knees while a leather-clad jackbooted madam is wielding a cat-o'-nine-tails, flogging my back and bare arse for not showing due deference to her exalted state as an all-powerful being. Can I get a tremendous hard-on then? You bet I can!

Other scenarios while fantasising include me being chained to a wooden whipping frame, arse bared for a thrashing from a riding crop by my secretary. In another fantasy, I'm bound hand and foot on a bed while a woman with a cunt like a mouth squats on my face, or even being shafted by a big dildo strapped to a muscled bodybuilder type woman. It is always a mature woman who dominates me in my masturbatory fantasies. It would be heaven to find such a woman in real life. My wife left me, and girlfriends have walked away, due to my nervous requests to be taken across a knee for a deserved spanking.

They wouldn't hear of it, calling me sick and a pervert. But I know I'm not, and have sympathy for other chaps like me. I mean those who desire being strictly disciplined and humiliated by a dominating mistress as the acme of sexual ecstasy. I don't force myself on reluctant women, rarely daring to mention what I seek from a partner; that I'd like to be whipped and humiliated. For a while I paid a dominatrix to degrade me by tying me up, walking over me and spanking me like a naughty schoolboy. I also did her housework at times, my poor efforts getting me further beatings. It was an extremely expensive time and I believe although paid, she really enjoyed thrashing me and making me eat humble pie, often before others. She was divorced and was having a lesbian affair during the period I visited her. Then she went back to her ex-husband and gave up her work as a dominatrix.

I saw a psychiatrist who put my masochism down to my upbringing as an unwanted child. I argued that I simply like to be dominated by strict females, made to bow to their will and be punished for not being worthy of them. She said that's what she meant, reminding me my parents had parted when I was a teenager and foster parents took me in. The mother treated me like a slave and gave me housework to do. I was regularly spanked and made to stand in a corner, or sent to bed without supper, and all for the slightest infringement of the house rules. Yet I worshipped her.

The bouts across her knee always gave me an erection, so I learned to equate the punishment and the resultant hard-on as being connected, giving me a nice feeling. I therefore often went out of my way to displease my foster mum, wanting the spanking because it got me aroused. Following a beating, crying and promising to be good, she would console me by cuddling me to her large comfortable bosom. This was the only show of love or affection given to me. In my time there she gave birth and fed her child with an ample supply of breast milk. I envied the baby at her nipple, nuzzled into those big swollen teats.

The front of her dress was often soaked with surplus milk, and she used a pump to drain off the excess after the baby had her fill. I knew she was aware her breasts fascinated me, feeding her kid and changing the nipple being suckled while I sat opposite her watching.

After one severe spanking across her knee for staying out late, as I blubbered and swore I'd be good in future, she drew my tear-stained face to her and made comforting sounds. Her arm cradled my head as she unbuttoned her cardigan and blouse. Giving up the wearing of a bra during nursing, she cupped one opulent bare tit in her hand and directed the rubbery nipple to my mouth.

Blissfully did I suckle on the teat and contentedly drew in sweet milk from both breasts. I heard her sigh as if in relief, and of course I was being used to drain off the surfeit of milk that was making her tits swollen and painful. I think, with the wisdom of hindsight, that she got a pleasant sexual thrill out of it all. Being fed by her became a regular occurrence while she was producing an excess supply of milk. Sometimes while suckling her I could sense her becoming agitated until she'd give a long sigh and would gently shudder. She would quickly push me from her whenever that happened. I still love to suck women's nipples if given the chance. The dominatrix I paid would let me suck her nipples after being whipped by her.

So good luck and many honest replies to your advertised appeal for letters relating to the bondage and correction scene. This is a sad one from a frustrated would-be male slave who would dearly love to find and devote himself to a strict mistress. I'd serve her faithfully and expect nothing in return except her contempt and discipline. There must be dominant ladies out there who would enjoy spanking, humiliating and teaching loyalty the hard way to a more than willing subject. Unfortunately, after weeks of being with new women and getting to know them, feeling it's safe to confess my special secret desire to be dominated, they stare at me for a moment then run a mile. I shall keep trying to meet one I'd gladly serve, with only her comfort and happiness in mind.

Willard, Somerset.

CHAPTER FORTY ONE
Wife's Black Master

Megan and I agreed we were better apart. I didn't blame her for no longer fancying me. In turn I thought she was cold, and I'd been getting my sex elsewhere without hiding the fact. But we remained friendly, acknowledging that we'd married too young and now were free to do as we liked. Financially we were forced to remain under the same roof, but in separate bedrooms until she or I found another affordable place. She was built curvaceously and pretty enough to get a boyfriend, so when she told me she'd met a nice young man I wasn't surprised.

I was in bed when she came home late, hearing what I thought were raised voices downstairs, and even a loud cry of what could have been pain. Thinking someone was cutting up rough, that Megan was in some sort of trouble, I rushed down into the living room in my pyjamas - and did a double take at what I saw. She was just getting off the lap of this big young black guy, and stood before him rubbing her reddened arse. Her dress, bra and panties were strewn on the floor, leaving her in nothing but elasticated stockings and high heels.

He'd obviously spanked her hard enough to turn the cheeks crimson and make her stand obediently awaiting his next command. He lolled back on the couch smirking confidently, with his jeans and underpants pushed down to his knees, his prick rearing free, a monstrous weapon both long and thick. I'd often felt like taking my wife over my knee for a good spanking when in one of her moods, so I had some admiration for the black lad. Seeing me, he said I must be Terry, her lodger. That was her way of explaining someone else was in the house, no doubt. He introduced himself as Carl.

'Has she ever sucked your cock, man?' he asked. Although she had in better days, I shook my head, supposing as a lodger it was unlikely. From the way she stood shivering nervously before her boyfriend, I reckoned she'd bitten off more than she could chew, if you'll excuse the pun. She was clearly scared and her look at me pleaded for help. But I was enjoying her discovering that all men were not so easygoing or considerate as me.

'Like it or not, she's going to suck my dick,' Carl announced. I saw Megan quail and brace herself to refuse, her eyes as big as saucers and fixed on the solid bar of black flesh rearing up from his groin.

'No, please, it's too big,' she whined. 'I could never get that in my mouth.'

To show he'd stand no nonsense, he drew the thick leather belt from the loops of his trousers and gripped it tightly in his fist. At once, not risking the belt's sting on her tender arse, Megan got down on her hands and knees between his legs, her eyes still glued to the upstanding prick. I'm sure he liked an audience to witness his dominance over her, winking at me as if we were old mates. He indicated a carrier bag full of cans of lager and told me to help myself.

Tilting a can to him, I said, 'Yeah, leather the bitch's arse until she begs to suck you off, mate,' and got a glare from my trembling separated spouse.

Her howls as the belt cracked across her rounded bottom were even louder than the slap of leather on her quivering flesh. Soon she was grabbing for his cock to greedily gobble it into her mouth to stop the flogging. On her knees as she was, I saw her vainly trying to get all of his thick inches beyond her lips. The purple knob and some six inches of the veined column was all she could manage. Cheeks bulging and tear-brimmed eyes popping, she sucked bravely as he gripped a clump of her hair in his right hand and tugged it to encourage her, at the same time working his hips to fuck her face. I thought with amusement, so this is the 'nice young man' she'd boasted about earlier.

I watched, fascinated by the horny scene, imagination working as I said I thought I detected Megan was becoming aroused too.

'She's liking it now,' Carl nodded, agreeing with me. 'You missed out, man,' he laughed. 'Living here with this horny slut and never fucking her mouth or cunt. Why don't you fuck her now while she's on her knees? Let's give it to her from both ends.'

I was all for that, made stiff as a poker by watching her face being fucked, arse raised nicely for penetration. But even with a mouth full of Carl's cock, she made noises to show she did not want that - or by me at least.

She clenched her bottom cheeks as if barring entry, so remembering a spanking had worked to soften her up a little, I gave her still blushing bottom a right good flurry of hard smacks. Howl though she tried with her gob stuffed by Carl's rod, her response to the spanking was to relax her bum. This let me see

119

the rear view of her quim. I inserted a finger to find she was soaking, her arse giving little twitches to show she was randy enough to be fucked. She sucked noisily on Carl's dong as I slipped a length up her tight snatch. Snug up there and in to the bollocks, I reached round to grasp her tits as I shafted her. Soon her arse was slapping against my belly, gyrating to get the cock reaching the different parts of her quim.

I know we all three climaxed at about the same time. As I shot my load deep up Megan's cunt, I saw Carl's face contort as he went into spasms and flooded her throat. Megan seemed to take leave of all her senses, bobbing her head at one end and grinding her arse at the other, exploding into violent orgasms. Carl had to support her as he drew her to her feet, glassy-eyed and weak-kneed from the sapping climaxes she'd enjoyed. He then led her off upstairs to her bedroom, saying he was going to fuck her all night. Hoping to get in on a threesome, I followed. Before the door was shut in my face, being told to piss off, he said next time I fucked her it would cost me money.

It seemed he was a pimp and she was now his working girl. Standing at the door, I heard Megan protesting that she wanted to sleep (how often had I heard that?), then I heard the noise of her being spanked. Soon after that I heard the rhythmic creak of the bed. With it came Megan's pleasurable moans and calls to be fucked harder, faster, deeper. She wanted it all night, urging Carl to fuck her all he wanted to, any time he wanted to. She was his woman, his slave, and he could beat her whenever she displeased him. I went to my lonely bed, certain she had found a soul mate.

I wondered what Megan had let herself in for. However, she stuck by Carl and she was there when his 'friends' came to visit, both men and women she entertained in her bedroom. There was no doubt they were earning money that way. One day, hearing cries from the bedroom, I went up to peer in. Megan was naked and tied down to the bed. Two men and two women were in the room with her, all naked and no doubt paying for the session. One of the women was sucking Megan while she in turn sucked one of the men. The other man and woman both had camcorders and were busy recording the scene.

Business being good, no doubt, Carl and Megan moved out to a much larger and more suitable house, leaving me to myself in my own place. Still awaiting a divorce, Megan visits if she's in town. She says that if I'd been more forceful and dominant when she'd made my life a misery, we might still be together. Maybe she's right.

Terry F., Birmingham.

CHAPTER FORTY TWO
Mexican Mistress

My girlfriend is a buxom trollop with jet-black hair and olive skin that shouts out that she's Mexican. I met her on holiday in Acapulco, a maid in my hotel where she provided room service. An absolute stunner with large shapely boobs and rounded arse, when tidying the room it always ended with us 'unmaking' the bed as we fucked lustfully. We spent time on the beach together in her off-duty periods, and I wined and dined her around town. One of the staff said I didn't need to pamper her, as she was a prostitute as well as a hotel employee.

But she never asked for money and we were stuck on each other. I was the lucky one. In her low-cut gown on nights out, or her tiny bikini on the beach with those mouth-watering tits overflowing the bra cups and threatening to burst free, I got envious looks for being the lucky bastard with such a superb specimen of womanhood.

I was married to Daphne, but separated because her parents still had power over her. Maybe I should have been more strict, especially about our sex life, which was virtually non-existent. Her parents had got her thinking it was a dirty thing, liked only by salacious men. It was not Daphne I blamed for her narrow-minded outlet. Looking back, for she was a sweet and lovely girl, maybe I should have put her across my knee and made her see my way. I know I'd have enjoyed that, and maybe a severe spanking would have rid her of those planted inhibitions about sex.

However, I was with my Mex spitfire and it was no holds barred with Carmen. On hot afternoons we'd lay naked on my hotel bed, with cold beer to sustain us between long slow bouts of sex. It sure beat the hell out of being married to a girl brought up to be a prude. We'd refresh ourselves by showering together. When turned away from me and leaning against the tiled wall of the shower cubicle, soapy suds cascaded down her back and funnelled into the valley of her magnificent arse. It became impossible for randy old me not to insert my rampant chopper between those ample brown cheeks and delightfully fuck whatever orifice my searching knob slid into first.

When I talked of my wife, Carmen insisted I should have been assertive. 'Like this, Rob,' she said one time after we'd fucked, rolling me over and giving my bottom a sound, no-nonsense smack that really stung. I was surprised how it turned me on, but it turned Carmen on even more. I was always devoured after she spanked me. I didn't need to be a sexologist to know she was into CP. She admitted her ambition was to go to America or Britain to work as a dominatrix in a house of correction. 'Practice on me,' I offered, and soon she was binding me to the bed, helpless while she had her wicked way. Or if I particularly displeased her, it was a cane instead of a spank. Once she even tried suffocating me with her big tits. What a way to go!

I got her to follow me to England, where she was soon employed in a rural mansion used as a house of correction, and proved well able to handle the situation. I saw a video of her with a client who was too eager nursing on her nipples, making them sore. She had a short leather strap and ordered the man across her knee to belt his arse until he begged for mercy. Although in demand, she wanted me to visit every chance, often staying all the weekend. On Sundays we'd drive to a country pub for lunch. She had never seen such places in Mexico, and loved it. We were about to leave for such a trip one Sunday when we saw a car draw up in the driveway. I noticed it was my wife Daphne getting out of the car. She was by herself and I'd made no secret to her where I spent my weekends.

Carmen said what a sweet girl my wife was. I didn't know if she was being sarcastic or meant it. Then I discovered she fancied her. 'How pretty, how innocent she looks,' she said meaningfully. 'I want to strip and beat her, have her submit to me completely. Make her beg for mercy, then seduce her. Begging this time for me to make love to her.'

I'd seen Carmen making spanked women as well as men kneel to tongue her cunt as an act of obedience. Because it was my wife, she said it would be more enjoyable to make her bend to her will, adding it would also be nice to have sex with her. She told me to hide before Daphne knew I was there. Intrigued, I did as asked, having nothing to lose by letting my wife fall into Carmen's clutches.

As Carmen went out to greet her, I went through the kitchen and out by the back door into the garden. I wondered how they were getting on, my wife and my girlfriend. Giving them ten long minutes to get to know each other, I stealthily peered into some of the correction lounges through the lace curtains. In one I was amazed to see Daphne bent across a table getting her pretty little arse warmed by Carmen and a whippy cane. I couldn't believe Carmen had ensnared her so quickly, but the reddened and striped bum Daphne presented was evidence enough. She took the punishment with muffled cries and flinching buttocks, no doubt the way she was used to when her father caned her. I couldn't hear properly, but she appeared to be apologising for something as she was punished.

The caning ended. Carmen then sat and took Daphne in her lap, cuddling and kissing away the tears that streamed down her cheeks. I went in and entered that room. Carmen said Daphne had called to make amends, to try to save our marriage, admitting she had been a wife that deserved to be deserted. She realised it was her parents' fault, and intended to change. She did not blame me for taking Carmen as a lover. That was when Carmen said Daphne should have the chance to make it up. We all went up to Carmen's bedroom and made love, a threesome romp that Daphne joined in with enthusiasm. Exhausting myself with fucking both girls, I then relaxed and watched them making lesbian love, with Carmen wielding a monstrous dildo. I'm sure it was the first time that Daphne discovered the joys of coming strongly and without inhibitions.

So my wife and I resumed our interrupted marriage on a good sexual understanding, the occasional spanking delivered more for sex play than to keep her in check. We visited Carmen and she visited us, so I was in the envious position of sleeping between my wife and girlfriend. Then an American client offered Carmen a fabulously paid management post in a house of correction of her own in Los Angeles. We've been over to visit and stay there for a holiday, enjoying the amenities of the place. Daphne even volunteered to help out with the dominating of male clients, the minx.

I was informed she soon became the most sadistic bitch in the place, therefore much in demand with the more masochistic clients. This, reckoned Carmen, when offering my wife full time employment, was because Daphne was making up for all her years of suppression. Whatever, I much prefer her as a wife the way she is. We're going back to L.A. for the Millennium celebrations, when by popular demand Daphne is going to be 'guest' dominatrix for our stay. She's looking forward to warming a few Yankee arses while we're there. And I'll be busy fucking my two women.

Rob, Cambridgeshire.

CHAPTER FORTY THREE
My Dream is a Thrashing

I left school ten years ago but I still have a thing for my French teacher. We always pass pleasantries whenever we meet. I've even followed her in the street to admire the splendidly jiggling bum she presents as she walks. She's still in her early forties, with a terrific figure. I've described the enticing wobble of her cheeky arse as she walks away, and coming at you her ample tits bounce invitingly with every movement. Her legs are fantastic too. I had a real crush on this most fuckable French madame when she taught me, and wanked buckets fantasising about her. And I'm still stuck on her. Wish I was hers to do with as she liked.

Once she had to discipline me in front of the class for being disobedient. Wanting attention from her, I gave her cheek. In return she gave me a glare that said she'd love to punish me physically, if only it was allowed. She gave me hundreds of lines to write, fuming as my classmates grinned. I was their hero, for Miss Lefarge was a strict mistress and extremely hot on discipline. Of course I'd actually wished she'd been allowed to cane my bare arse while bent over before her, or spanked with her hand while held across her knee. It was the stuff of my fantasies at the time. Another favourite was being ordered into her study for punishment.

Miss Lefarge would be wearing a low-cut white blouse showing the deep creamy cleavage dividing her gorgeous full breasts. The short black mini-skirt she wore showed her stocking tops and a tempting glimpse of white thigh. I'd imagine I'd refused to do a French exercise and boldly told her I wasn't going to do it. Furious, not caring what was allowed, she ordered me to drop my pants and bend across her desk, grabbing me by the scruff of the neck to make sure I obeyed. Then she produced a whippy cane, swishing it through the air to scare me as I waited with trembling buttocks.

She'd proceed to give me a merciless thrashing, striping my quivering posterior and shouting insults with each downward blow. I screeched with pain, begged abjectly, pleading for her to stop, so turned on that I'd soon shoot my load. The fantasy would always end as I was in the dying throes of coming, grovelling before her as the spasms subsided and shamed for not controlling my lustful urges. I'd swear undying love and servitude, kissing the cane she had used to thrash me. If I could last out long enough before shooting my load in the fantasy, I'd be ordered to fuck her or picture her astride my face ordering me to lick her out, to tongue her cunt clean after she'd been with a lover.

This lurid female domination fantasy became so fixed in my subconscious that I actually dreamt it some nights, waking with a massive hard-on subsiding, a damp patch on my sheet and a sticky mess coating my belly.

It was at a New Year party given by a fellow teacher at my school, that I found myself in the company of the one woman I adored. Miss Lefarge was surprised I'd made it as a teacher, informing my friend I was the most undisciplined youth she had ever taught. I wondered how she'd feel or what she would think if she'd known I still fantasised and masturbated over her!

Later that evening, in the kitchen making coffee with the host, he asked me what I thought of Yvonne Lefarge. I said never mind her academic skill as a teacher, to me she was my ideal of a real woman, that as her worst pupil I wished she'd been free to cane me. I'd have enjoyed the pain as long as it was coming from her. I was surprised by my friend's answer. 'If you're into that sort of thing, Tim, she'd have enjoyed herself dishing it out,' he said. 'It's her party piece, acting the bitch, dominating weaker souls.' He went on to relate how a fellow teacher he knew had been engaged to her, years ago when she first arrived from France. He'd broken it off because her idea of foreplay was to tie him up and whip him.

She was into the strict correction of men, he assured me. His friend was even forced to go across her knee and be spanked if he displeased her. All that made me incredibly envious of the silly bastard who couldn't stand the heat and called off the engagement. 'Better believe it's true that she's an amateur dominatrix,' my friend went on in case I didn't believe him. 'Such people do exist, believe me.'

She even took her fiancé on holiday to France just before the wimp chickened out, I was told, and introduced him to a club for sadists and submissives. It no doubt made up his mind to get out after getting his arse warmed a few times by the dominant Yvonne.

Intrigued, I chatted up my former teacher, daring to risk a rebuff for introducing talk of punishment. She'd had a few drinks, and although chatty, was in no way intoxicated. I told her I was ashamed of my bad conduct at school, that I'd deserved physical punishment and it was a pity it was no longer allowed. 'I ought to have been thrashed by you, Miss Lefarge,' I fished hopefully. She took the bait, agreeing I should have been.

'And would you have preferred a cane, or the whip, Timothy?' she asked lightly. We both laughed, but I took a chance that what I'd heard was true. I admitted to still having a strong desire to be put across her knee and spanked like the naughty boy I was in her class. I saw her interest in me increase; a potential submissive.

She asked would I drive her home to save calling a taxi. Once there and invited in, I did drink because I hoped to stay the night and not need the car. She asked was I serious about my desire to be punished by a strong and dominant woman. I then took the risk and confessed my fantasy, going into lurid detail about what I'd like her to do to me. She listened with her face colouring. Then she patted her knee and signalled I was going across it once I'd lowered my trousers and underpants and discarded them. Although more than eager to comply, the shock of my wildest fantasy coming true made my response slow. She snapped out that I must obey at once when ordered. If I desired to be controlled as I claimed, I'd learn how strict she could be.

I kicked off my trousers and pants, bending across her strong thighs and assuring her this was the stuff my dreams were made of and couldn't thank her enough for understanding. It was the wrong thing to say, for severe mistresses don't allow light talk, in fact they don't allow talk at all unless permission is given. She told me sternly that instead of being a dream, I might well find my sessions with her more of a nightmare. Reminding me I'd been a horrible and obnoxious youth, she then smacked my upturned bottom with what I can only describe as venom. The force was such that it must have hurt her hand, for it certainly stung my backside. I loved every strike, every smarting blow, picturing myself bare-arsed across this comely woman's lap and being spanked like a naughty boy. Of course I kicked, hollered, cried and begged, doing the whole bit to please the sadistic bitch walloping me. I got terribly turned on, certain she was too.

I got the biggest hard-on imaginable, my stiff cock straining against her leg as she thrashed me, a terrific turn-on for us both. This was her chance to humiliate me as well. I was called names like 'dirty-minded filthy boy', and told I should be ashamed of having that disgusting erection. A fully deserved punishing and later I'd be whipped and made to stand in a corner until I apologised.

I was also interrogated about my fantasies. In my very horny state I was delighted to admit all, including the scene where I was made to lick her cunt clean. Feeling I'd been spanked enough, or more likely she was randy for sex, I was pushed off her knee onto the carpet.

'For thinking such thoughts, Timothy, I'm going to make you lick me to show you how disgusting that sort of thing is.' I got on my knees before her parted thighs, watching her peel off her panties to let me have access to eat her, my prick rearing like a flagpole. Lolled back in her chair with both feet placed on my shoulders, she tilted up her inviting cunt.

Directing me, remaining dominant of course, I was instructed exactly how she wanted it, ordered where to lick and probe, and how she expected her clitoris to be sucked. She went on giving such detailed commands until she lost control. Her whole frame shuddering as she came, her grip tightened painfully in my hair as her hips bucked frantically, crying out in French that she was climaxing, blaming me as the beast who had made her do so.

Proud as I was to have brought such a fine mature woman to that convulsive orgasm, I was not to get thanked for my services. In fact I was cursed for being a lecherous swine, a cunt-licking pig, and one who had no respect for women. It was evident I was going to be taught to know my place as her slave. I felt that was rich, as I'd just given her such orgasmic pleasure with my tongue, but I humbly begged her forgiveness and swore obedience to my mistress.

It was the start of a mutual relationship that's still going strong, one I intend to continue as long as Yvonne doesn't tire of our twice-weekly sessions. There's no doubt she's dedicated to dominating and humiliating her men friends; quite a few before me, it seems, including the wimpish fiancé who got out before being flogged or fucked silly by such a dominant woman. From that first night I was made to be subservient to her in every menial way imaginable, and Yvonne has a great imagination. I thrive on each ordeal.

She's had dominant women friends visit for dinner, using me as her maid in wig and make-up, wearing only a short frilly apron as I serve the food and drinks. Always I'm mercilessly insulted and abused by all the females present. This year we'll holiday in France, where my mistress is a founder member of a CP society near Cannes. She assures me I'll be put through my paces.

Oh yes, that straining erection I always get when being spanked or otherwise disciplined is never wasted, but always put to good use. As a treat I'm allowed to give my mistress a good rogering once she's satisfied her desire to inflict punishment, with the usual result of making her super horny. That's what it's all about really, isn't it? Power over us weak-willed males gets the sadistic bitches all hot and bothered, with an itchy cunt needing a prick, even if they claim they can't stand us. Being dominant is why they get randy, and wanting to be fucked turns the tables on them for a while, being on the receiving end for a change. Mind you, I'd never dare suggest that to her as an explanation.

Happy spankings out there, guys!

Tim, Hereford.

CHAPTER FORTY FOUR
Older Woman

I couldn't get my mum's nice new friend out of my mind. Before falling for her I'd been a normal eighteen-year-old. I chatted up the girls at college, fondled their tits, touched up their tight quims, and had fucked four of the most willing ones. A randy teenager always on the hunt for cunt, I considered girls my age on this earth for young rams like me to make use of their bodies. But after seeing Margaret for the first time I became a lovesick prat.

Mum's friend was more than twice my age, and I'm sure she was lonely and neglected. Why was she always at our house if she wasn't? Her husband was an engineer on an oil rig supply vessel. When at home he was at the pub every night, and I'm sure he was treating her badly. I knew she'd be better off with me. Call it a crush I had on her, but I was on another planet over the lovely Margaret. With her lovely tits and bum, Margaret was the cause of many a wank.

I learned that on Sunday mornings she took her two young kids to the local indoor municipal swimming pool. I started to go along, kidding on I was keen on teaching the girls to swim while eyeballing their mother in her bathing suit. It was a black one-piece that strove to contain her voluptuous figure, the upper part overflowing with creamy tit. Below, at the fork of her thighs, her mound bulged prominently, a delightful curve I could imagine with a forest of soft brown hair surrounding the lips of her cunt.

But my obvious crush on her was becoming apparent to others, my mum and dad included. Worse, they shamed me when Margaret was in our house, teasing her that she had a secret admirer. My burning cheeks and anger gave me away. I ran out of the house, furious with my parents, greatly embarrassed that my true love had discovered my secret and now would laugh at me.

The next day my parents were out working on their allotment when Margaret came from taking her kids to school. I was not at college, having a dental appointment later. When I answered the door I blushed again, reminded how my parents had been joking about me getting so besotted over an older woman, old enough to be my mum, in fact.

Seeing my flushed face, Margaret smiled and raised a cool hand to gently stroke my cheek. At her touch my dick immediately became painfully stretched. I also knew instinctively that she'd been aware of my feelings for her. 'You're so sweet, Robbie, so don't feel bad about liking me,' she murmured, moving closer to press a light kiss on my cheek. 'It's good for any woman to know she's admired. I think you're such a nice young man, and so handsome...'

Her closeness made her very prominent breasts rest against my chest, accidentally on purpose, I fervently hoped. The feel of their soft warmth was so erotic that my head spun, my erect prick responding by threatening to shoot a load in my pants.

Soon her sweet womanly smell and the touch of her lips on my cheek did prove too much for a lovesick lad to endure. With a low moan and professing my undying love for her, I embraced her tightly to my body, kissing her long and lingeringly on the mouth. At once I realised my erection was pressing snugly against her upper thighs.

Margaret responded by letting the kiss proceed and increase in its intensity, our lips opening wetly and tongues snaking together. Her arms encircled my neck as if drawing her face closer as our mouths fused, while her groin ground against mine. I rejoiced inwardly as she began strong pelvic movements against the hard cylinder of my rampant prick. With her lower body making such obvious fucking motions into me, I replied by lowering my arms and using my hands to firmly grasp the cheeks of her arse to pull her harder into me as our thrusts matched.

It was heaven, as good as a fuck. So my jeans and her dress separated my prick and her cunt, but the sensation was ecstatic and not bad for starters! As she worked her crotch to meet my forward lunges, I heard her mumbling agonisingly against my lips that we shouldn't be doing this, it was so wrong. I was a boy and she a grown and married woman, old enough to be my mother. Such talk only excited me further. I'm sure it aroused her more too, for her frenzied thrusting against me continued, and I lost control and came in my underpants.

Then I heard soft moans, whimpers and sighs change abruptly into swift grunts as she was grinding into me with wild and helpless abandon. Her voice became strained and hoarse as she cried out loudly that she was coming. 'You've made me come,' she screamed. 'Damn you, you made me do this, you dirty little sod!'

She thrust me from her, slapping my face in the shame and fury at what she'd allowed or couldn't control. The slap was stinging my cheek, but I didn't care. I'd soaked my underpants but was elated to think I'd made this extremely nice lady climax when rubbing against my prick. As I tried to kiss her again she smacked my face once more. She ordered me to let go of her, that I'd taken advantage of her, and finally that she never wanted to see or have anything to do with me again.

In her anger, more at herself than at me, I hoped, she went past trying to maintain her dignity, but stopping at the door she looked back at me. It was obvious from her mussed hair, flushed face and dazed eyes, that here was a woman still shaken by having a tremendously violent orgasm.

Left alone, I did a little dance of triumph. No longer was she the worshipped from afar wife and mother, but a woman who'd been brought to orgasm and shown to lust after it, therefore fair game. My crush on her was gone; now my desire for her was purely sexual. I intended to fuck her.

I was cleaning myself up in the bathroom when she phoned to say we must have a serious talk. Mentioning she was in the house alone, she said I should go round there.

I walked to her bungalow where she was desperate to make me promise I'd never reveal to a soul what had happened between us. As if I would, I promised, revelling in the thought of boasting to my mates in college. Margaret said she was as much to blame. We'd got carried away with our strong feelings, but it must never happen again. As she appeared calm and we talked quite openly, I risked asking if it had been nice for her.

'You know it was, you wicked boy,' she answered, even allowing a little wry smile. Seriously, she added her husband had never given her an orgasm. She'd only experienced one, until that morning, she added shyly.

'Then let's do it again,' I said, and held her in my arms, kissing her like before. At first she protested and tried to push me away, then she returned my kisses. Every time our lips parted she scolded me for being persistent.

'Can't you control that naughty penis, you bad lad?' she said as my cock rose, hardened, and pressed into her. Again she muttered it was wrong, that she was a married woman and me a mere teenager. I'm sure by the responses coming, the body language, the thought of a youth having sex with her, was erotically stimulating enough for resistance to vanish.

We found ourselves kissing into a nearby bedroom, propelled there by Margaret. Without need for discussion or permission, our kissing and fondling led to our clothes being discarded in a heap on the carpet. I stood in awe of her naked womanly charms.

'Do you like me, Robbie?' she asked shyly as she turned round to let me see her rear view too. Stripped and with my dick straining upward, I nodded feebly. Who wouldn't have liked those awesome breasts, thick nipples, and curved hips and thighs?

We fell on the bed together. Guided between her thighs, it was a moment to die for as my prick slipped up her moist and clinging channel.

To my delight Margaret was vocal, urging me to fuck her hard, to fuck her and make her come and come. 'It's been so long,' she moaned, adding that she'd forgotten how hard young men could get, sighing about how lovely it was with my prick deep inside her. Then I was coming in her and as we both convulsed, her right hand began smacking my bottom harder than I'd thought possible. I kept yelling and spurting my load, finding the spanking timed with our jerking and adding to our excitement.

Intrigued, and once recovered, I asked if she was into spanking like I'd read about. She joked that I'd soon find out if I ever talked of our affair. Pressed on the matter, she said she'd put me across her knee and wallop me for revealing our secret.

At once interested, I asked her to show me. Sitting up with her legs over the edge of the bed, she ordered me to lie over her lap. Excited by the idea, I did so. Margaret immediately gave my bum a hard slap to show she meant business. I howled with pain as she continued smacking my backside until it felt to be on fire. It was obvious she was getting a kick by spanking me, her free hand below my stomach stroking my dick, which was again spectacularly rigid. Ordered to stand and show her, she nursed my prick in her soft cleavage, giving it a few slurpy sucks each time it bobbed out.

Rolling over, bottom lifted, she told me to fuck her again. Asking if this was to be a regular thing, she turned to look at me and said she'd be eternally damned for what we'd already done, so she might as well give in and enjoy herself.

Our meetings were to be secretly conducted for seven more months before Margaret returned to her home town of Aberdeen. Moving back with her husband who'd taken a shore job with a refinery, she was by then heavily pregnant. Never outright saying it was mine, when naked with me she'd stand with a belly like a full moon and say teasingly, 'Look what you've done to me, you randy young sod.'

We carried on our spanking and correction games, for it always made her eager to fuck. She whacked me with a cane, belt, or slipper.

All that was a few years ago now, but I still get the desire to be punished at times. I'll never marry until I find a girl who'll enjoy being dominant with me, but genuine Margaret's are hard to find.

Now I gladly pay a local housewife to administer the cane or a spanking before we fuck. I get my rocks off and a striped arse to keep me satisfied for a day or two. She, with a few other clients she serves as a visiting masseuse, makes enough to send her son to a private school. So everybody's happy, including her husband who doesn't know how his wife does it. He thinks she's just thrifty. Anyway, more power to your CP research project. I'll look forward to reading the results.

Robert, Greenock.